Books by A

McIntyre Security, Inc. Bodyguard Series:
Vulnerable

Fearless

Shane (a novella)

Broken

Shattered

Imperfect

Ruined

Hostage

Redeemed

Marry Me (a novella)

Snowbound (a novella)

Regret

With This Ring (a novella)

Collateral Damage

A Tyler Jamison Novel:
Somebody to Love

Somebody to Hold

A British Billionaire Romance:
Charmed (co-written with Laura Riley)

Audiobooks by April Wilson

For links to my audiobooks, please visit my website:
www.aprilwilsonauthor.com/audiobooks

Hostage

McIntyre Security Bodyguard Series
Book 7

APRIL WILSON

This novel is a work of fiction. All places and locations mentioned in it are used fictitiously. The names of characters and places are figments of the author's imagination. Any resemblance to real people or real places is purely a coincidence.

Copyright © 2018 by April E. Barnswell/Wilson Publishing LLC
Cover by Steamy Designs

All rights reserved.

Wilson Publishing
P.O. Box 292913
Dayton, OH 45429
www.aprilwilsonauthor.com

With the exception of short passages to be used for book review purposes, no part of this publication may be reproduced, scanned, or distributed in any printed or electronic form without written permission from the author. Please do not participate in or encourage piracy of copyrighted materials.

Visit www.aprilwilsonauthor.com to sign up for the author's e-mail newsletter to be notified about upcoming releases.

ISBN-13: 978-1719275378
ISBN-10: 1719275378

Published in the United States of America
First Printing July 2018

Dedication

To Lori... You're not just my sister; you're my BFF, and you've put up with me for a very long time.

To Laura Bonacker, whose insightful guidance into premature babies and the NICU made *Hostage* a much better book.

1

Beth

Sitting across from me at a table for two, Lia lifts her glass in my direction. "A toast to baby Luke! It won't be much longer now, little dude. Make your appearance! Aunt Lia is waiting."

Laughing, I raise my glass of ice water to join my sister-in-law in her toast. "He's not due for six more weeks, Lia. Please don't rush him."

As if hearing his name, the baby in my burgeoning belly does a cartwheel and sticks the landing right on my bladder—his new favorite pastime. He's been restless lately, awake more often than not, turning somersaults inside his increasingly cramped quarters and sticking his feet into my ribs. I have to admit, I'm anxious to get him out of my womb and into my arms. I'm *so* ready to have this baby. Scared, yes. Terrified actually, as he's my first, and I really don't know what I'm doing. But also *so* ready.

I've read a ton of books on pregnancy, childbirth, and newborn care. I own a bookstore, so of course my first impulse is to turn to books, but no matter how much you read about something, until you actually experience it for yourself, it's impossible to really know what it's like.

Lia takes a sip of her Coke and sets her glass down to reach for a taco. "He's going to be such a hellion," she says, laughing. She grins at me. "I guarantee it."

Based on the stories I've heard about his daddy as a youngster, I can believe it. "If he's anything like Shane...."

Lia wags her finger at me. "He'll be worse than Shane. I'll make sure of it. I'll teach him everything I know."

I can certainly believe Lia's prediction, as she's the biggest hellraiser in the McIntyre clan. "Please, Lia, have pity. I'm the one who'll have to chase after him. Go easy on me. Don't corrupt him too soon."

Lia shakes her head. "Go easy on you? Where's the fun in that?"

Despite Lia's merciless teasing, I lean back in my seat and sigh with contentment. It feels so good to be out of the apartment, even for just a few hours. For the past few months, I've been working mostly from home, rarely going out. I'm lucky to leave the penthouse these days. Shane's been watching over me like a deranged hawk ever since we found out I was pregnant. He doesn't want me to overwork myself, or get too tired, or... pretty much do anything. I know he means well—he's just trying to protect me—but sometimes it's smothering. Like right now. I've got cabin fever so bad I could scream. Getting away for lunch today with Lia feels like an indulgence.

Lia frowns at me over the top of her glass. "Hey, are you okay?"

I shrug. I really shouldn't complain. I have everything I could possibly need, and Shane spoils me rotten. I'm married to my knight-in-shining armor, and we're about to welcome our first child into the world. Yeah, I have nothing to complain about. "I'm just a little stir crazy. I was holed up in the apartment almost all spring, and now it's nearly summer and I just want to get outside, you know? I want some fresh air and sunshine. I want to do something, go somewhere, anywhere, before this little guy turns our lives upside down."

I lay my hands on my belly, molding them to the firm round shape of my abdomen, smoothing the fabric of my sundress over the bump. When I feel the undulating ripple of movement inside, I smile.

Lia studies me for a moment underneath her lashes. Then she takes another sip of her drink and shrugs. "Okay, let's do something. If you could do anything, what would it be?"

"I don't know. Maybe get out of town for a little while? Even a short trip would be great."

"Like a road trip?"

"Yes! That sounds like fun."

"Why don't you and Shane go up to Jake's cabin this weekend and spend the night? Just a quick road trip. I'm sure you could talk him into it."

I frown, thinking the odds of that aren't good. But her suggestion gives me an idea. "How about a double date? You and Jonah could come with us."

Lia considers my suggestion. "Sure. Why not? We don't have anything planned this weekend. Jonah doesn't have any performances scheduled, and I'm always up for a road trip."

"We could go to Lucky's Tavern," I suggest. "Jonah promised Hal he'd perform there again, and you know how Jonah loves to play small venues." The more I think about it, the better I like the idea. "Come on! It'll be fun." Then I frown. "That's if I can talk Shane into agreeing to an overnight trip right now."

"Your due date is still weeks away," Lia says. "I'm sure you can talk him into it. You won't know unless you try. Sweet talk him a little. He'll cave, trust me."

I reach for my phone. "I'll call him now."

Lia catches my hand and shakes her head. "No, don't call. Ask him in person. Let's head over to the office right now so you can ply your feminine wiles on him. *In his office. On top of his desk.*" She gives me a suggestive look. "Do I have to spell it out?"

My face heats up at the thought of having sex in Shane's office... on his desk, to be exact. I have to admit, it's one of my favorite fantasies. And, I don't know what it is about being pregnant, but lately I want sex all the time. Shane's not complaining—not in the least—but these days I can't get enough of him. Morning, evening, middle of the night... my body aches for him. Even now, the thought of a little afternoon nookie in Shane's office is making me flush all over. I can feel the heat building between my legs, making me want to squirm. "I'll do it."

"Ladies, can I get you anything else?"

I smile up at our server, a handsome young guy with dark hair hanging low on his forehead. He flips his head back, tossing his bangs out of his eyes, and gives me a megawatt smile as his gaze lingers on my cleavage.

"Forget it, pal," Lia says, snapping her fingers at our server to redirect his attention. "Eyes off, unless you want me to break your arm."

"What?" he says, his eyes directed to Lia. He thrusts our check into her hand as he sputters a denial. "I wasn't doing anything. Honest! I—"

"Save it, buddy." Lia hands him a credit card. "She's *so* not available."

* * *

A taxi drops us off in front of the McIntyre Security, Inc. office building, and we walk inside, glad to get out of the stifling heat.

As we pass the front desk, the security guard on duty gives me a friendly smile. "Good afternoon, Mrs. McIntyre."

Mrs. McIntyre. Shane and I have been married for nearly six months now, but I'm still not fully accustomed to hearing people call me that. "Good afternoon, George."

As we head toward the bank of elevators, I catch my reflection in the mirrored wall. My gaze catches on my obviously pregnant belly, as well as the diamond ring and gold band on my ring finger. I never expected to find myself married and pregnant at twenty-five. Good grief, I'd never even had a serious boyfriend before I met Shane.

Just thinking about my new husband puts a smile on my face. I fell so hard for him, and not because of his looks or his wealth. And not because of his hot CEO persona and the way he fills out a suit and tie. No, I fell hard for him because he *gets* me. And he loves me in spite of all my flaws and insecurities.

From the very beginning, he accepted me for who I am. He got my anxiety, and he made things right for me. He also eliminated the monster who had loomed over my life like a sinister, dark cloud. He *killed* Howard Kline for me, when that cretin broke into my home with the intent to kill me as payback for the fact that he'd spent nearly two decades in prison for abducting me when I was a young child. Shane made sure that he himself was the one to pull the trigger and put an end, once and for all, to my lifetime of fear and anxiety.

Lia rides up to the twentieth floor with me, where the executive offices are located. She'll drop me off on Shane's floor, and then she'll head down to the third floor, where the martial arts studio is located so she can hang out with her twin, Liam, while

I'm plying my wiles on my unsuspecting husband.

When the elevator stops at my floor, she shoos me out. "Have fun. And remember, he's putty in your hands."

Before heading to Shane's office, I make a quick detour to the ladies' room. I want to freshen up first, brush my teeth, and—here's the most important part of my plan—slip off my panties and tuck them into my purse. For what I have in mind, a bare bottom will work wonders.

Walking half-naked beneath my billowy sundress feels strange to say the least. It's actually pretty daring of me, as I'm not the most sexually confident woman in the world. I almost chicken out before I reach the executive suites, but Diane Hughes, Shane's executive assistant, sees me through the glass walls and waves me inside. Before I can think better of my plan, and get cold feet, I walk through the door and stop at her desk.

"Don't you look pretty," she says, giving me a bright smile. Her pale blue eyes crinkle at the corners as she looks me over. She rises from her chair to give me a warm hug. "Pregnancy becomes you, dear girl. How are you feeling?"

When she releases me, I lay my hands on my belly. "I'm as big as a house, Mrs. Hughes, but I feel great."

She grins. "You're going to be such a fantastic mother. I just know it! And Shane! Good Lord, that little baby is all he talks about these days. That, and how beautiful you are."

My cheeks pinken as I glance toward Shane's office door, which is closed. "Speaking of Shane...do you know if he's busy at the moment?"

"You go right in, honey. His next appointment isn't until three o'clock."

As it's only one-thirty, that gives me plenty of time for what I have in mind.

"He's all yours, dear," Diane says, waving me toward Shane's door. "I'll hold his calls until further notice."

I smile guiltily, wondering if she's a mind reader. Am I that transparent? "Thank you."

I knock on his door, steeling myself with a deep breath.

"Come in."

I open his door, popping my head through the opening, and see Shane seated at his desk.

He looks up, and his demeanor changes immediately as he leans back in his chair with a pleased expression. "Sweetheart! What are you doing here?"

"I hope I'm not interrupting anything." I step into his office and shut the door behind me, turning the lock to ensure our privacy.

He raises an eyebrow, but he doesn't comment.

"I went out to lunch with Lia today," I say, setting my purse on one of the black leather chairs positioned in front of his desk. "Since I was in the neighborhood, I thought I'd stop by and say hello."

He looks very much like the corporate CEO in his charcoal gray suit and white dress shirt. I could stare at him all day in his *GQ* finery. His short, brown hair and trim beard frame his handsome face perfectly, making me weak in the knees just at the sight of him. And those electric blue eyes...they can go from gentle and smiling to hot and intense in a heartbeat.

He crosses his arms over his chest and looks at me pointedly. "Where's Sam?"

"Sam and Lia switched places today so Lia and I could have a girls' day out. I didn't think I needed *two* bodyguards."

He relaxes a smidgen. "Then where's Lia? I assume she accompanied you here."

"She's downstairs with Liam."

"I see." His smile brightens.

Before I can lose my nerve, I round his desk and swivel his black leather chair so that he's facing me. He raises an eyebrow, his curiosity piqued. I know I have his full attention when his gaze darts down to the V-neckline of my dress, which shows off my new cleavage, and then back up again. Having cleavage is a relatively new experience for me. I've always been pretty flat-chested, but pregnancy has given me a temporary boost in that department. I finally have something to show off, and I intend to put it to good use.

"Are you busy?" I say, gripping the arms of his chair and leaning in to brush the tip of my nose against his.

His hands grip my waist. "I'm never too busy for you. What do you have in mind?"

I can tell from the glint in his eyes that he's getting ideas of his own. There's a very good reason why I never play poker with Shane and his brothers. I'm terrible at hiding my hand, and I'm sure he already suspects I'm up to something. "Diane said she'd hold your calls."

"Really?" His lips quirk up in a grin, and he looks decidedly intrigued. And aroused. "Go ahead. I'm listening."

I step between Shane's knees, standing as close to him as I can. His long fingers flex on my plus-sized waist. "I like this," he says, his fingers clamping down on my flesh. "There's more of you to grasp."

I laugh as I lean forward to kiss him, thinking I'd better do this before I lose my nerve completely. I raise one knee and slide it onto his chair, on the outside of his right hip. My initial plan was to straddle his lap, unzip his pants, and ride him like a cowgirl, but now I'm wondering if that's even possible with my belly in the way. And then there's the question of whether or not his chair can hold our combined weight.

Before I can do a quick mental calculation, he slides his hands beneath my dress and up the backs of my thighs, pausing when he reaches the juncture where my thighs meet my bare butt cheeks.

"Where the hell are your panties?" he says, sounding almost scandalized. His gaze shoots up to meet mine. "Did you leave the house like this?"

"No! I took them off a few minutes ago in the ladies' room. I'm not about to walk around downtown Chicago half-naked!"

He relaxes, apparently mollified by my answer, as he proceeds to slip his fingers between my legs from behind—something he knows is guaranteed to turn me on. His fingers tease the seam of my labia, making me squirm. Then he dips a long finger into my wetness and groans deep in his throat. Immediately his expression tightens, and his nostrils flare with arousal.

"Jesus, sweetheart," he says, touching me more intimately, sliding his finger deeper inside to stroke me deliciously. He leans forward and presses a kiss to the shadowy valley between my breasts and groans. "You're so wet."

Before I can even think about attempting my cowgirl position, he sweeps his arm across the surface of his desk to clear a spot right in front of his chair. Then he lifts me up and sits me on his desk, bare bottomed, and turns his chair to face me. I shiver when he pushes my dress up around my waist, exposing my nakedness to his hot gaze. His cheeks darken as he looks his fill.

I run my fingers through his short, chestnut brown hair, making the short strands stand up in tufts. "Um, do you have anything planned for this weekend?"

He glances up at me, his brow furrowing incredulously. "You're sitting half-naked on my desk and you want to talk about our weekend plans?"

I grin guiltily, knowing full well how inept I am at this. "I was thinking we should go away for a night this weekend, the two of us and Lia and Jonah. It would be fun." I rake my nails against his scalp, and he closes his eyes, giving me another heart-felt groan. "You know, one last bit of fun before the baby arrives."

He frowns, looking like he's resigned himself to having this conversation. "What exactly did you have in mind?"

I shrug, continuing to stroke his hair as it's an excellent way to distract him. "Just a quick little road trip. We could drive up to Jake's cabin in Harbor Springs tomorrow morning and stay the night. It's only a two-hour drive. It'll be fun. An overnight double date."

He frowns. "Honey, I really don't want to go out of town so close to the baby's due date."

"He's not due for another six weeks!"

"But what if something happens? I don't want to be so far away from your doctor."

"Nothing's going to happen. Besides, the cabin's only two hours away. That's not so far."

Shane leans back in his chair and crosses his arms, a frown marring his handsome face. "Beth, no. It's too risky."

"Oh, come on, it'll be fun. We could go to Lucky's Tavern for dinner. Jonah could play a few sets—he promised Hal he'd perform there again. That would be fun. Come on, please? This might be the last chance we'll have to do something like this for a while. And I have cabin fever so badly! I feel like I've been stuck at home for months."

"I really don't like the idea of you being so far away from your doctor."

"I'll be fine. I promise. Please?"

"Beth—"

I lean forward and kiss him, my fingers in his hair as I tease his lips apart. I draw his lower lip into my mouth and gently suck on it, which I know drives him crazy. Actually, he likes it when I suck on anything of his. "Please?"

He sighs, clearly exasperated. "Beth."

"Please?"

He lays his warm hands on my bare thighs and spreads my legs wider, exposing me to his hot gaze. "You don't play fair, do you?"

I smile, sensing victory. "We can make out at the cabin. Remember the last time we stayed there?"

He laughs. "We don't have to leave Chicago to make out. In fact, isn't that what we're *trying* to do right now?"

"Yes, but it'll be fun to go somewhere with Lia and Jonah. Shoot, we live in the same building and hardly go out together. Come on. Let's do something spontaneous and crazy."

"You want something spontaneous and crazy?" He reaches for the hem of my dress and pulls it up and over my head, dropping it to the desktop, leaving me sitting bare-ass naked on his desk, dressed in nothing but a white lacy bra. My heart starts pounding, and I glance behind me at the locked door. I know no one can see us, but still... I feel so exposed. It's unnerving. "Shane."

He unhooks my bra, and the cups spring free. My bra straps slide down my arms, leaving me uncovered.

"You wanted spontaneous and crazy," he says. "Does this count?"

2

Beth

Rationally, I know his office door is locked, and that Diane is holding his calls—that means no visitors, too—but still, I feel so exposed. Since he has the corner office, the two exterior walls are nothing but glass, providing a nearly panoramic view of the downtown Chicago skyline. Right now, it's all clear, sunny skies and glass-and-steel office buildings as far as the eye can see. I know the windows are tinted for privacy, but from where I'm sitting, it doesn't feel very private to me.

Suddenly, I feel chilled, and my confidence takes a nose dive.

"Shane."

"What's wrong, honey?"

My gaze shifts toward the windows.

"Sweetheart, the windows are tinted on the outside. No one can see into this office."

"I know, but—"

"But what? No one can see us. I promise."

I sigh. "All right."

"Honey." He frames my face in his hands. "Do you honestly think I'd let anyone see you naked?"

"No." I feel a wave of emotion welling up inside me, making my eyes mist. I'm sure the pregnancy hormones are to blame—I cry at the drop of a hat lately—and I can't seem to help it. I love this man so much. No matter what I need, he's always there for me, patient as a saint as he puts up with my many insecurities.

He peers down into my face, looking a little baffled. "Honey? Why the tears?"

The concern in his voice sends me over the edge, and now the waterworks are flowing. And even though I'm wearing waterproof mascara, I'm afraid I look like a raccoon now.

"Beth?" He crouches down at eye level, a hint of a smile on his face. "What's wrong, honey?"

"Nothing's wrong!" I barely manage to get the words out between sobs. "It's just that I love you so much." And then more sobs come, and I know I'm a hot mess now, and I'm embarrassed. "Stupid pregnancy hormones."

Shane bites his lip to keep from smiling as he pulls me into his arms and rubs my back. "I know. I love you too."

We both laugh then, mine more of a watery spluttering, and he pats me on the back.

He hands me a tissue and I dab at my face, checking for mascara streaks. So far, so good. "I'm so sorry. I'm ruining everything."

He tips my chin up so that I'm looking him in the eye. "You could never ruin anything." Then he takes the soggy tissue from me and hands me a clean one. "Here. Blow."

I blow my nose. "Falling apart like this wasn't part of the plan. I was going to use my feminine wiles to get you to agree to the road trip. And I've botched everything."

He chuckles. "You really want to go on this trip that badly?"

"Yes. I thought it would be fun to do something with Lia and Jonah…. sort of our last fling before we become parents, you know?"

He sighs. "All right. We'll go. But only if you promise to take it easy and not stress yourself out, like you're doing right now."

I nod, wadding up the damp tissue. Shane holds out his hand, and I place the crumpled tissue in his palm, and he drops it in the wastebasket under his desk.

"Now," he says, running his hands down my bare arms, "the burning question is… do you really want to have sex now? Or was this all just an elaborate ploy to get me to agree to the road trip?"

I grin at him, my cheeks flushing hotly. Of course I want him! "Yes."

"Yes, what?"

"Yes, I want to have sex now. Right here on your desk."

"We could take this into the bedroom, you know," he says, nodding at the door that leads to his private office apartment. "I think you would be far more comfortable on a bed."

I reach for his tie and pull him closer. "I want to do it right here on your desk."

He grins. "You won't get any complaint from me."

I loosen his tie, pulling it free from his collar, and lay it aside. Then I slowly unbutton his fine dress shirt, letting it fall open to reveal his bare chest, which is a genuine work of art with its taut golden skin, muscled ridges, and light dusting of chest hair. Once I'm done, I run my hands down his torso, my fingers skimming over the ridges of his muscles. "Leave the rest on," I say. "It feels naughtier this way, when you're still partly dressed and looking very much the CEO."

Shane gives me a crooked smile as he cups one of my breasts in his hand. He brushes his thumb across the nipple, watching as it puckers into a tight bud. Then he draws the tip into his mouth and suckles my flesh, swirling his tongue around the tip. I can feel the wet heat of his mouth and the soft tug of his lips all the way down to my core as liquid desire pools between my legs. He moves to my other breast and gives it the same treatment, increasing the ache between my legs until I'm squirming.

"Shane, please."

He grasps my hips and pulls me to the edge of the desk, nudging my thighs apart. "Don't rush me. I'm just getting to the best part." Then he drops down onto his chair and rolls it toward me, glancing up at me with a heated gleam in his eyes. I know exactly what he wants—his mouth, on me—and it makes me shiver. He's insatiable.

He leans in and begins trailing teasing kisses up my inner thigh, heightening my arousal until I'm practically panting. When he reaches the apex of my thighs, he nuzzles my mound, breathing me in and stealing my sanity.

"Oh, God." My thighs are trembling now, and my breasts are aching. All of me is aching. "Shane, please."

"Shh. Patience, sweetheart." He pries open the lips of my sex, exposing my opening and my clit to his hot gaze. Then he proceeds to lick me, so thoroughly, his tongue swiping through my slit. He takes his time, and the feel of his tongue on my flesh sends a frisson of desire through me. I gasp and reach for him, my fingers gripping his head.

Shane always brings me to climax before he penetrates me, so that I'm soft and wet enough to take him without discomfort, but right now he's clearly in no rush. Heat and desire are pooling between my legs as he dips his tongue inside me, then slides it up to flutter against my clit. He torments me until I'm a quivering mess and desperate for release. I tug sharply on his hair, but if I'm hurting him, he doesn't complain.

"Shane—" My words are cut off with a whimper as he lashes my clit with his tongue. His finger slides into me, thrusting gently in and out as he opens me up and strokes me deep inside.

Panting shamelessly now, I find myself petting his head, encouraging him with loving strokes. His relentless tongue drives me higher and higher, and his finger rubs my sweet spot deep inside me. The pleasure is so intense I can't hold back my cries. My legs stiffen, signaling that my climax is imminent. Still, he continues his wicked torment, pushing me over the edge, until I arch my back and cry out in a breathless, shaking voice, "Shane!"

He shoots to his feet, wiping his wet beard and mouth on the tail of his shirt. His belt hits the floor with a loud thunk, and he wrenches open his trousers, shoving them and his boxer briefs down just far enough to free his erection. Fisting his thick length, he steps between my open thighs.

With one hand he raises my left thigh, and with the other he guides himself into my opening, which is drenched now thanks to his attentions. He positions the big head of his cock against my opening and presses in, groaning loudly as he works himself inside me, one slow inch at a time.

He fills me so beautifully it makes me gasp. "Shane!"

"I know," he breathes, his mouth pressed against my temple. He dips down to kiss my lips as he pulls out a little, then presses deeper inside me, rocking into me a little farther each time. "Sweetheart." He groans, pressing his forehead to mine as he looks down at where we're joined. "My God, you feel so good."

Once he's fully seated inside me, he spreads my thighs wider so he can press closer against me, melding our bodies together. He holds himself still for a moment, giving me a chance to adjust to the size of him. We're both breathing hard now, and I grab his arms to hold myself upright.

"Reach back to brace yourself," he says, his voice rough now with arousal.

When I do as he says, he slides his forearms beneath my knees, spreading my thighs and tilting me back so he can open me up further. He pulls almost free, then slides back in slowly, his cock stroking hotly through my wet flesh, creating the most delicious friction. Over and over he strokes in and out of me, setting off little fireworks deep inside that make me gasp and whimper with pleasure.

"Okay?" he says.

I can do little more than gasp. "Yes!"

I brace myself as Shane picks up the pace, his strokes powerful and yet so controlled as he tempers his strength.

"I want to feel you come on me," he says, his voice deep, almost a growl now. "I want to feel you squeeze me."

"I can't come again. It's too soon."

"Yes, you can." He reaches between my legs to rub firm little circles on my clitoris. He presses his lips to mine, both of us panting. "Come for me, sweetheart."

His voice, his words, the tremors in his arms, his thumb on my clit... it all sends me over the edge a second time. I gasp as a second orgasm hits me, biting my lips to keep from crying out. He holds himself deep inside me, motionless as my walls clamp down on him, his arms shaking. When he erupts inside me, sending wave after wave of scalding heat into my body, his hoarse shout fills the room, echoing off the walls.

Oh, my God! Diane must have heard that. I bite my lip to keep from laughing and press my hot face into the crook of his neck.

After his last pulse into my body, he gently pulls out and lowers my thighs to the desktop before capturing my face with his hands and leaning in for a gentle kiss. "You're going to be the death of me," he breathes, smiling as he touches his nose to mine. Then he leans down and kisses my taut, round belly.

Shane grabs a tissue and cleans himself up, then rights his clothes. Then he says, "Let's get you cleaned up." He grabs my dress and bra, sweeps me up into his arms, and carries me through the door to his private office apartment. We head straight for the bathroom.

Once I've washed up, I slip my arms into my bra straps, and he reaches in front of me to fasten it. He lays his hands on my big belly, catching and holding my gaze in the mirror. "I love seeing you like this." He skims his hands over my abdomen. "So round with our child. You look beautiful."

I laugh, laying my hands on his. "I look like I swallowed a basketball."

He grins, shaking his head. "No, you look stunning. We made this baby together. Part of me is inside you, growing, thriving." He skims his lips down the side of my neck and across my shoulder. Just then, the baby kicks, and we both feel it. His expression grows serious. "I'll do my very best to be a good father and a good husband. I don't have a lot of experience at doing either, but I'll try."

I turn my face to kiss the edge of his jaw. "You're a wonderful husband, and I know you'll be an equally wonderful father. You don't do anything half-heartedly. Luke's a lucky little boy."

"Yes, he is, because he has you for a mother."

I laugh. "I have even less experience than you do when it comes to parenting. At least you had six younger siblings. I'm sure you changed more than your share of diapers and patched up countless boo-boos. I've never even babysat."

"We'll figure it out as we go. And we have our parents to help us. Between them, they raised nine kids. I'm sure they'll have plenty of advice for us."

Shane helps me into my dress, and as he smooths the fabric over my hips, he gives me a look. "We need to retrieve your panties." He slips his hand underneath my dress and clutches a bare butt cheek. "You are not walking out of my office with a bare bottom."

I smile. "I wouldn't dream of it."

3

Shane

As I gaze at Beth's reflection in the bathroom mirror, I have to fight the urge to sweep her up into my arms and carry her to the bedroom for another round. This time it would be slow and relaxed, so I can worship her the way I want to. While I don't think she'd object to the idea, I don't want to wear her out. She's always been a little physically fragile, but this pregnancy has taken its toll on her. She tires so easily lately.

I can't wait until our baby is born. Of course I want to hold our son, but the truth is, I won't rest easy until she has delivered. Even with the benefits of modern medicine, there's always a risk of something going wrong. I ruthlessly slam a lid down on that thought. Beth needs me strong, not freaking out.

Beth frowns at her reflection in the bathroom mirror. Her pale blonde hair is mussed, numerous strands having come lose from her ponytail, and her blue-green eyes are bright. "I look like I've been rolling around in bed."

I grin. "You do have a well-fucked look about you."

She reaches back and swats at me, laughing. "I do not!" Then she returns to studying her reflection, her finger tips dancing over her slightly swollen lips. "Do I?"

"You look like a beautiful, expectant mother." I lean down and kiss the side of her neck, skimming my lips across her skin and breathing in her scent.

The baby kicks, and we both feel it beneath our hands. As her gaze meets mine in the mirror, she gives me a sweet, satisfied smile and it hits me hard.

I tighten my hold on her. "This baby can't get here fast enough." I bury my face in the crook of her neck and shoulder. When she rests her head against mine, I trail kisses along her throat to her lips, finally giving her a gentle kiss.

She kisses me back, then straightens and pulls the elastic tie from her ponytail. "I have to fix my hair or everyone will know what we were up to." She shakes her hair free, the blonde strands flowing like pale silk over her shoulders.

When she reaches for a hairbrush on the bathroom counter, I beat her to it. "Let me." Then I proceed to brush her hair, loving how the soft strands slide through my fingers. When she groans, I smile.

She loves it when I brush her hair. I swear, it's tantamount to foreplay for her. I take my time, watching the bristles separate and smooth the strands. She closes her eyes and practically melts into me when I carefully work the brush through a few tangles. Every time she moans, my dick hardens a little more, and I have to fight the urge to abandon the brush completely and carry her off to bed.

Finally, I have to stop, or else we'll be here all day. I lay the brush down and gather her hair into a sleek ponytail, securing it with her hair band. "There. Now no one will know what we were up to."

Forcing myself to refrain from asking for a second round, I walk her out of the apartment and back into my office, where we locate her purse. She retrieves her panties, and I hold her steady as she bends over to slip them on beneath her dress. Then we're through my office door and heading toward the elevators.

We stop at Diane's desk. "I'm going to walk Beth down to the martial arts studio. I'll be back shortly."

Diane nods, smiling at us as she consults her desk calendar. "Don't forget, you have a three o'clock meeting with Frank Elliot."

Frank Elliot. I would have gladly gone the rest of my life without ever hearing that man's name again. After what he and his wife did to my brother Jake, I have no interest in talking to him.

But the man called me this morning, sounding frantic as he begged for a meeting today. Out of curiosity, I made time for him, but I can't imagine what he could possibly have to say to me. The Elliots burned their bridges with the McIntyres a decade ago, and I have no desire to reopen that old wound.

I nod at Diane, masking my distaste at hearing that man's name. "Believe me, I haven't forgotten."

I grab Beth's hand and lead her toward the elevators.

"Is everything okay?" she says, glancing up at me as we step into an available car. I push the button for the third floor.

The elevator doors close, and we begin our descent. I pull her into my arms. "Yes. Why?"

Her smooth brow furrows. "You didn't sound very happy when Diane reminded you about your three o'clock appointment."

I shrug. I don't want to expose her to my family's dirty laundry—at least not until I know what Frank Elliot wants. I don't believe he's coming here to dredge up old history regarding Jake, but I can't be sure until I talk to him. I sigh, knowing I have to tell her something. "I'm meeting with someone I never thought I'd talk to again. It's fine, just a little distasteful."

"What does he want?"

"I have no clue. It must be serious for him to swallow his pride enough to speak to me. Years ago, he made it perfectly clear he thought the McIntyre family beneath him."

"What?" she gasps, clearly affronted on our behalf. "That's ridiculous!"

"Thank you for the unambiguous vote of confidence." I smile as I kiss the top of her head, fully aware of how she's vibrating with indignation on my behalf. "It's all right, sweetheart. There's nothing you need to worry about."

* * *

When we arrive at the martial arts studio, we're greeted with a vigorous display of physical fighting skills, courtesy of my two youngest siblings. They're two peas in a pod when it comes to fighting, and they're dedicated to each other, despite their differences in temperament. Lia's a snarky little pistol, while Liam is a gentleman and probably the mellowest of all my siblings.

Like the rest of the McIntyre brothers, Liam is tall—six feet. And he's a lean, mean fighting machine. He's not nearly as brawny as Jake or as lethal as Jamie, but he's got mad skills with his hands and feet. He's won Jiu-Jitsu and kickboxing championships all around the world. When he's not traveling around the country or overseas competing, he teaches martial arts and self-defense to McIntyre Security employees and clients.

Lia, on the other hand, is dwarfed by her twin. She's tiny in comparison, although you'd be sadly mistaken if you assumed she was any less lethal than her twin. She barely tips the scale at a hundred pounds, but she can flatten a man twice her size without breaking a sweat.

There's obviously a class in session when we approach the viewing window. From our vantage point in the hallway, we can see the dozen or so women seated in a circle on the mats, and inside the circle Liam and Lia are squaring off with each other, apparently in the process of demonstrating self-defense moves to the class.

"Ooh, this will be good," Beth says, slipping her arm around my waist and leaning into me as we watch.

Lia stands in the center of the circle, looking bored out of her mind, and Liam is positioned a few feet behind her. Liam is talking, undoubtedly giving the class some instruction, but with the door closed, we can't hear what he's saying.

"What are they doing?" Beth says.

"This looks like a self-defense class, and since Liam is behind her, I imagine they're going to demonstrate how to get out of a choke hold."

Liam walks up behind Lia and grabs her, wrapping one arm around her neck, putting her in a secure choke hold. Immediately, she drops one shoulder, raising the other, and twists to dislodge his grip. With that little bit of an opening, she pivots to the side and pantomimes slamming her elbow into his stomach. Then she mimics shoving her knee into his groin, then hitting him in the face with her elbow, twice in rapid succession.

After the slow-motion demonstration, they repeat the moves in real-time, moving swiftly and decisively, and Lia doesn't bother pulling her punches.

Even in training, Lia plays hard. She's fast and vicious—that's her MO. I don't think Liam is faking it when he steps back and tries to catch his breath after they demonstrate a few basic moves.

The ladies in the class hoot and holler when Liam raises his hands in capitulation, signaling surrender to his pint-sized opponent. Then he smiles at Lia and reaches out to muss her blonde braids. Frowning, she knocks his hand away and steps out of his reach.

When Lia steps out of the circle, Beth knocks on the window and waves for Lia to join us in the hallway.

"I see Liam roped you into doing some demonstrations for his class," I say when my sister joins us, closing the door behind her.

"Yeah, well, somebody's got to show them how to do it right." Lia looks Beth over, then glances at me expectantly.

"So?" Lia says, eyeing me as she crosses her arms over her chest. "Are we going on a road trip or not?"

That's my baby sister... getting right to the point.

"Yes, we're going," Beth says, grinning.

"Jonah agreed to this little road trip?" I say.

Lia shrugs. "He doesn't know about it. He's at the recording studio working on his new album—Sam's with him. I'll tell him this evening."

I pull Beth closer, tucking her under my arm. "If you're done here, take my wife home, will you? She's tired."

Lia rolls her eyes at me, giving me a knowing smirk. "Gee, I wonder why."

"That is none of your business," I say. My baby sister is far too observant for her own good. "Just take her home so she can relax. If we're going away tomorrow, she needs to rest up."

Lia salutes me. "Whatever."

* * *

After seeing Beth and Lia off, I head back up to my office, debating whether or not to tell Jake that I'm meeting this afternoon with Frank Elliot. I can't imagine what Frank wants with McIntyre Security. I doubt his visit has anything to do with Jake, and I don't want to upset Jake needlessly, so I'll hold off on telling him anything until I know more. I'll meet with the man in private first. If it doesn't involve the man's daughter, then Jake doesn't need to know a thing. I sure as hell don't want to do anything to remind Jake of the girl who broke his heart.

Two minutes before three, there's a quiet knock on my office door. "Come in."

Diane opens the door partway and pokes her head inside. "Mr. Elliot's here to see you."

I sigh, shaking my head and wondering for the umpteenth time why I ever agreed to this meeting. If he needs help with security, he could easily go to another firm. We're certainly not the only game in town. "Thanks, Diane. Send him in."

Normally, I'd get up and greet a potential client on my feet, face to face, so we can shake hands and exchange pleasantries, but honestly, Frank Elliot doesn't deserve any such consideration. Yes, I'm holding a grudge—a big one—and I'm not necessarily proud of that fact. It's unprofessional of me. But family is family, and this man hurt my brother, badly, and I can't let that go. I'll listen to what he has to say, and then I'll kick him out of my office and tell him to look elsewhere for help.

Frank walks into my office looking haggard well beyond his sixty-two years. His suit fits him badly, practically hanging off his shoulders, and it's clear he's lost weight. His dark eyes are framed by shadows, making him appear haunted. For the longest time, he stands a few feet in front of my desk and stares at me, his expression a mix of defiance and resignation.

I figure I might as well get this over with as quickly as possible, for both our sakes. "Frank." He nods curtly. "Shane."

The man really doesn't look well. "I think you'd better sit down before you fall down. You look like shit."

The corner of his mouth quirks up at my blatant assessment, and he laughs bitterly. "Yeah, I guess I do," he says, taking one of the chairs in front of my desk. "Thanks for seeing me on such short notice."

"Why are you here, Frank?"

He scoffs, but there's no amusement in his tone. "Right to the point, eh?" He shakes his head. "Even as a youngster, you never were one to beat around the bush. I guess it's for the best."

"I have plans with my wife this evening, and you're keeping me from them. Get to the point."

He flinches at the mention of my *wife*, which is fitting considering his history with my brother. Then he nods. "I heard you got married last year. Congratulations. And I understand there's a baby on the way."

I'm not interested in making small talk with the guy, let alone wondering how he knows so much about my private life. "Just tell me what you what, Frank."

He sits up a little straighter, as if resigned to say what he's come to say. "Look, I'm sorry for what Sharon and I did to break up Annie and Jake. In hindsight—"

"Skip the apology and get to the point. Or get out of my office."

His eyes narrow, but he manages to swallow his ire. "All right. Fair enough. I'm here because I need your services."

"To do what?"

"I need to hire a bodyguard." He meets my gaze head on, defiant despite his obvious unease. "I need someone to protect my daughter."

"Annie?" Of course he means Annie. Frank and his wife only have one child. "Why does she need protection?"

"Because her husband is threatening to kill her—*ex-husband*, I should say. They divorced three months ago."

I cross my arms over my chest and take a deep breath, fairly reeling from the news. I hadn't known about the divorce. But instead of focusing on that, I focus on the rest of his revelation. The one thing I cannot abide is violence against women and children. I've seen far too much of it, and I won't tolerate it. "I'm listening."

"You recall that Annie married Ted Patterson, a junior partner in my firm?"

"Yes. Actually, I recall that Annie was engaged to marry my

brother, until you and your wife managed to talk her out of it. She married Patterson just weeks later."

At least Elliot has the decency to look abashed. "I—we're—sorry about what we did. In hindsight, it was a mistake."

"No kidding." I remember Annie. She and Jake were inseparable. He doted on her, and she worshipped the ground he walked on. If any two people were destined to be together, it was these two. At least until her parents started meddling.

I remember Annie as a quiet, mousey girl. I can picture her back in high school—brown hair, with bangs in her face, intelligent brown eyes hidden behind a pair of glasses, always a book in her arms. She was a bookworm, a nerd, one of the smart kids, while Jake was a jock through and through, big for his age and muscular even then. As a hotshot quarterback on the football team, Jake could have had any girl in that school with a snap of his fingers, but he only had eyes for the quiet little bookworm.

They got engaged the summer after they graduated. A year later, while Annie was a freshman in college, Jake was working at a hardware store, trying to figure out what he wanted to do with his life. A week before the wedding was scheduled to take place, she broke their engagement, effectively breaking his heart. Shortly after, she married Patterson, one of her father's employees. At the ripe old age of twenty, my brother found himself jilted. She wrecked him, and he's been pining for her ever since.

I want to tell Frank Elliot to get the hell out of my office. I want to kick his ass to the curb and tell him never to return. But

I can't. I keep picturing that quiet little girl from high school. She wouldn't have been able to protect herself from a fly, let alone an abusive husband. The thought curdles my stomach.

"Just give me the facts," I say, reaching for the small digital recorder on my desk. "I'm going to record our conversation."

Elliot nods eagerly, suddenly looking more relaxed. "Yes, I'll tell you anything you want to know. Just please, promise me you'll protect my daughter." Elliot meets my gaze head on. "And my grandson."

"I'd heard there was a child."

Frank nods. "Yes. Aiden is five, hardly more than a baby." The man swallows hard. "Annie isn't the only one Patterson abused. Aiden has bruises too."

Too.

Shit.

There's no way in hell I can keep this from Jake. "All right, Frank. Start talking, from the beginning. Tell me everything."

4

Beth

When Lia and I arrive back at the penthouse, Cooper's already home from the shooting range where he supervises weapons assessment and training for company personnel. We find him in the kitchen mixing up a marinade for chicken breasts. The air is redolent with rosemary and garlic, making my stomach growl. Cooper has mad skills in the kitchen, and luckily for all of us, he loves to cook.

"Damn, that smells good," Lia says, hopping up onto a barstool at the kitchen counter. "Why, yes, Cooper!" she says, mimicking Cooper's gruff, baritone voice. "Jonah and I *are* free for dinner tonight. Thanks for asking."

Cooper glances back over his shoulder at Lia and raises an eyebrow. "Wow, that was subtle. Lia, would you and Jonah like to join us for dinner tonight?"

"Yes, as a matter of fact, we would. I'm tired of take-out. I want a home-cooked meal."

"You could learn to cook," Cooper says, turning back to his culinary work.

Lia rolls her eyes. "You're funny."

I walk over to my adopted father, who looks very handsome with an apron draped over his well-worn blue jeans and T-shirt, and put an arm around his waist, leaning in to kiss the side of his arm. "How was your day?"

"Good," he says, pouring the marinade over the chicken breasts. "How was yours?"

"Great. Lia and I are making plans to go away for the weekend. To Jake's cabin."

Cooper looks skeptical. "Just the two of you?"

"The guys are coming, too," Lia says, reaching for a bowl of fresh strawberries. She bites into a berry and chews. "Princess has cabin fever—who can blame her? We could all use a change of scenery."

Cooper still doesn't look convinced. "And Shane agreed to this?"

I laugh, bumping him with my hip. "Yes, he did. Don't sound so surprised."

Cooper washes his hands and dries them on a paper towel, then he gives me his paternal face. "Honey, I don't think you should go out of town so close to your due date."

I lay my hands on my belly. "It's not *that* close. I still have another six weeks."

"Besides, we're not going far," Lia says, reaching for another strawberry. "It's only two hours away. If something happens, we'll hoof it back home in plenty of time."

Cooper shakes his head, obviously not impressed with Lia's argument. But before he can respond, the elevator chimes, and a moment later, Jonah and Sam walk into the penthouse.

"Something sure smells good," Jonah says, as he heads straight for Lia.

"That's our dinner you're smelling," Lia says, pulling Jonah close for a kiss. "We've been invited to stay for dinner. Oh, and by the way, we're going out of town tomorrow—just for one night. 'Kay?"

Jonah shrugs as he cups the back of her neck and leans in for a second kiss. "Hey, I go where you go."

Sam heads over to Cooper and me, tossing me a quick smile. "Hey, princess," he says, giving me a fist bump. Then he stops directly in front of Cooper, grabs him by the apron, and pulls him close for a kiss. "Hi, babe. How was your day?"

"It was good," Cooper says. "How about yours?"

"Oh, my God!" Lia says to Cooper. "Are you blushing?"

Cooper gives her a flat stare. "No, I am not. And you'd better stop that right now if you want to stay for dinner. It's not too late to uninvite you, young lady."

Lia hops off her barstool and drags Jonah by the hand to the seating area by the hearth. "I'm not saying another word."

While Cooper sees to dinner, Sam and I join Lia and Jonah on the sofas. Positioned strategically in front of a towering stone hearth, two sofas and two armchairs surround a huge coffee table. Sam and I crash on one of the long sofas. I kick off my sandals and tuck my feet up under me, and Sam stretches out beside me.

"So, where are we going?" Jonah says, pulling Lia onto his lap.

"To Jake's cabin," she says. "It's our last wild fling before the baby comes."

Sam laughs. "You mean my godson, don't you? Lucas *Samuel*."

Lia rolls her eyes at me. "Oh, for God's sake, why did you name your baby after Sam? He's never going to let us forget it."

I laugh as I reach over to pat Sam's back. "Oh, maybe because he saved Luke's life. And mine." I lean over and kiss his cheek. "He's my hero."

Lia groans. "Oh, please stop. Sam's head is big enough already."

The elevator pings, announcing a new arrival, and we all turn our heads as Shane walks through the foyer door. I heave my cumbersome body up off the sofa and rush to meet him. "You're home early!"

He pulls me close for a kiss. "I thought I'd come home so we can pack for our trip."

Cooper stalks out of the kitchen, slinging a hand towel over his shoulder as he parks himself in front of Shane. "I can't believe you agreed to let her go out of town right now. Are you crazy?"

"Most likely, yes," Shane replies, biting back a grin as he heads for the refrigerator to grab a beer. "Don't blame me. I succumbed against my better judgement during a fit of passion."

Cooper frowns at Shane. "What if she goes into labor early?"

Shane eyes me stoically as he answers Cooper. "We'll leave the helicopter on standby all weekend in case we need an emergency evac."

"I don't think this is one bit funny," Cooper says, reluctantly accepting the cold bottle of beer Shane offers him. "She's weeks from her due date. I hardly think this is the time to go out of town."

Shane claps his hand on Cooper's shoulder, giving it a squeeze. "My wife doesn't ask me for much. I think I can give her this."

Cooper shakes his head. "You are so pussy-whipped, my friend."

"You just wait," Shane says, wagging his finger at Cooper as he glances across the room at Sam, who's watching their exchange with great interest. "Your time will come, *my friend*. And frankly, I'm going to enjoy watching you squirm."

* * *

I follow Shane to our private suite to watch him change out of his suit and into something casual. Standing just inside the closet, leaning against the door jamb, I enjoy one of my favorite pastimes—watching my husband undress. Partly it's because he has a body that never fails to make me weak in the knees. But I love simply watching him strip out of his CEO attire. In his suit and tie, he makes my pulse race. But in jeans and a T-shirt, he instantly becomes a big, sometimes scruffy teddy bear, and I just want to wrap myself around him.

He's not looking at me, but he's perfectly aware that I'm watching him undress. It's not exactly a strip-tease, but personally I find it just as mesmerizing. After tossing his shirt in the hamper, he steps out of his slacks, flashing me his taut, muscular thighs and his sexy, black boxer briefs.

My hungry gaze follows him as he walks across the closet to grab a pair of jeans and a T-shirt.

I can't believe my good fortune and where my life has taken me. I think back to the person I was before I met Shane, just a shell of who I am today. It seems like a lifetime ago that I lived quite happily in a townhouse in Hyde Park with my best friend, Gabrielle. My life was simple. I spent my days working as a reference librarian at the medical school library, and I came home every evening to an empty house and ate dinner alone as Gabrielle, a sous chef, worked the coveted evening shift at Renaldo's. I was afraid of my own shadow back then, afraid of meeting new people, especially afraid of men. I was more or less a hostage of my own fear and anxiety.

My life changed almost overnight when I met Shane at Clancy's Bookshop. I smile now at the memory. I can almost hear his rough, sexy voice, when he said, "Do you like what you're reading?" Of course, he had to catch me reading an anthology of spanking stories. I was so mortified, I wanted to crawl in a hole and die. But, he didn't let me.

He introduced himself and asked for my name, setting off all kinds of warning bells in my head. I tried to retreat back into my quiet, safe world and hide, but he didn't let me run. He gave me the courage to stay, to *try*, and he made everything all right. He always makes everything all right.

"Beth?"

I shake myself out of my reverie and glance at my husband, who's in the process of zipping up his jeans. "Hmm?"

"Is everything okay, sweetheart?"

I nod, blushing. "Fine. I was just thinking about the night we met."

Dressed only in jeans, he approaches, towering over me, and my heart races. My God, he's everything to me now, and that frightens me sometimes. The thought of losing him sends me to a very dark place, and suddenly, old memories come crashing back. I remember that damp, musty cellar, ice cold and pitch black. I remember lying naked on the ground, shivering uncontrollably, my arms bound behind me. I was so terrified I could barely breathe. And, my God, that monster! Rationally, I know Howard Kline is dead. Shane killed him, *for me*. But what if he hadn't? The thought of Kline coming after me *now*—after our *baby*—horrifies me.

My breath catches in my throat, and I choke on a sob.

"Hey, what's wrong?" He wipes the trail of tears from my cheeks and peers down at me, searching my face for answers.

I close my eyes and shake my head, trying to chase away the chilling remnants of old memories. *Kline is dead. He's dead! There's nothing to be afraid of.* "I'm sorry. It's nothing."

"It's not *nothing*, Beth," he says, drawing me close. "You're shaking. Come here." He leads me across the room and pulls me down beside him on the sofa. Then he grabs a tissue from the box on the coffee table and hands it to me. "Talk to me, sweetheart. What just happened?"

"It's nothing, honestly." I laugh shakily and take a deep breath. "It's these darn pregnancy hormones."

He narrows his gaze. "You were on the verge of having a panic attack. Why?"

I lean into him, hiding my face. "I was thinking about Howard Kline. And the baby." Just putting those two names together in a single thought horrifies me.

"Oh, sweetheart." Shane tightens his arms around me, and I close my eyes when I feel his lips in my hair. "Kline's gone. He can't hurt you anymore. I won't let *anyone* hurt you or our child, I promise."

We sit there together, holding each other, until a quiet knock on the door brings us back to the present.

"Yes?" Shane calls.

Cooper's voice comes loud and clear through the closed

door. "Dinner's ready. Are you guys coming?"

"We'll be out in a few minutes," Shane says.

"Sure. Take your time."

Shane kisses my forehead. "Everything's okay, right?" he says. "We're okay. The baby's okay. There's nothing to be afraid of."

I nod, wishing it were that easy. I take a deep breath and force myself to ignore the low hum of anxiety coursing through me. "Right. Everything's okay."

* * *

Dinner is a joyous affair, surrounded by good friends. Not just Cooper and Sam, but Lia and Jonah as well. These people are part of my family now, and I love them all dearly.

The meal is delicious—the chicken breasts are flavorful and tender, and Cooper made my favorite sides. Everyone's relaxed and enjoying a bottle of white wine, except for me. I stick to water. For dessert, Cooper brings out a hot berry cobbler, which he serves with scoops of vanilla ice cream.

Lia and Shane plan our itinerary for tomorrow's little excursion. We'll meet here in the penthouse at ten o'clock. We should hit Harbor Springs by noon, where we'll have lunch at the diner, and then we'll walk around the little downtown and maybe visit the marina and look at the boats. That evening, we'll go to Lucky's Tavern for dinner and see Hal. Jonah will bring his guitar and do a few live sets at the tavern.

Cooper frowns throughout our impromptu planning session, clearly unhappy with our plans, but he refrains from saying anything more. He made his concerns known to Shane already, and he's said his piece.

Sam seems rather subdued, and I wonder if he's remembering the horrible shooting that took place in the woods near Jake's cabin when he and Cooper visited there a few months ago. The shooting that nearly took Cooper's life. If Sam hadn't been there to take care of Cooper and take out the shooter, Cooper would have bled out.

"Are you okay?" I ask Sam, reaching over to touch his arm.

He gives me a sad smile. "Sure. Fine."

I slide my hand down to his and give it a squeeze.

* * *

After dinner, Lia and Jonah head down to their own apartment to pack and relax for the rest of the evening.

Sam and I do the dishes, while Shane disappears into his home office to make some work calls.

"Where's Cooper?" I ask Sam, as I hand him a plate to put in the dishwasher.

He shrugs. "Probably in our room."

"He's not happy about the trip."

"No, he's not. Frankly, Beth, I'm not happy about it either. You shouldn't be leaving town right now."

Sam leans against the kitchen counter, crossing his arms over his chest. "I'm surprised Shane agreed to this."

"I asked him to. Actually, I sort of begged him. This will probably be our last chance to get away for a while before the baby comes."

Sam frowns. "That man can't say no to you, but that doesn't mean this is a good idea."

Guilt is weighing me down, and I certainly can't argue with Cooper's and Sam's concerns. Maybe this trip is a mistake. Maybe we should cancel our plans, stay home and play it safe. I can't help thinking I'm taking unfair advantage of Shane by asking for this.

"Just promise me you'll be careful," Sam says. "Shane and Lia will be with you, so you'll be in good hands. But still, I can't help worrying about you. As I'm your bodyguard, it's in my job description."

5

Beth

After we finish the dishes, Sam excuses himself to go in search of Cooper. As I watch him head down the hallway toward the suite he shares with Cooper, I can't help wondering what those two are getting up to in the privacy of their own room. I'm so happy for them both—happy that they found each other, happy that Cooper feels able to open himself up to Sam and to the rest of us. I love these two men dearly—they're every bit as much my family as the one I was born into.

Shane is still holed up in his office, probably making plans to clear the way for him to be out of town this weekend. As the boss, he's always on call and constantly fielding client calls and text messages from operatives in the field.

With nothing else to do, I head to our suite and begin packing an overnight bag for the two of us. We won't need to bring much—just some PJs, a fresh change of clothes for Sunday, and our toiletries. I leave the oversized duffle bag on the bench at the foot of our bed in case Shane wants to add anything.

My thoughts are interrupted by a brisk knock at the door. "Come in."

The door opens, and Cooper's standing there with a grin on his face. "Special delivery," he says, nodding to the nursery, which is right next to our room. "A package just arrived for you."

I follow him eagerly into the nursery, smiling when I see Sam using a wickedly sharp pocket knife to cut the tape sealing the massive box lying on the floor. On the front of the box is a picture of the gorgeous mahogany baby crib we ordered from an online boutique. "The crib!"

Cooper stands aside, ushering me into the room. Sam has the box open now, and he's pulling pieces of the crib out, along with what looks like a complicated installation diagram.

"You want us to put it together for you?" Cooper asks as he helps Sam haul more heavy pieces of wood out of the box.

"Would you mind?" I say.

The nursery is pretty much ready for the baby's arrival. I have a matching mahogany changing table already in place, along with a super cozy, padded rocking chair and matching footstool. The walls have been painted a pale blue with white trim, and there's a plush blue rug on the gleaming wood floors. The closet is filled with outfits for a newborn baby boy, and the changing table is stocked with diapers, sleepers, socks, knit caps, and other baby paraphernalia. A small bookcase holds a selection of baby books, and a trio of darling teddy bear prints decorates the wall above.

"You sit down and relax," Cooper tells me, pointing at the rocking chair.

I take a seat and watch as Cooper and Sam lay out all of the crib pieces and the hardware. Apparently, Sam is in charge of reading off the instructions, while Cooper puts the pieces together.

"Which bolt do I use here?" Cooper says, staring at the wide array of options.

"That one," Sam says, pointing. "The big one with the flat head."

"Which one? This one?"

"No, the other one. The one with the flat head, to the left of that one."

"This one?"

"Yeah, that one. You should have eight of those."

"You guys should sell tickets," says a baritone voice coming from the doorway. I look back to see Jake leaning against the door jamb, a highly amused expression on his face.

"Hi, Jake!" I say, waving my brother-in-law into the room. "The crib arrived today."

"Yes, I can see that." He grins at the guys. "You two need some help with that?"

"No," Cooper grumbles as he uses a wrench to tighten a bolt. "We're doing just fine, thank you."

"Hey, what am I missing?" Shane says, brushing past his brother as he enters the nursery. He studies the partially-completed crib. "Do you guys need some help?"

"No!" Cooper says. "Why does everyone keep asking that?"

"Take it easy," Shane says, lifting his hand in a peace offering. "It just looks a little complicated, that's all."

Sam rises to his feet, offering Cooper a hand. The guys lift two sides of the crib and position them. "Here, hold this," Sam says to Shane, "while we attach it to the back."

An overwhelming sense of contentment fills me as I watch the guys, all four of them now, assembling my baby's crib. I rub my belly, feeling grateful that Lucas will be born into a big, loving family. He'll be surrounded by aunts and uncles and grandparents who will love him unconditionally. When I was growing up, it was just me and my mom. My brother, Tyler, was grown and out of the house before I was old enough to walk. My family is really close, but there are just the three of us. Being part of a large, extended family is such a joy.

As if summoned by my thoughts, Lucas performs a somersault in my womb, sending a ripple through my abdomen and making me smile. My baby is strong and healthy, growing just as he should, and in little over a month, he will join our family.

I watch Shane as he holds one side of the crib upright so

Cooper can attach it to the back panel. The four men, all dear to me, work together to attach the remaining sections. When they're done, they position the crib against the wall and stand back to admire their handiwork.

"How does that look?" Shane asks me. "Do you like it?"

"I love it. Thank you, guys."

Cooper leans down to kiss the top of my head. "You're welcome, honey."

The room is perfect now, everything in place and ready for Lucas. The baby rolls again, this time managing to kick my bladder. I let out a breathy "oof!" as I press my hand to my abdomen.

"Are you okay?" Shane says, eyeing me quizzically.

"I'm fine. Your son just kicked my bladder."

Shane presses his hand against my bump. "Settle down in there, pal," he says, drawing amused glances from the rest of the guys. "Take it easy on your mama."

Jake grins as he shakes his head at Shane. "Watching you playing daddy is going to be quite entertaining."

* * *

After the crib construction project is completed, the guys celebrate with a round of beers. And while the guys entertain themselves at the bar, I curl up on the sofa with a well-worn copy of *What to Expect When You're Expecting* and a blanket. As the evening wears on, my energy wanes, and I find myself yawning. When I read the same paragraph three times and still can't make any sense of it, I realize it's time for me to call it a night. With a sigh, I lean my head back and close my eyes, just for a few minutes.

The next thing I know, Shane is sitting on the coffee table in front of me, taking the book from me and setting it aside. "Time for bed," he says, smiling at me. "If we're going to the cabin tomorrow, you need a good night's sleep tonight."

He stands and pulls me to my feet. When I look toward the bar, I realize that Jake is gone and someone has turned down all the lights. It looks like the impromptu party is over.

"Good night, guys," Shane calls to Cooper and Sam, who are cleaning up at the bar.

On the way to our suite, I pull Shane into the nursery and flip on the light. "Isn't it perfect?" I pick up a newborn sleeper that's been laid out on the changing table and hold it up, amazed at its tiny size. "Can you believe he'll fit in this?"

Shane wraps his arms around me from behind, his hands splayed out over my belly. "I can't wait for our son to be born. I want to watch you hold him, rock him." He nuzzles my neck, and then his voice drops, becoming huskier. "I want to watch you nurse him."

When I melt into his embrace, he kisses my temple, and then he swings me up into his arms. "Come on. You're exhausted."

He carries me the few yards to our room and sets me on my feet in front of the bathroom door. "Get ready for bed. I'll join you in a few minutes."

As I brush my teeth, I hear echoes of Cooper's and Sam's misgivings about the trip, and I wonder if I'm making a big mistake. Pregnant women travel all the time, don't they? I'm not asking to do something unreasonable or risky, am I?

Automatically my hands go to my belly, and I'm hoping to feel Lucas stir. It comforts me to feel him moving inside me. Sure enough, he humors me with a kick, making me smile.

Shane joins me in the bathroom and reaches for his toothbrush. I leave to get undressed. To surprise him, I put on a pale pink, baby doll silk nightie and matching panties—one of his favorites. By the time I come out of the dressing room, he's already in bed, lying shirtless, looking relaxed with one arm tucked behind his head.

When he sees me, his eyes widen appreciatively, giving me more than a hint of what he thinks of my choice of nightwear. "You're asking for trouble, you know that, right?" he says, grinning at me.

I smile back, hoping he's right. I feel like getting in a bit of trouble right now. "What did you have in mind?"

"Come here, and I'll show you," he says, pulling me onto the bed.

6

Beth

Shane draws me across his lap so that I'm straddling his hips. Even though the bedding is between us, I can easily feel his erection swelling beneath me. His warm hands slide up beneath my nightgown and stroke over my belly. At first, I tense, feeling self-conscious about my body, but when he pushes my nightie up, exposing the taut, rounded shape of me to his heated gaze, the look in his eyes is all the reassurance I need.

That is desire on his face, plain and simple. He finds my body attractive, even heavily pregnant.

Despite the arousal coursing through me, lingering doubts and worries crowd their way into my brain, pushing away thoughts of sex. "Is this trip a mistake?"

"You are so beautiful," he says as he frames my belly with his big hands. He leans forward and kisses my baby bump.

I laugh, laying my hands on his. No matter what he says, I can't help feeling self-conscious about my body, how it has changed over the pregnancy. I'm happy that my breasts are larger, but not so happy about the other changes, including a greatly expanded waistline, a spidery network of stretch marks on my abdomen, and swollen ankles and feet. "I'm as big as a whale. And you didn't answer my question."

He gazes up at me, serious now. "I wouldn't call it a mistake, exactly, but there is some risk involved, yes. I would categorize it as a calculated risk."

"Cooper and Sam think it's a mistake."

Shane nods. "I know. Cooper's already given me an earful on the subject. Yes, it's possible you could go into labor early, but not likely. And we're not going far. If anything happens, I can have you back in Chicago pretty quickly."

He lies back on his pillow, his hands sliding down to gently caress my thighs. "Sweetheart, if I had my way, I'd keep you locked up in the penthouse twenty-four-seven. But I realize that's not reasonable. I've got to give you room to breathe, to have some fun. I figure this overnight trip is a reasonable risk. Plus, I'll be by your side the entire time. At the first sign of trouble, I'll whisk you back here so fast your head will spin."

I want to go. I want to get some fresh air and have a change of scenery. The drive to Harbor Springs is idyllic, mile after mile of countryside, pastures, and horses, with the occasional glimpse of Lake Michigan. And yet, I can't shake these misgivings.

I reach for his hands and link our fingers together. "I would never do anything to endanger our baby."

"I know that, honey." He squeezes my hands. "Don't worry. I'll take care of everything. I promise."

He releases my hands and slides a finger inside the gusset of my panties to tease my clitoris, essentially putting an end to the conversation. I'm already wet and swollen. His touch sends a shock of pleasure through me, making me arch my back and gasp. Positioning the pad of this thumb right over the slippery knot of nerves, he starts rubbing lazy, determined circles.

I immediately begin squirming and let out a breathy moan, followed by his name. "Shane."

"Just relax and let me make you feel good."

I brace my hands on his chest and close my eyes, over-whelmed by the rush of pleasure surging through me. He knows my body so well. He knows exactly how to drive me crazy and how to make me come hard. "I want you inside me."

He smiles. "I want that, too, but be patient. I want to watch you come first."

I feel so vulnerable like this. As the pleasure mounts, and my moans escalate into whimpers, I close my eyes, trying to hide from his watchful gaze.

"Open your eyes, sweetheart, and look at me."

When I do, his beautiful blue eyes lock onto mine, holding me fixed. He works my clit, faster and faster, ratcheting up the exquisite pleasure to the point I'm panting and squirming on him. My thigh muscles tighten, and I know I'm close. "Shane."

He watches me closely, this thumb doing diabolical things to my clitoris. I want to close my eyes and hide, but I can't look away from his gaze. There's so much heat there, so much need. He's just as desperate for me as I am for him. The thought sends me over the edge, and I fall forward, crying out loudly as I'm inundated with waves of intense pleasure. The sensations ripple through me, and I'm practically panting when he leans forward and locks his lips on mine, drinking in my cries.

Even through the sheet, I can feel the heat and the strength of his erection. He helps me slip off my panties and pulls my nightgown over my head and tosses it to the foot of the bed, exposing every inch of me. He shoves the bedding aside, uncovering his thick erection, and he guides me over him so that the tip of his length is poised right at my opening. He lifts his hips, nudging the head of his cock inside me, making us both gasp with pleasure. Even though I'm already soft and wet, the size of him still makes me catch my breath.

"Doing okay?" he grates out through gritted teeth.

I know he's trying to hold back, to keep himself from shoving inside me too quickly. I let gravity do the work as my body sinks onto him, driving him deeper inside me. This late in my pregnancy, missionary position is out of the question. It's much easier if I'm on top, like this, or if he takes me from behind. But he prefers to be able to see my face when we're together, so he can gauge my response and my frame of mind.

"Yes, fine," I gasp, as I sink down another inch. I can feel my body opening for him.

His thumb returns, circling my clitoris, distracting me from the stretch of him inside me, from the aching fullness.

I start to move then, and he helps me by gripping my hips and raising and lowering me on his erection. I'm so wet that he thrusts easily now, lifting his hips to meet my downward movements.

I love to watch his face, so beautifully expressive. It's all there to see, the tension, the pleasure, his need to come, which is tempered by his restraint. He's always so careful with me, sometimes at the expense of his own pleasure.

"Behind me," I say, my voice barely audible as I roll off him and onto my hands and knees.

"Jesus, Beth," he says, his voice rough with need as he surges onto his knees behind me. He slams back inside me, harder than he intended to I'm sure, sending me face down onto my pillow. "Shit, I'm sorry, sweetheart."

He starts to pull out, and I reach back with one hand to grasp his thigh, holding him to me. "Don't stop."

"Beth—"

"I'm fine." I push back against him, driving his erection deep, and my body clamps down on him like a fist.

A rough groan escapes him as he clutches my hips. "I don't want to hurt you."

But his need finally supersedes his desire to be gentle, and he rams into me, thrusting hard and deep. Several more thrusts follow in quick succession, and the sounds coming from him are low and guttural.

His powerful thrusts and obvious pleasure send me over the edge, making my body tense and shake as I come once more. I press my face into my pillow to muffle my cries. Shane follows right behind me, shouting hoarsely as he bucks into me, filling my body with spurt after spurt of liquid heat.

His movements slow as his orgasm wanes, until he finally slides out of me. He rolls me onto my side and spoons with me, wrapping his arm around me, nestled just below my big belly.

"Jesus, are you okay, sweetheart?" he says, his breath coming hard and fast. He cups his hand gently over my sex.

I'm so boneless and replete now from *two* mind-shattering climaxes that I can barely speak. "Mm."

He gives me a shaky laugh. "Is that a *yes?*"

"Yes."

"I'm sorry. I shouldn't have been so rough."

The mattress shifts as he rises from the bed. "I'll be right back." A few minutes later, he returns with a warm, wet washcloth.

My dear, sweet, chivalrous husband. When he's done cleaning me up, I roll onto my side and snuggle with my pillow, feeling deliriously happy and so physically satisfied. I can still feel the echoes of pleasure moving through me. "Thank you."

"You don't need to thank me."

He returns to the bathroom to clean himself up, and then he climbs into bed and spoons with me. "Sweet dreams," he murmurs into my hair, and then he kisses the back of my head.

I feel a tender twinge deep inside me, and it makes me smile. I like it when he lets himself go like that. He always feels guilty afterward, but I love feeling his incredible strength and raw passion.

* * *

Sometime in the night I awake, shaking and cold. That makes no sense. I'm never cold when I'm in bed with Shane. He's like my very own electric blanket, his body radiating heat all night long and keeping me toasty warm. I roll onto my back to discover that the bed's empty.

"Shane?"

But there's no reply.

I get up and head for the door, thinking he might have gone to his home office just down the hall, but when I open the bedroom door, I suddenly find myself on the first floor of the medical library where I once worked.

No!

It's the same nightmare scenario that has terrorized me for years. Alone in the library, with that monster stalking me in the darkness, his dogged footsteps and his heavy breathing growing louder and louder as he comes closer. And his voice—it sounds like crushed gravel. Just the thought of it makes me shake uncontrollably.

"It's just a dream," I tell myself. "Wake up!"

I close my eyes, squeezing them hard, hoping to wake myself from this nightmare before it gets worse. But when I open them again, I'm still in the library, still in the dark.

I look down at my naked body, my breasts swollen and heavy, and my belly protruding. My hands go immediately to my abdomen, covering it protectively. Shivering, I search desperately for something to wear. Anything to keep me from feeling so horribly exposed.

And then I hear the footsteps—the same heavy, dogged footsteps that have haunted me since I was just a child. "No!"

I run for the bookshelves, row after row of towering shelves, hoping to hide in the dark spaces between them. I know this library like the back of my hand. I can run. I can hide.

As I run deeper into the shadows, his heavy footsteps and ragged breaths grow louder. No matter how fast I run, it seems like he's always just a few steps behind, keeping pace with me.

"Beth!"

Oh, my God! "Shane!" I cry.

"Where are you?"

"In the shelves! Hurry!"

Please find me, please find me, before it's too late. Before he gets us. Us. This time it's not just me who's running.

"Beth? Where are you, honey?"

Shane's voice seems farther away now, so distant, but the footsteps and the heavy breaths draw closer.

"Shane! I'm here. Please hurry!"

"Beth? Where are you?"

Even farther away... he's heading in the wrong direction.

No! I suck in a deep breath and scream his name as loud as I can.
"Shane!"

Strong fingers grip my shoulders, crushing and bruising. "You think you can escape me?" That awful, horrible voice. It can't be Kline, though. He's dead!

The monster's hands reach around me, embracing my pregnant belly, sending chills down my spine. "What do we have here?" the monster says, and then he laughs.

Sobbing, I scream. "Shane!"

"Beth, damn it, wake up!"

I shoot up into a sitting position, my arms flailing madly as I fight him off.

Shane catches my hands, holding them still. "Honey, it's okay. You're safe."

I stare at him as my heart beats frantically, and I start wheezing.

Shane reaches into the top drawer of my nightstand and pulls out my rescue inhaler, holding it to my mouth. I latch onto the device, and he administers the medication.

"It's all right," he says, his voice low and soothing. "Just relax and breathe."

As the fear and panic begin to recede, I lie back on the bed, trying to steady my breath. It's been so long since I've had a panic attack bad enough to trigger my asthma, and so long since I dreamed about Howard Kline. I thought that was behind me, but apparently I was wrong. Even after his death, that monster continues to haunt me.

I close my eyes in an attempt to stem the hot tears streaming down my temples. My throat is so tight I can barely speak. "I'm sorry."

"Shh," he croons, wiping my face with a tissue. "You have nothing to apologize for." He climbs back into bed. "Do you want to talk about it?"

A long time passes before I can bring myself to answer him. "It was the same dream, in the library at night. Kline was there. Only this time, you were there, too, calling for me, searching for me. I called to you, over and over, but you couldn't find me. You kept moving farther and farther away. And then Kline grabbed me. He touched me." I shudder. Then my hands go to my belly, covering it protectively.

Shane's gaze locks with mine in the haze of the early morning light. "I will always find you, Beth. I will always come for you."

He brushes my sweat-dampened hair back with a hand that seems less than steady. "Go back to sleep, sweetheart. I won't leave your side until you're ready to get up."

I shift my position to ease the dull ache in my lower back. Then I let out a long, heavy sigh and close my eyes, drawing Shane's arm beneath my breasts and holding him tight.

7

Shane

I awaken again after a couple fitful hours of sleep and realize that sleep is pointless for me now. I can still hear her terrified cries, her rasping breath. She's come so far since I met her, but every once in a while the nightmare returns, and it breaks my heart to see her hurting like that. If I could kill that bastard Kline again, I would. Gladly.

I gravitate toward her soft, warm body, like a moth to the flame. Cooper's right—I am pussy-whipped. But you won't hear any complaints about it from me.

I resist the urge to skim my hand down her side to palm her

sweet ass as I don't want to risk waking her this early. She needs all the sleep she can get, especially after that nightmare.

I'm often up and out of bed long before Beth, but this morning I'm loathe to leave her side. I promised I'd stay with her until she woke up, and I'm sure as hell going to keep my word. As I'm a workaholic, though, I have to do something productive while I wait. I slip quietly from bed, pull on a pair of shorts to prevent accidently flashing Cooper—another early riser—then head to my office down the hall to grab my laptop.

I settle back into bed and get to work. One of my priorities is to e-mail Jake to let him know there's a client meeting scheduled for Monday that he needs to attend. I'm not going to tell him that the meeting is about Annie. Not yet. I don't want him dwelling on it all weekend.

I use this quiet time to catch up on reading field reports and e-mails, doing as little typing as possible so I don't wake Beth. An hour later, she begins to stir.

I set my laptop aside and watch her wake up. Every movement she makes, every sound, every breath is sensuous. She stretches first, still half asleep, and her accompanying soft sounds make me hard. She instinctively turns to face me, her arm stretching out over my hips, and she shifts closer. Then her eyes open slowly, and she frowns at the bright morning sunlight streaming into the room.

"Good morning," I murmur, leaning down to kiss the top of her tousled head.

Not quite fully awake, she mumbles something unintelligible and presses her face into my hip, which makes me smile.

My wife is definitely not a morning person. I can't wait to see how she handles having a newborn baby, who will presumably have an erratic sleep pattern and will be waking us up at all hours. I have a feeling I'll be handling most of the late night and early morning feedings. Unlike my wife, I don't require a lot of shut-eye. In the military, I had no choice but to learn to function on just a few hours sleep.

Beth arches her back and stretches, making a pained whimper.

"What's wrong?" I ask her.

"My back hurts."

"I was too rough with you last night. I'm sorry."

She smiles. "I'm not. It was worth it."

She gasps as she presses her hands to her abdomen, her eyes widening.

"What?" I say, instantly going on red alert.

"I think I just felt a contraction."

I lay my hand on her belly and frown. She's had Braxton Hicks contractions before, on and off, so they're nothing new. The first couple times she had them, I insisted she go to the hospital to get checked out, but each time they sent us home telling us to relax. "Do you think they're Braxton Hicks?"

She nods. "I'm sure they are. It's nothing to worry about. They're not very strong."

"We definitely overdid it last night," I say, wanting to kick myself. I clearly remember the firm grip I had on her hips as I plowed into her. I wouldn't be surprised if she has some bruises this morning.

She sits up gingerly, and the sheet slips down, baring her breasts and their lush, pink nipples. *Damn.* My dick hardens instantly.

"Last night was amazing," she says with a sigh. "A little back-ache is a small price to pay." She grimaces as she swings her feet around to the floor. "I'd better get in the shower."

"Wait." I catch her arm. "Are you sure you're all right? If you want to stay home...." I let my words trail off, not wanting to in-fluence her response, but wanting to give her an easy out if she feels like staying home.

"I'm okay." She stands, gloriously nude, and arches her back cautiously, as if testing it. "I'm just a bit sore. It'll pass."

The sight of her standing there naked, with all her glorious new curves on display, and her blonde hair mussed from sex and sleep, makes my pulse speed up. I'd love nothing more than to coax her back into bed. But that's obviously out of the question now.

I shut down my laptop and throw back the covers. "I'll join you in the shower."

She grins at the sight of my inevitable morning erection. "It looks like you need a cold shower."

I fist my cock and give her a rueful grin. "I doubt even a cold shower will help with this."

She surprises me by climbing back onto the bed, crawling toward me on her hands and knees with a wicked gleam in her eye. "Maybe I can help you with that."

Before I can protest, she pushes my hand aside and wraps her slender fingers around my erection. She bends down to kiss the tip, her tongue swiping a drop of pre-come.

"Sweetheart, no," I say with a low groan. "You don't have to—"

"Of course I don't *have* to. I *want* to."

I fall back onto the mattress, groaning as I reach out to stroke her hair while she reduces me to an incoherent mess.

* * *

After my wife makes me see stars and shout to the rafters—something else for Cooper and Sam to rib me about—we take a joint shower, where I return the favor, kneeling before her beneath the spray of hot water, gently licking and sucking on her until her legs are shaking and she comes with a breathy, keening cry.

Seeing to my wife's needs is my greatest pleasure on Earth. Tasting her, seeing the evidence of what I do to her, hearing her soft whimpers and breathy cries—those are my rewards. As her orgasm reverberates through her, she pulls me up and leans into me, our bodies plastered together beneath the hot water. Her lips tremble as they cling to mine.

While she stands boneless in the water, I grab her shampoo and squirt some into my hands, creating a lather so I can wash her hair. I love the feel of those long, wet strands in my hands.

We take turns washing each other, exploring and teasing each other's bodies, and eventually rinsing off.

Finally, we dry ourselves off and dress, then head to the kitchen in search of breakfast.

Sam is seated at the breakfast counter plowing through a mound of pancakes. Wearing only a pair of shorts, he looks like he just rolled out of bed, his red hair mussed and his eyes at half-mast.

Cooper is mixing eggs in a glass bowl. "Good morning, sleepyheads," he says to us, nodding toward the barstools. "Have a seat. Coffee, eggs, and sausage coming right up."

Beth hops up on the barstool next to Sam and elbows him in the side. "Good morning, studmuffin," she says, grinning at him.

He practically chokes on a mouthful of food as he reaches for a glass of orange juice. He elbows her back gently. "Good morning, princess. Did you sleep well?"

She blushes. "Yes."

"I'll bet you did. We heard you all the way down the hall."

"You did not!" she cries, swatting at him.

He raises his brow at her. "Did so."

Cooper stares Sam down. "Don't embarrass her."

I head for the Keurig machine to make Beth a cup of her favorite French Vanilla decaf. While her cup is brewing, I watch Cooper out of the corner of my eye as he observes the interaction between Beth and Sam.

To be honest, when Cooper first approached me with the

idea of Sam coming to live here in the penthouse with him—*with us*—I wasn't sure. I didn't have any particular objections, but I worried that adding a new person on a permanent basis would change the dynamics of our living arrangement. But then again, adding Beth to our living arrangement had changed things, too, for the better. Cooper had someone to dote on finally, which satisfied his need to nurture. And since he'd become Beth's adopted father, more or less, I worried that Beth might feel slighted if Sam moved in with us and Cooper's attention was diverted from her to his lover.

When I initially asked Beth what she thought of the idea, she'd immediately given it her full endorsement. "Oh, my God, yes! That would be awesome," she'd said, practically jumping up and down in her excitement. "Our family is growing!"

Now I realize she was exactly right. Sam is part of our family, just as much as Cooper is.

When Beth's coffee is ready, I set it on the counter in front of her. "Sam, how about you?" I say, glancing at the empty coffee mug in front of him. "Want a refill?"

"Sure, thanks," he says, handing me his cup.

I make him a cup, then one for myself.

Cooper plates up eggs and sausage for everyone, while I retrieve the toast. I take the empty barstool beside Beth, and Cooper eats standing at the counter, facing the three of us.

"I love the four of us together like this," Beth says, smiling contentedly.

"Soon to be five," Sam says, hopping off his seat. He pats

Beth's belly. "Don't forget about my little namesake—shoot, what is he to me?" Sam looks at Cooper, considering. Then he starts laughing. "If you're essentially Luke's grandpa, what in the hell does that make me?"

* * *

After we eat, Beth and I head back to our suite to brush our teeth and collect our overnight baggage. We're not bringing much—just one large duffle bag that we share and a toiletries bag.

"How's your back feeling?" I ask her, as she collects the last few items she needs from the bathroom.

She sighs, reaching around to lay a hand on her lower back. "It still aches. I might have pulled a muscle last night."

"And that would be my fault. What about the contractions? Still feeling them?"

She frowns. "Not really. I think they stopped."

"Good."

Once we have what we need, we head out to the great room. Lia and Jonah are there waiting for us, their bags in the foyer.

"Ready for a road trip?" Lia says, offering Beth an eager fist bump.

"You bet," she says.

"We're as ready as we'll ever be," I say, trying to suppress my own misgivings about this outing, which I keep to myself as I don't want to spoil this for Beth. I'm sure everything will be fine.

Cooper comes out of the kitchen drying his hands on a towel. He tosses the towel onto his shoulder and props his hands on his hips, eyeing us critically. I know he's still not happy about this trip.

Sam comes up behind Cooper and puts his hands on Cooper's shoulders, squeezing them. "Looks like you and I get the whole place to ourselves for the weekend."

Cooper smiles, looking a bit self-conscious, and I have to give Sam credit for skillfully defusing the situation.

I step forward and offer my hand to Cooper, and we shake. "Hold down the fort while we're gone, okay?"

Cooper nods, eyeing me with his steely gaze. "You take damn good care of our girl."

Our girl. That makes me smile. I squeeze his hand. "I will. I promise."

He nods, then releases my hand.

"Oh, puh-lease!" Lia says. "We're going to Harbor Springs, not the ends of the Earth. Can we stop with all the drama? And what about me? Who's going to take care of *me*?"

"I will, babe," Jonah says, laughing as he hooks his arm around Lia's neck and pulls her close. "Don't worry, I'll take good care of you."

Lia rolls her eyes as she heads for the foyer, Jonah close on her heels. "You'd better."

Sam hugs Beth and kisses the top of her head. "Be safe, okay?" he says. "Remember to use the buddy system. Don't wander off anywhere alone."

She laughs at him, returning his hug. "I will."

I pick up our bags and steer Beth toward the elevator where Lia and Jonah are waiting. Down in the parking garage, we load our gear into one of the Escalades. Lia sits in the back with Beth, and Jonah and I climb into the front seats.

"Let the road trip begin," Lia says.

I glance into the rearview mirror and see the small smile on Beth's face.

Here's hoping for a quiet, uneventful weekend.

8

Beth

As we head north on Lake Shore Drive, skirting along the edge of Lake Michigan, I lean back in my seat and sigh with pleasure, feeling the effects of weeks of cabin fever slowly eek out of me. My gaze is locked beyond my window as we speed along the freeway. The sky is a clear, bright blue, punctuated with white clouds, and the lake is calm today, stretching out as far as the eye can see. Sailboats in a multitude of shapes and sizes skim across the horizon as if they're racing the sun. Massive yachts churn effortlessly through the water as they head for destinations unknown. We pass several beaches filled with tourists and locals alike sunbathing on the sand and frolicking in the surf.

Once we leave the city skyline behind us, any lingering stress melts away. I'm so looking forward to a night at the cabin, just the four of us sequestered away in the woods. We can relax, grill out on the back deck, and maybe watch a movie tonight.

I shift in my seat in an attempt to get more comfortable. My back still aches, and sitting in a moving vehicle isn't helping. The baby kicks, and I rub my belly, wondering if he can feel me. I love to feel him moving—it means he's okay. When he goes silent, when he naps, I worry. I know he has to sleep sometime, but I can't help feeling reassured when he's active. Just six more weeks and I'll be able to hold him in my arms.

"Baby moved?" Lia says, her voice low.

There's a small smile on her face as she watches me. She tries to act nonchalant, but I have a sneaking suspicion Lia is looking forward to becoming an aunt. As if on cue, Lucas rolls once more, making my abdomen ripple. "He's doing somersaults."

She lays her hand on my belly. "Can I feel?"

I reposition her hand and press it against me. "Of course you can. He's right here."

Sure enough, the baby rolls again, this time kicking my bladder, making me jump with the force of it. The little guy sure is strong. He does it again. "Ow!" At Lia's questioning look, I explain. "He kicked my bladder. Twice."

Lia shakes her head. "That's just too weird. I don't think I could ever do that."

"Do what?"

"Be pregnant."

"Sure you could. If you wanted to." I lower my voice so that it doesn't carry to the front seat. "Do you guys want kids? Have you talked about it?"

Lia shakes her head. "Not really. He's brought it up a couple of times, but I always change the subject. I mean, we're not even married, right? Anyway, I don't think I'd make a good mother. I'm far too impatient."

I feel a pain deep in my chest at her quiet remark. She's not being snarky this time. It's an honest self-assessment, and it makes me sad to think she feels that way. "Lia." I squeeze her hand. "You'd be a fierce and wonderful mother. You and Jonah would both be fantastic parents."

She shrugs again, trying to appear unaffected, but her lips turn up in a small smile.

We pass Old Town, and then the exit to Lincoln Park Zoo. I have such fond memories of Mom and Tyler taking me to the zoo when I was young. I can't wait until Lucas is old enough to go on family outings.

I relax in my seat and watch the cyclists making their way along the Lakefront Trail, with the lake as their backdrop. Then my eyes migrate to the front seat, to the back of Shane's head, and I feel a surge of emotion run through me, making me shiver. How did I ever get so lucky?

The farther north we go, concrete and steel give way to green landscape. Shane eventually exits the highway for a smaller

thoroughfare, and the landscape becomes more rural, trees re-
placing houses, pastures and horses far outnumbering other
signs of human habitation. We pass a few small towns.

"How much farther is it?" I ask. My bladder feels like it's
about to burst. One of the downsides of being pregnant is an
almost constant need to pee.

"About forty-five more minutes," he answers, meeting my
gaze in the rearview mirror. "Are you doing okay?"

I shrug. "I'm fine, but my bladder's about to explode."

He chuckles. "I guess that means we need to make a stop."

Reluctantly, I nod. I hate being a party pooper, but if Luke
sends one more well-aimed kick to my bladder, I'll wet myself.
"Yes, please."

"Not a problem," Shane says, laughing. He turns left, off the
main road, and follows the signs to a small town about five
miles to the west.

When we reach the center of the town, which doesn't
amount to more than four blocks of two-story buildings dating
back more than a century, my hopes sink as there don't seem to
be any recognizable places to stop.

"This looks like our best bet," Shane says, as he pulls into
the parking lot of a small gas station and convenience store. He
pulls the Escalade up to an available gas pump. "I might as well
fill up the tank since we're here."

I grab my purse, open my door, and hop out. "I'll be right
back!" I call as I jog across the pavement toward the store's front
entrance.

I hear the other car doors open behind me, then Shane's voice.

"Go with her, Lia," he says.

"I know," Lia says, following after me.

An elderly man holds the door for me as I dash inside. It's a typical convenience store, shelves filled with everything from chips to candy bars to nuts to batteries and motor oil. There's a small line of customers waiting to pay at the check-out counter. I'm tempted by the self-serve coffee station, but first things first. I need the restroom.

I ask one of the young men standing behind the check-out counter where the restrooms are.

"Through that door," he says, pointing to the back of the store. "Then turn left. It's the first door on the left. You can't miss it."

As I head toward the back of the store, Lia falls into step beside me.

"Slow down, princess. Where's the fire?"

"I've got to go!" I say, pushing through a swinging door that leads to a large storeroom filled with mountains of boxes, a worktable, and a fridge that looks like it has seen better days. Just as the guy said, there's a door immediately to the left marked RESTROOM. I head straight for it, relieved to find it unlocked. I yank open the door and step inside the rather squalid, single toilet room. Doesn't anyone ever clean in here? But beggars can't be choosers, and I'm just grateful they have a restroom.

Lia pokes her head inside the bathroom, making a quick visual sweep. "I'll wait out here."

I close the door, not bothering to lock it as I know Lia will plant herself outside the door like a guard dog. Thank goodness there's a hook on the back of the door where I can hang my purse because there's no where else to put it.

Just as I'm done emptying my bladder and reaching for the toilet paper, I hear a series of sharp pops. Three more cracks in rapid succession come from the front of the store, followed immediately by frantic shouts and screams. My heart leaps into my throat as I stand and put my clothes to rights.

The restroom door crashes open, hitting the back wall with a jarring clang, making me jump. Lia steps into the room and flips off the light, casting us in near darkness. She grabs my hand in a vice grip and pulls me out of the room. "Follow me, and don't make a fucking sound!" she grates.

"What's going on?" I whisper.

"Those were gunshots."

My heart kicks painfully in my chest. "What!"

"Quiet!" I can barely make out her movements in the dark as she reaches behind her back and pulls out a handgun from the waistband of her jeans. I hear the click of the safety as she disengages it.

"Stay close," she says, pulling me along behind her.

9

Shane

Standing beside the Escalade, getting ready to pump gas, my gaze follows the girls as they disappear inside the convenience store. I have to fight the urge to accompany Beth inside, but I know full well she's in good hands with Lia.

The convenience store is located at one end of a downtown block. Most of these old buildings have been turned into cafes, antiques shops, and clothing boutiques. Who knows what the two-story building that now houses a convenience store and gas station used to be? On the other side of the convenience store is an Italian restaurant with quaint red-and-white check-ered curtains hanging in the windows.

I check my watch, making mental note of the time. I'll give them ten minutes. If they're not out by then, I'll go in.

"Relax," Jonah says, grinning at me from across the hood of the Escalade. "She's fine."

I smile, feeling a bit chagrined to be caught fretting over my wife. I can't help it, though. Beth brings out my protective instincts. And the fact that she's nearly eight months pregnant with our child only makes it that much worse. I don't just have one person to worry about now; I have two.

The gas pump shuts off when the tank is full, and I return the nozzle to its cradle. The peace and quiet of this Saturday morning is shattered by the unmistakable report of three handgun shots in rapid succession. My gaze snaps to the front of the convenience store, and through the front windows I can see a figure dressed in black sweats and a hoodie pointing a handgun at the two young men behind the counter. A second figure, also dressed in black, blocks the doors, holding off a crowd of frantic shoppers at gun point. He raises his handgun and fires three times at the ceiling.

My heart slams into my ribs, throwing me instantly into high alert. I pull my Glock from the back waistband of my jeans and grip the handle with white knuckles.

Jonah's halfway across the parking lot, running toward the store.

"Jonah!" I yell. "Get back here!"

He turns, confusion clouding his expression. "That sounded

like gunshots!"

"Get back here. It's a robbery."

I watch in horror as one of the gunmen lines up the hostages along the glass front, using them as human shields. The fucking cowards. Three men, four women, and one child are visible through the windows, their hands pressed flat on the glass, their faces shell shocked. My heart in my throat, I scan those frightened faces, searching for Beth and Lia, but they're not among them. I don't know whether to be relieved or scared out of my mind.

I pull out my phone and dial 911, giving the operator a succinct description of the situation. "Two perpetrators are robbing the convenience store at 126 Main Street at gunpoint. Shots fired. No word on casualties. At least eight hostages that I can see through the glass storefront, possibly more."

I check the magazine in my gun, popping it out and back in.

Jonah grabs my arm, looking as frantic as I feel. "What do we do?"

"Nothing yet. We need to figure out exactly where the girls are before we can help them."

Reality sinks in, and my blood pressure spikes through the roof. There's a deafening roar in my ears. I lean back against the driver's door, my chest heaving. My heart is pounding so hard I'm having trouble thinking straight. Honest to God, I've never been so scared in my entire life. I can't bear the thought of Beth and Lia being in there. And I have no idea of their status. I don't know if they're hurt or not.

The wail of sirens alerts us to the arrival of local law enforcement. Two police cars screech to a halt in front of the convenience store, lights flashing, sirens blaring. They cut the sirens and step out of their cars, taking defensive positions behind their open car doors.

"Coming to you!" I yell, crouching down and making my way to the side of one of the police cars. "Two perpetrators, both armed," I say. "Eight hostages visible, but there are at least two more souls in that building that are unaccounted for. My wife and sister."

The deputy at my side looks me over, his gaze hesitating on my handgun.

"Shane McIntyre of McIntyre Security," I tell him, reaching into my back pocket for my wallet and identification. "Former military special forces. What kind of tactical capabilities can you muster?"

The deputy, a young man barely out of his twenties, shrugs, looking more than a little overwhelmed. "It's just the two of us on duty today. We can call on the county or state forces. There's a SWAT team in Blanchard, but they're an hour away, longer if they're already deployed."

"That's too long," I say. "I can have a tactical response team here before that."

The deputy shakes his head. "This is our jurisdiction."

"Not if you lack the resources. I have the resources."

"You can't just—"

But I've heard enough. I'm not going to sit here arguing with a junior deputy. I make my way back behind the Escalade to Jonah. "Any sign of Beth or Lia?"

He shakes his head. "No. Where could they be?"

I call Jake, and he answers quickly. "Listen carefully. I need a full tactical response team to my location, 126 Main Street, Galford. Pull out all the stops and get a team here. There's an armed robbery in process, with hostages, at a convenience store. Beth and Lia are in that building, exact whereabouts unknown. I need a team here, ASAP."

"Jesus," Jake says, falling silent for a moment. "All right." I can hear him typing rapidly on a keyboard. "Hold on." There's a moment of silence, then he returns. "Okay. There's a private air field ten miles to your west. I can have a team there in forty-five minutes."

Forty-five minutes seems like a lifetime to me. "Hurry, Jake. I don't think we're going to get much support here from the locals. This is a small town. Their capabilities are limited, and the nearest SWAT team is at least an hour away."

"I'm on it. I'm sending out code red alerts now to Cooper, Sam, Killian, Cameron, and Jason Miller."

"Jason?"

"He's a former combat medic and a former paramedic. We might need him."

He's right, of course. Shit! The thought of Beth needing medical attention makes my vision go dark around the edges. I feel myself listing to the side.

Jonah grabs me, propping me up. "Are you okay?"

"No, I'm not okay!" I bark at him. "My pregnant wife is in there!"

10

Beth

M y pulse is thundering in my ears, and I feel sick when Lia presses me into a dark space between a metal cabinet and a stack of cardboard boxes.

"Wait here," she whispers.

As she steps away, I grab her arm. "Where are you going?"

"I need to find out what's going on," she whispers. "Stay here." And then she's gone, leaving me alone with my mounting panic.

I press myself against the wall, trying to hide in the shadows as my mind races. *Where's Shane? And Jonah! Dear God, let them be okay.* The last I knew, the guys were outside pumping gas, but they might have finished and come inside looking for us. I have no way of knowing. I heard at least six shots fired. Had someone been hit? One of the customers? Or an employee?

When I hear more gunshots in rapid succession, followed by more shouts and screams, my stomach roils. This can't be happening!

Lia returns in a flash, grabbing my wrist and hauling me toward the back of the storage room into a dark corner behind a coat rack and more stacks of boxes.

"Can't we go out the back door?" I say, pointing at the metal door on the back wall.

"No good. It's padlocked, and I can't find the key. Wait here." She pushes me down to a sitting position on the wood floor.

Then she's gone again, leaving me to drown in my frantic thoughts. God, I want Shane! Where is he? Surely he heard those shots, and the screams. He has to be beside himself, worrying about me and Lia. And Jonah too! *Oh, my God.* My eyes sting with tears, and I have to grit my teeth to hold back a sob. The baby kicks at that moment, hitting my ribs and nearly knocking the breath out of me. In my panic, I'd forgotten all about the baby. My hands go to my belly, covering the mound as best as I can, as if my poor pathetic hands would be enough to protect the tiny life inside. My heart sinks. *This can't be happening!*

I squeeze my eyes shut and lay my forehead on my arms, which are braced on my knees. When I feel a hand clamp down on one of my wrists, I jump, poised to scream.

"Shh!" Lia whispers, holding her finger to her lips. "Follow me."

She hauls me to my feet, and I follow her through a maze of boxes and palettes filled with cases of beer and water bottles and soft drinks. We stop when we reach one of the walls, and before I can ask her what she's doing, she opens a door and pulls me through it. Lia closes the door behind us, and it's so dark I can't see a thing. My skin starts to crawl until Lia flips on a penlight and shoves it between her teeth. Then she grabs my wrist again and leads me across the small dark space.

I can barely make out the outline of an access panel about four feet high. She slides open the panel and pushes me through it, then follows behind me, sliding the panel back into place. It's even darker in here, and I nearly scream when I walk into a cobweb. When she shines the penlight on the walls around us, I see bare wooden studs and exposed electrical wiring covered with more cobwebs.

"Where did you get a flashlight?" I whisper.

"Shh!"

Lia sweeps the small space with the flashlight until she spots a steep, narrow staircase that goes...up up up. She starts climbing, pulling me after her. All I can see are open studs, fraying electrical wires, and an obscene amount of cobwebs. Obviously no one has been up here in decades, if not longer. I stumble on the too narrow steps, just catching myself from falling face down.

She doesn't answer me. Instead, she trudges up the steps,

dragging me along with her, until we reach a small landing at the top. Up here, the air is hot and stale, and I can barely catch my breath. There's a door to our left, and when she tries the old-fashioned knob, it turns with a rattle. She pushes open the door and shines her flashlight inside, making a quick sweep of the cavernous room.

Lia pulls me into the room and shuts the door behind us.

"Where are we?" I say, my voice no more than a whisper.

"In the attic."

"Lia, what's going on down there? And where are Shane and Jonah?"

"Armed robbery," she says, leaving me to make a quick circuit of the room, shining her flashlight into dark corners and crevices behind more boxes and a wide assortment of cloth-covered furniture. "Two men armed with handguns and assault rifles. I don't know where the guys are, but I didn't see them inside the store. Hopefully they're still outside."

The attic is huge, extending the entire width and breadth of the building. There are small round windows on the three exterior walls, each letting in a modicum of light...just enough for us to realize we've stepped into an old storage room, most likely long forgotten. The room is musty and dank and hot, with no apparent ventilation. The air is thick with dust motes that dance in the air as we pass. Immediately I start coughing, covering my face with my top to muffle the sound. This place is an asthmatic's worst nightmare. There's dust everywhere, most likely mold, too, based on the smell.

Lia steps up to one of the tiny circular windows and rubs some of the grime away with the side of her fist, letting in a tad more light. "I see them," she says, as she peers down at the ground.

I make my way through the maze of discarded furniture to Lia's side to glance out the window. Down below, our Escalade is still parked at the gas pump, and I can see the tops of Shane's and Jonah's heads as they crouch behind the vehicle. They're in a heated discussion, and Shane's keying something into his phone.

I sigh, relieved to know they're safe.

Lia's phone vibrates in her pocket and she pulls it out, checking the screen. "It's Shane." She reads his message, then holds her phone out to me so I can see.

Shane: Lia, do you copy? Is Beth okay?

She texts him back.

Lia: She's fine. Two gunmen, male, caucasian, early twenties. Strung out. Prob drug addicts. Armed with Glocks and assault rifles. Both carrying backpacks. Extra ammo? Explosives? Look up. Attic window.

She hits the send button, and a moment later, Shane and Jonah both crane their necks upward to study the window near the top of the roofline. I wave, not sure if they can see me through the dirty glass.

Lia's phone buzzes, and we both glance at Shane's reply.

Shane: We see you. Stay up there. We'll get you out. How much batt power do you have?

Lia: 86%

When her phone vibrates with an incoming call, Lia spares me a quick glance. Then she answers the call. "Shane, go ahead." She watches me as she listens to him. "Yes." A pause. "No, she's not hurt." Another pause. "I know. I will. Here she is."

Lia holds her phone out to me. "He wants to talk to you. Make it quick. We need to conserve the battery."

My hand shakes as I hold Lia's phone to my ear. "Shane?"

"Listen to me carefully."

I'm stunned by how cold and detached he sounds.

"You're safe up there. Just don't make a sound. Do what Lia says. She'll keep you safe. Do you hear me?"

"Yes. Shane—"

"You're going to be fine. Sit tight. I'll get you out of there."

"Shane—"

"I don't have time to talk. Hand the phone back to Lia."

My throat tightens and my heart aches as I hand the phone back, trying not to dwell on how distant he sounded. Not one word of comfort, not a single note of compassion or even affection in his voice.

Lia studies me for a moment, her brow furrowing, then speaks into the phone. "Jesus, Shane, what the fuck did you say to her?"

My eyes flood with tears, and my body starts quaking. I feel light-headed and dizzy. Lia continues to scowl as she listens to Shane. Then she looks at me and points to a cluster of upholstered recliners a few feet away, her message clear. *Go sit down before you fall down.*

Failing miserably to mask my disappointment, I head for one of the chairs and sit down, causing a cloud of dust to waft up from the material. Immediately I start coughing again, trying my best to muffle the sound.

The ache in my back is intensifying, the physical pain matching the emotional pain that's swamping me. I have to look away from Lia, who's reading Shane the riot act, and try not to cry. I know he's worried about us, but he didn't have to sound so cold...or cut me off so quickly. He could have at least said *something.* Even an *I love you* would have sufficed. Instead, he came across like a complete stranger, cold and indifferent. And then it occurs to me—he's angry. At me? Oh, my God. Does he blame me? I was the one who wanted this trip in the first place. If it weren't for me, we wouldn't be in this predicament. He's right, though—it is my fault.

A cloud of dust particles sends me into another coughing fit, and Lia shoots me a dark look that is easy enough to interpret. *Be quiet!*

I lean back in the chair, squeezing my teary eyes shut as I try to steady my breathing. A ripple in my abdomen brings my attention back to the baby, and I cradle my belly with both hands, stroking the firm mound as if my touch can comfort him. My chest tightens painfully, constricting my lungs, and my breaths come shorter and faster. With a sense of dread, I realize I'm headed for a full-blown asthma attack.

I automatically reach for my purse, needing my rescue inhaler, but I come up empty handed. *Oh, crap! Where did I leave my purse?* I think back. The last time I saw it was in the restroom downstairs. I left it hanging on the hook behind the door. *Lia's going to kill me.*

I start wheezing, unable to get enough air.

A single gunshot breaks the silence, making me jump. Horrified screams erupt from the ground floor. I glance at Lia, who's scowling at her phone screen. "Shit! Shane says they shot one of the hostages."

I freeze, sitting as still as a statue, and all of a sudden everything catches up with me. *Oh, my God, there are actual gunmen downstairs–criminals.* Numbness settles over me as my body starts shaking. *We're trapped up here, and there's not enough air.*

I can't breathe!

My heart starts pounding and my entire body seizes as a crushing weight presses down on me, sucking all the air out of my lungs, leaving me gasping.

"Beth?"

I can't breathe!

"Beth!" she snaps, more sharply this time.

Suddenly, Lia is in front of me, crouching on the floor, holding my hands. "Look at me! It's okay. Calm down." She scans my body and frowns.

I barely manage to wheeze out a couple of words. "Can't... breathe..."

"Where's your purse?"

I shake my head frantically, pointing down below.

"Downstairs?" she says, scowling. "Shit! In the bathroom?"
I nod.

Lia stands. "I'm going downstairs to get your purse."

"No!" I grab her wrist. She can't go down there! They might see her.

She twists easily out of my hold and grabs my hands, holding them securely. "Beth, listen to me. You need your inhaler. I'll be right back. Try to stay calm."

The sound of yet another gunshot coming from downstairs makes us both jump. Right on the heels of the gunshot are renewed screams.

"Shit! Those fuckers are unhinged." She pats my leg. "I'll be right back."

And then she's gone, slipping out the door and closing it quietly behind her.

I sit in my chair, shaking, and try not to cry. I feel like screaming, and I would give anything to be with Shane right now. I need to feel his arms around me. And then I think about what he must be going through right now. He's got to be worried sick.

My heart hammers painfully in my chest, and my lungs are heavy as lead. Tighter and tighter, my chest contracts until I can't get enough air. I start gasping, fighting against outright panic. This room is closed up tight! There's no ventilation! There's not enough air!

I jump up from the chair and run to the window that overlooks the parking lot, frantically trying to open it, desperate for some fresh air, but the window is clearly not designed to open. I can see Shane and Jonah crouching behind the Escalade, out of the line of sight of the gunmen. Shane's talking on his phone, his expression tense.

I lift my hand and lay it against the dirty glass, willing him to look at me. When his head snaps up, his gaze latches onto mine, cold and stark. He stares at me, looking like a stranger. Gone are the gentle smiles and teasing glances. In their place is a cold-minded intensity I've never seen before. I stare at him, transfixed, and he never once looks away, not even when Jonah says something to him, tugging on his sleeve to get his attention.

I don't know how long I'd been standing there, staring at Shane, when hands clamp down on my shoulders, making me jump. I turn to see Lia behind me, holding my purse and a plastic shopping bag filled with loot.

"Sit down," she says, leading me back to the recliner.

Once I'm seated, she hands me my purse. I pull out my inhaler and administer the medication. Then I grab my phone out of my purse, desperate to see if I have a message from Shane. Anything. But there aren't any. I try not to feel hurt, because I know he's stressed right now, but it's impossible not to.

Lia takes my phone from me. "You're down to forty-four percent," she says, scowling at the screen. She powers off my phone and tucks it back into my purse. "Leave it off. We'll save your phone as our backup."

Lia pulls a bottle of spring water out of the shopping bag, screws off the cap, and thrusts it into my hands. "Drink."

I don't realize how parched I am until the water hits my tongue, and then I can't get enough. I end up drinking half the bottle in one go before she takes it from me and screws the cap back on. "Pace yourself. We could be here a while. And remember, what goes in must come out. I'll scout around for a bucket, or something we can use as a makeshift toilet."

The thought of peeing in a bucket is more than I want to contemplate right now, so I focus on the immediate priorities. "Thanks for getting my purse. And for the water."

She nods as she reaches into the sack and pulls out a protein bar, handing it to me. "Eat."

The last thing I feel like doing is eating, but as she went to all that trouble, I can't refuse. I unwrap the bar, and as I take my first bite, an abdominal cramp hits me, making me crumple forward with a cry. I press my free hand to my belly, which feels hard as a rock, and pant through the discomfort.

"What's wrong?" Lia says, her voice sharp.

I shrug, not sure what to make of it myself. "A cramp, I think."

"Is that normal?"

I force myself to breathe through it, finally relaxing when it subsides. "I guess. I've had them before, but they're usually not that bad. I'm fine now. It's gone."

Lia eyes me skeptically.

"I'm fine, Lia, really."

"Finish your food," she says, rising. "I figure we've got enough food and water to last us at least two days, longer if we ration."

"Two days? Are you serious?" I'm horrified at the prospect of being up here that long.

She shrugs. "There's no telling how long this will go on. We need to be prepared for the worst."

ᕽ 11

Shane

*B*reathe, I remind myself. *Just fucking breathe. You're no help to the girls if you can't keep it together.*

I stare hard at the attic window, willing Beth to reappear. I just want to see her face once more. Knowing that she's up there, out of harm's way, is a comfort. If they can remain quiet up there in the attic, they'll be perfectly safe. As soon as this hostage situation is resolved, I'll be the first one up there, breaking down her door and carrying her off to safety.

My only consolation is knowing that my sister is with her. Lia won't let anything happen to Beth. I know that. Still, it's...

difficult for me to be out here, when Beth is in there. I can't even let myself think about how scared she must be. Jesus, I'd give anything to have her here with me, in my arms, where I can protect her with my own body if necessary.

It's taken me a while, but ice has finally settled into my veins, thank God, chasing away the fear, the gut-wrenching panic that threatened to choke me the minute I heard those gunshots. In the first few minutes of the siege, it was nearly impossible for me to think straight, knowing that Beth and Lia were somewhere in that building, possibly at the mercy of those drugged-out lunatics. And our baby! He's in danger too. They all are. The thought makes me burn.

It's my fucking job to keep my family safe, and right now, they're in there, and I'm out here. I would trade places with them in a heartbeat. I would walk into that building and trade myself for them if I thought it had a chance of succeeding. I take a deep breath, steeling myself for what's to come.

Jonah turns to face me, a mix of fear and compassion in his gaze. "You okay?"

I nod. "Jake and his team are on their way. ETA thirty-seven minutes by helicopter. Add ten minutes for unloading the chopper and securing ground transportation to our location. Cooper hired two SUVs from the airfield."

Jonah nods, looking as shell-shocked as I feel.

At the first sign of trouble—a series of rapid gunshots coming from inside the convenience store—I felt the Earth shift beneath my feet. I'd never been so scared in my life. I spent over ten years in the Marines, as part of Force Recon—special ops—and never once during those years had I ever felt such hopeless fear as I did today. In the Marines, I'd feared for my life dozens of times, sure, but never once was it as crippling as this fear I have for Beth and Lia.

At the beginning of the standoff, I'd assumed that Beth and Lia had been rounded up at gun point with the rest of the customers. But when the gunmen lined the hostages along the front glass windows, and I didn't see any sign of them, I was able to take my first breath. *But where the hell were they?* Knowing my sister, their whereabouts was anyone's guess.

Jonah and I waited for twenty agonizing minutes before I caught sight of Lia peering out of a small round window in the attic. I would have bowed down at my sister's feet at that moment, if I could have. She'd somehow managed to sneak Beth out of harm's way.

If they could stay up there in the attic, undetected, there was a damn good chance they'd get through this ordeal unscathed. And frankly, that was my primary objective. I'd do what I could to assist with the hostage situation on the ground floor, but if push came to shove, my allegiance would be to my family.

In the meanwhile, I have a tactical team *en route*. But there are other people who need to be notified. Beth's family—her mother, Ingrid Jamison, and her brother, Tyler. And my family—my parents and my siblings.

Dreading the news I have to deliver, I bring up Tyler's contact info on my phone and press the call button.

Two rings later, he picks up, answering in his usual clipped, brusque tone. "Jamison."

Tyler and I have known each other in a professional capacity for years, but it wasn't until I met his sister that our association became personal, not to mention complicated. Tyler was eighteen years old when his sister was born, and he more or less helped their single mother raise her. Beth's father, a Chicago street cop, died in the line of duty when she was an infant, leaving her mother a widow and Tyler suddenly a teenaged father figure to a baby girl. Tyler's a controlling son-of-a-bitch, and he didn't take kindly to me entering the picture and assuming a significant role in his sister's life. He didn't like me usurping his place, but that was too damn bad. The minute I met her, Beth's life intertwined with mine, and she became *mine* to protect.

"What is it, Shane?" he says. "Is something wrong?"

The news I have to deliver sits on my tongue like acid, burning me, but I have no choice. He needs to know. "There's no easy way to say this, so I'll just come out with it. Beth and Lia have been caught up in an armed robbery at a convenience store in Galford, forty-five minutes north of the city. They're safe at the moment. They're in hiding, and the perps don't know of their whereabouts. But the situation is volatile. I'm working on a plan to extricate them from the building. I have a tactical team on the way, their ETA approximately thirty-five minutes."

At first, there's nothing but dead air on the line, making me wonder if the call had been dropped. But then I hear a muffled curse. Tyler's voice comes hard and fast, which tells me he's already on the move. "Send me your location. I'm on my way. Who has jurisdiction?"

"Galford has a police department, but it's small. There are two deputies on site, and they've called in a third. But that's all they've got. The deputy in charge has already requested a SWAT team from Blanchard—they're the closest jurisdiction with a tactical response team. In the meanwhile, I've got a team of my guys on the way. My objective is to get the girls out of the building without the gunmen knowing."

"How many assailants?" Tyler says.

"Two armed males. We've seen handguns and assault rifles. The perps are erratic, possibly high. They've shot at least one hostage that we know of."

"Shit. I have no jurisdiction there, but I can help on the ground."

I hear the engine of Tyler's pick-up truck turn over, followed by a loud squeal as he peels out into traffic.

"What about your mother? Do you want me to call her?"

"No. I'll do it. You just focus on getting Beth and Lia out of there."

After ending the call with Tyler, I call my parents, explaining to them what's going on, as objectively and succinctly as I can. They're obviously shaken, but they do their best to keep it together, promising to inform the rest of my siblings.

The third deputy arrives just as the officer-in-charge raises a bullhorn and addresses the gunmen, demanding that they release the hostages and put down their weapons. One of the gunmen opens the front door, holding a sobbing middle-aged woman in front of him like a shield, and jeers at the officer's demands. I can tell from the sound of the perp's voice that he's in physical and emotional distress, likely suffering from withdrawal. These two perps are drug addicts, and they're desperate for cash and their next fix. That's never a good combination.

I lay my hand on Jonah's shoulder. "Stay here and watch for our people to arrive. I'm going to see if I can help with the negotiations."

Keeping low to the ground, I make a dash for the officer with the bullhorn, plastering myself close to the vehicle once I reach his side. "I have extensive negotiation experience," I tell him, craning my neck to see over the hood of the police cruiser. The perp at the door is shaking badly as he presses the muzzle of his gun to the woman's head. He's completely unstable, which means this situation could go from bad to worse any time. "I can help you."

The officer shakes his head at me, looking more than a little frazzled. "This is official police business, sir. Stay back, or I'll have you removed from the vicinity."

I have to bite back a derisive laugh. Who's going to remove me? He and his two buddies are up to their eyeballs in this shit-storm. Besides, I'd like to see them *try*.

I return to the far side of the Escalade, where Jonah is staring hard at his phone, a frown marring his expression.

"What's wrong?" I say, my heart immediately jumping into my throat.

Jonah looks from me to the little attic window high over-head, then back to me, hesitating as if he's not sure what to say. But I don't have time to pussy foot around. "Just spit it out, Jonah."

ᑌ 12

Beth

What started out as a few cramps has turned into what feels like contractions. At first, I thought it was more of those Braxton-Hicks contractions, which I've had before—like I had earlier this morning. But the contractions continue to come, and each one seems stronger than the one before it.

I'm starting to think I might be in labor for real, and it scares me to death because it's too early. Way too early. Luke's not ready to come out. And the conditions here, as I look around at the hot, dusty room, are far from sanitary.

I finish the water bottle Lia gave me, and the protein bar, but the food is sitting like a rock in my stomach, making me nauseated. I get up and go to Lia, who's standing by the window overlooking the street. "What are you doing?" I ask her.

"Texting Jonah."

I peek out the window and see Jonah crouched behind the Escalade. He's alone. "Where's Shane?"

"Over there." Lia points to one of the patrol cars parked in front of the convenience store.

I spot Shane crouching behind the patrol car, talking to one of the police officers. "What's he doing?"

Warm water starts trickling down my leg, and I look down in horror, staring at the spreading puddle beneath me. "What in the world?"

My first thought is that I wet myself. After all, I did just drink an entire bottle of water. But I think I would know if my bladder just decided to let go.

Lia looks down at the floor. Then her gaze shoots up to my face. "Did you just pee?"

I shake my head and press my hand between my legs. My clothes are soaked. "I don't think so."

Her eyes widen as realization dawns. "Shit!" She grabs my arms and walks me back to a recliner. "Sit down."

"I can't sit down! My clothes are wet. I'll ruin the chair."

Rolling her eyes at me, she pushes me down onto the chair. "Sit down! You're in labor, for fuck's sake!"

I wrap my arms around my abdomen. "I can't be. It's too

soon."

Lia starts pacing, keying something furiously into her phone. "Well, I don't think you get a say in it."

After she finishes doing whatever she's doing with her phone, she crouches down in front of me and rests her hands on my knees. She looks calm now, like it's nothing out of the ordinary for someone to go into labor. "It's going to be okay," she says with a forced smile on her face. "You're going to be fine. The baby's going to be fine."

Another contraction hits me, and I double over, gasping for breath. My mind races as I try to recall everything I've ever read about labor. "I think we're supposed to time the contractions."

Lia brings up the stopwatch on her phone. "Let me know when the next one starts."

The liquid has slowed to a trickle, but my clothes and the chair are soaked through.

Lia pats my leg. "We need to get you out of your wet clothes and find someplace where you'll be comfortable. Hold on, let me see what I can find."

She makes a quick circuit through the attic, moving quietly and efficiently as she searches every inch of the room. She ignores all the chairs and focuses on a group of sofas in the back corner of the room. Then she locates a stash of bedding sets, selects one, and pulls out the contents. She lays a sheet over the sofa, and then she stuffs an accent pillow into a pillowcase and props it against the arm of the sofa.

"Here you go," she says, waving me over. "A bed."

I rise gingerly and cross the room to the makeshift bed. She eyes my clothing and frowns. "You should take those wet clothes off."

"But I don't have anything to wear."

She frowns, then grabs another of those packaged bedding sets and pulls out a sheet. "Wrap this around you like a skirt. I'm afraid it's all we've got."

Lia helps me undress, remaining calm and clinical as she peels the wet clothing from my skin. My shorts hit the floor, followed by my panties. Even my sandals are soaking wet, so I kick those off and shove them under the sofa. My bra and top are still dry, thank goodness.

She helps me double up the sheet so it's not so long and wraps it around my torso, tucking it in to secure it on my body. "Sorry," she says. "That's the best we've got for now."

"It's fine. Thank you."

"Has the water stopped?"

"It's down to a trickle now."

Lia folds a blanket and lays it on the sofa. "Why don't you sit on this for a while, just in case." She brings over the bag of provisions and hands me one of the bottles. "You should drink more water."

I look at her like she's crazy. "I can't. I already need to pee."

"Oh, right. Let me see what I can come up with."

Lia continues searching the room for something we can use as a toilet. As horrifying as that idea is, my bladder is really starting to complain. I'm not going to be able to hold it forever, especially if I keep drinking more water.

"I've got something," she says, carrying over an industrial-sized, white plastic bucket. "It's not great, but it will have to do." She sets the bucket on the floor in the nearest corner. "Want to give it a try?"

With Lia's help, I manage to squat over the bucket and take care of business without making too much of a mess. "I don't suppose we have any toilet paper?" I say, hopeful.

She frowns. "Well, shit."

"That's okay. I'll make do without it."

When I sit back down on the sofa, another contraction hits me, making me double over. "Another one," I say, rather unnecessarily, as Lia is already checking the stopwatch on her phone. "How long since the last one?"

"Fifteen minutes," she says. "Shit. This is really happening."

13

Shane

J
ust spit it out, Jonah," I say, my voice hard.

The look he gives me is filled with pity. "Lia thinks Beth is in labor."

My face grows cold as the blood drains south, making me light-headed. "What? No! She can't be in labor. It's too soon."

Jonah hands me his phone, and I read Lia's text message.

Lia: I think princess is in labor. She's having contractions. At first I thought it was those fake contractions, but her water just broke. Don't tell Shane. He'll freak.

Freak? Freak doesn't even begin to describe how I feel. I slide down the side of the Escalade until my ass hits the concrete. My mind is reeling. A really bad situation just got a thousand times worse.

If she's in labor, our timetable just shortened dramatically. The girls could have stayed up there a good long time as long as they had food and water. But if Beth's in labor... then no. I need to get her out of there ASAP. If she goes into active labor, they'll *hear* her. And Jesus! The baby is six weeks premature. I'm not sure exactly what that means for him, but it's easy to assume he's going to need emergency medical assistance. "Fuck!"

I text Jake, who's *en route* to our location.

Me: You've got Jason Miller with you, right?

Jake: Yes

Me: Good. Beth is in labor.

Jake: Fuck

Me: Exactly. Hurry.

Right now, Jason is the best chance Beth has. I don't know the first thing about birthing babies, other than what I learned watching some YouTube videos with Beth. We had signed up for birthing classes at the hospital, but those weren't scheduled for another week. I think back to the videos we watched and my gut clenches. I can't imagine her going through that without me at her side.

I close my eyes and lean my head back against the vehicle.

"Hey," Jonah says, laying his hand on my shoulder. "It's going to be all right. Lia will take care of her until help arrives."

But even if help arrives, it won't do the girls any good if we can't find a way to get help up to them.

I shoot Lia a text.

Me: When the hell were you going to tell me my wife is in labor?

Lia: How about now? Dude, your wife is in labor. Contractions are about 15 mins apart.

Me: Find us another way into that goddamned attic.

❧ 14

Beth

I'm trying not to cry. I'm trying to hold it together. I know Lia's doing everything she can for us, and I'm grateful to her. But I'm so scared I can barely think straight. I lay my hands on my baby bump and stroke the firm mound, feeling a fleeting sense of relief every time he moves.

My pulse is galloping like a horse. I'm finding it difficult to breathe, but I don't know if that's my asthma kicking in, or anxiety, or if that's part of labor. Every time a contraction hits me, I feel a crushing weight descend on my abdomen, making it harder to breathe, harder to think straight.

Lia brings the shopping bag with our loot over to the sofa and sets it on the floor within easy reach. Then she sits beside me and pats my leg. "How do you feel?"

I let out a heavy breath when the current contraction ends, finally able to relax. "Better. I don't know if it's my imagination or not, but it feels like each contraction gets stronger."

"That would make sense." She hands me a bottle of water. "Please drink some more. You should stay hydrated."

"But we don't have any toilet paper."

"You're in labor, and you're worried about toilet paper?"

"I don't like to feel wet."

"All right. I'll find something."

Lia resumes scouring the attic for anything useful, missing nothing. She brings back a hammer, a screw driver, a crowbar, and—thank God—a half-used roll of paper towels. She holds the paper towels up in the air. "Voila!" she says. "Toilet paper! Or at least the next best thing."

I smile at her, grateful. "Thank you."

"You're welcome. Now will you drink more?"

My abdomen seizes up, signaling another contraction. Lia's eyes are on me, alert, and she reaches for her phone to check the stopwatch.

"Twelve minutes since the last one," she says. "They're getting closer. Let me know when this one stops."

I force myself to pant through the contraction, like I saw in a childbirth video, and I try not to panic. It doesn't hurt exactly. It feels like there's an elephant sitting on me, which makes it hard to breathe. When the sensation finally subsides, I look up at her and nod. "Done."

Lia's phone vibrates with an incoming message. "Shane says there's a paramedic on the way." She pats my leg. "Good. The cavalry is coming. Now we need to find a way to get you out of here without alerting the morons downstairs."

At the mention of Shane's name, my tears start flowing again. "Stupid pregnancy hormones," I say, wiping my face on the sheet.

"I know. They're a bitch. That's why I'm never getting pregnant. I refuse to do weepy or hormonal."

I grab her hand and squeeze it. "I want you and Jonah to have a baby. Our kids would be cousins."

Lia shrugs, but I catch the hint of a smile on her face. "Maybe I'll adopt," she says. "Yeah, adoption sounds really good right now."

* * *

"Breathe, Beth!" Lia says, squeezing my hands. "Try to relax and breathe, like they do in the movies." And then she proceeds to demonstrate, panting violently, like she's just finished a full marathon. If I weren't seized up at the moment with a powerful contraction, I would have laughed.

"Not funny," I manage to eek two words past my clenched teeth, but just barely. Each contraction is worse than the one before, and each time they're coming faster and lasting longer.

This is happening so fast! I'm not ready.

Lia holds my hands throughout the contraction, squeezing my fingers so tightly that they're numb.

When the contraction finally subsides, I exhale a slow, heavy breath and lower my sweaty head back onto the pillow. "It's over."

Lia releases my hands and checks her phone, undoubtedly looking for an update on when the cavalry will get here. How long has it been? But even when they arrive, they can't get to us up here.

I close my eyes and try to rest while I can. The contractions are stronger and coming more frequently. This isn't happening how I had envisioned it. And I guess this means I won't be getting an epidural like I'd planned.

Lia starts pacing. This waiting is killing her, I know it. She goes to the window at the front of the building and gazes outside. "They're here!" she calls over to me. "I see Jake and Cooper talking to Shane. Now we just need to figure out how to get them up here."

She starts making another circuit through the attic, stopping to look out all of the windows, front, side, and rear. I can just see the wheels turning in her head as she tries to figure out a way for us to get out of this building without attracting any unwanted attention.

When she lingers by the door to the staircase leading downstairs, I get nervous. She can't go downstairs again. It's far too dangerous. The gunmen could see her, catch her, and then she'd be in the same predicament as the other hostages. "Lia! What are you doing?"

She gives me a dismissive wave, shushing me. Then she quietly opens the door and shines her skinny flashlight into the narrow stairwell, seeming to study the walls, the ceiling, the floor.

When she walks through the door, disappearing from sight, I get really nervous. "Lia!"

From my vantage point on the sofa, I watch her shine the flashlight against the walls in the stairwell. "What are you looking at?"

"Our way out of here," she says, turning back to me with a huge grin on her face. She steps back into the attic room and closes the door. "We're getting you help," she says, as she keys something into her phone.

15

Shane

The SWAT team from Blanchard arrives, and a swarm of activity takes place in the street outside the convenience store. They brought one armored vehicle with them and six tactical officers outfitted with full body armor and loaded with firepower. The apparent leader of the team converses with the deputies up front who have been attempting, without success, to negotiate with the gunmen. The coward at the door is still holding a woman in front of him as a human shield.

Along with the arrival of the SWAT team, two ambulances

pull up to the crime scene perimeter, presumably on call for casualties.

Moments later, another two SUVs pull up to the police barricade, and I see my guys spill out of the vehicles. Jake, Cooper, and Sam head straight for me, behind the Escalade. Cameron Stewart, Killian Deveraux, and Jason Miller, the medic, quickly disappear behind the convenience store to do reconnaissance.

As I watch the guys approach, my phone vibrates with an incoming message from my sister.

Lia: Dude! The interior walls up here are bare wood planks. If you can get into the attic of the adjacent building, you can pry the planks off the frame and access this attic. Easy peasy. Get your asses up here. Things are progressing quickly!

The guys hunker down with me and Jonah beside the Escalade. Jake appears focused and ready to rumble. Cooper looks fit to be tied. He's absolutely seething, and I know he wants to rip me a new one over this debacle. Well, he's going to have to wait.

"I know!" I say when Cooper glares at me, cutting him off before he can say *I told you so*. I glare right back at him, daring him to give me shit. "I know I fucked up. I don't need you throwing it in my face. The only thing that matters right now is getting Beth and Lia out of that building."

"Sit rep," Jake says, taking charge as he pointedly moves in between me and Cooper. He hands me an ear comm piece.

I insert the comm device into my ear and attach the throat mic to my shirt collar. Then I give him a situation report, rattling off what we know so far to everyone on our team, what we know about the gunmen and the hostages. I tell them Beth and

Lia are ensconced up in the attic over the convenience store, and that Beth is in labor.

Cooper's eyes narrow at me, and I swear to God he wants to beat the living shit out of me. Fine. He can get in line. I'm sure Tyler will fight him for the privilege when he gets here. And then I'm sure I'll have Sam to contend with at some point, not to mention Beth's mother and my folks. The list is endless.

"Lia says the wall separating this building from the adjacent one is made of wood planks. If we can get up into the attic next door, we can pry the planks off the frame and slip through to the room they're in. Then we can evacuate them through the adjacent building."

Cooper and Jake both crane their necks to see past the hood of the Escalade at the Italian restaurant next door.

Sam and Cooper take off, heading for the alley behind the building.

"That'll work," Jake says, nodding. Then he activates his throat mic. "Guys. Meet me behind the Italian restaurant adjacent to the convenience store. I think we've identified our entry point." Then Jake addresses me. "I'll go talk to the restaurant manager. Once we have access to their upper floor, we should be to our target in no time."

Another text comes in from Lia.

Lia: You guys had better figure something out quick. Her contractions are coming closer.

Fuck.

Me: We're working out our evac plan now. Hold tight.

Lia: We need the paramedic up here NOW dammit.

My stomach sinks at the thought of Beth giving birth up there.

I can't stay out here any longer. I've got to get inside that attic. I look at Jonah. "I'm going in with them. You stay here, out of the line of fire. If things get hairy, seek shelter across the street, in the hardware store or the diner."

Jonah nods. "Don't worry about me. Get up there. Beth needs you."

Just as I'm about to move out, Jonah grabs my arm. "Tell Lia I love her, and I'll see her soon."

"I will." I study Jonah, who's been a tower of strength throughout this whole ordeal. He's maintaining his cool, but I know it has to be difficult for him. In the short time they've been together, he and Lia have become inseparable. She's his whole world now.

I make a wide sweep around the vehicles parked in front of the convenience store to access the rear of the buildings. Two of the SWAT team members are guarding the rear door of the convenience store, but they let me pass with a curt nod when I flash them my McIntyre Security Inc. identification. I'm sure they've already seen our tactical team disappear inside the rear of the adjacent store. Fortunately, they're giving us a wide berth and not interfering in our activities as long as we don't interfere with theirs.

I continue along the alley past a row of reeking trash dumpsters and a mountain of empty cardboard boxes to the back door of the restaurant, where Sam is standing guard.

At my approach, Sam opens the door and points up a back staircase. "Go up the stairs, turn left. You can't miss them."

I charge up the stairs and reach a landing where Cooper is waiting for me. He motions me through a door that leads into a storage room.

"On the far side," Cooper says, pointing across the room.

But it's unnecessary. I can see Cameron and Killian working on the far wall. Jason Miller is standing nearby, loaded down with medical gear as he waits for access to the other room.

Cameron and Killian work together as they systematically pry six-inch wide wooden planks off the building's ancient wooden frame. Thank God this building predates modern building codes, or this would have been a whole lot harder.

Jake is organizing a small arsenal of automatic weapons, handguns, and other tactical munitions, including flash-bangs and hand grenades. They clearly came prepared for all contingencies.

Cooper comes up behind me and lays his hand on my shoulder, undoubtedly offering an olive branch. "I spoke to the restaurant owner, explained the circumstances. He's fine with whatever we need to do. I told him we'd reimburse him for all damages."

I nod as I wait impatiently for the guys to create an opening in the wall big enough for us to get through. Fortunately, the studs are placed far enough apart on these old buildings that we'll be able to walk between them once the planks have been removed.

"What's the plan?" Cooper says, including Jason in his question. "We get them out and transport Beth to the nearest hospital, right?"

"That depends on how far along she is in the delivery process," Jason says. "If she's close to pushing, we may not be able to move her. She's better off delivering here than in a moving ambulance. We can get hot water and clean towels from the restaurant downstairs, and I brought a full med kit. Since the baby is premature, we'll need a NICU transport. They'll have specialized equipment that he might need."

I nod and look to Jake.

"I'll call it in," he says, pulling his phone out of his pocket.

"How about she delivers in a fucking hospital?" Cooper says, getting in Jason's face. "There are two ambulances parked out front. We can use one of those to transport her to a hospital right now, before she gives birth."

I lay my hand on Cooper's shoulder, giving it a squeeze as I ease him back. "Let's wait and see what we're dealing with."

Lia appears suddenly on the other side of the wall, her face visible through the narrow gap between two boards. "Any time now, guys," she says, clearly sounding strained and more than a little breathless.

"We're working on it, Lia," Cameron says calmly, as he and Killian pry a second board loose and quietly lay it on top of the first. In all the years I've known him, I've never seen Cameron lose his cool.

A quiet cry comes from the darkened room behind Lia, and she turns and bolts back to where she came.

When the third board comes down, opening up a two-foot wide gap in the wall, I'm the first one through and across the narrow stairwell to enter through the door on the other side.

The dimly lit room is filled with discarded furniture and boxes, and it takes me a few precious seconds to locate the girls in all this clutter.

It's not until I get closer that I can make out Beth's shape lying on the sofa. Lia and Beth are holding hands, and Beth is straining upward, her chin tucked close to her chest. She's grimacing silently, her face flushed a deep red, her teeth gritted in soundless distress.

"Jason, get in here now!" I say, trying to keep my voice down. "Cameron, Killian, guard this stairwell. Cooper, I need you with me." There's no question in my mind about where this child will be delivered. Our baby is going to be born here.

Cooper follows me through the opening, and he's right on my heels as I make my way through the discarded furniture across the room to Beth.

"Breathe, Beth," Lia is telling her in a low, firm voice, as she stares hard into Beth's wide eyes, holding her attention by sheer force of will. "Breathe."

Dropping to my knees on the wood floor beside the sofa, I reach for her, brushing back her sweat-soaked hair. She's burning up. "Sweetheart."

She turns to stare at me with wide, frightened eyes, tears

streaming down her pale cheeks. Her jaw is clenched tight, and she's obviously holding back cries of pain. My heart slams in my chest. My own eyes prick with tears as I put my arm around her to support her.

My throat tightens, making speaking difficult. "Oh, God, baby. I'm so sorry."

"Not. Your. Fault," she gasps.

Yes, it is. It's my job to protect her, and I fucked up royally.

Cooper moves around to the back of the sofa, and Jason appears beside me, setting his medical kit on the floor and gently nudging me aside. He opens his kit and begins pulling out an assortment of medical instruments, starting with a blood pressure cuff, which he hands to me. "Put this on her left arm, right above her elbow, and cinch it tight."

Beth gives out a low moan, sounding pained and afraid, then sinks back onto the damp pillow, her chest heaving as she draws in air. Seeing her like this breaks my heart. It wasn't supposed to happen like this. She should be in a hospital, getting the best medical care possible, not giving birth in a dusty, sweltering attic.

Once I get the blood pressure cuff on her, I lean close, pressing my lips to the side of her head. "Sweetheart, I'm here," I murmur quietly, stroking her hair. My heart hammers in my chest, and I feel almost paralyzed with fear.

I don't know how to help her. For the first time in my adult life, I don't know what to do. I make it my number one job to make her life as easy as possible, free from fear and strife, and now she's in agony and I'm helpless to fix this.

She lifts her hand blindly, as if searching for mine, and I take it, cradling it against my chest. "Shane. I'm scared," she whispers, her voice barely audible. "It's too soon."

"I know, baby. I'm here now, and so is Cooper. And Jason. We're going to take good care of you, I promise."

Cooper leans over the back of the sofa and brushes Beth's hair away from her damp face. "We're here, kiddo," he says, his voice low and tight. "Everything's going to be all right."

After taking Beth's blood pressure, Jason takes her temperature by swiping a wand across her forehead. Then he pulls on a pair of sterile gloves. "Hi, Beth," he says. "My name's Jason Miller, and I work for your husband. I'm going to help you deliver your baby. Is that okay?"

She glances up at him, and then at me.

"Jason's a medic, sweetheart. He's delivered babies before. He knows what he's doing."

"Okay," she says.

Jason gives her a reassuring smile. "I need to check your cervix, okay? To see how much you're dilated."

"Okay." Beth nods, looking wary.

Jason looks at me, as if asking permission to touch my wife. I nod curtly. "Do what you need to do."

Lia moves back to give Jason room to work, hovering at the far end of the sofa. Her gaze remains locked on Beth. I've never in my life seen Lia so worried.

Jason discretely lifts the sheet from the lower half of Beth's body, exposing her bare thighs and hips. She has a loose top on, but she's clearly bare below the waist. I hate seeing her exposed like this, but it can't be helped.

He reaches between her thighs. "I'm going to touch you now. Can you open your legs more?" His voice is very low and gentle, very professional. "I'm going to check your cervix."

"You've done this before?" Cooper demands, glaring at Jason. "Delivered babies, I mean."

"Yes, sir," Jason says, his concentration remaining on Beth as he moves his hand between her legs. "I worked ten years as a paramedic after serving as a medic in the Army. I've delivered over a dozen babies in the field."

Cooper makes a grunting sound, but doesn't reply, instead watching Jason's every move like a hawk.

I study Jason's expression as he examines Beth, looking for any indication of what we're up against. Beth closes her eyes and turns her face toward mine, her nose brushing mine as she whimpers quietly.

Jason meets my gaze, his expression carefully neutral. "Nine centimeters."

"Which means what, exactly?" I say.

"It means we're having a baby. Soon. I'm sorry, but it's too late to move her."

16

Shane

Jason glances up at Cooper. "Tell the guys to bring up a pot of boiled water and some clean towels. I'll need a basin, plastic or metal, it doesn't matter as long as it's clean, and a trash can."

Cooper reaches down to caress the top of Beth's head. "I'll be right back, kiddo."

Jason helps Beth lower her legs, and then he covers her with the sheet. "Beth? Have you felt an urge to push yet?"

She shakes her head. "No." Her voice is little more than a rasp. "I feel a lot of pressure on my abdomen. When the contractions start, it's hard to breathe."

Jason pulls a wooden chair close to the sofa and takes a seat. "You're well into active labor. Your cervix is dilated to nine centimeters, so it won't be long before you'll feel the need to push. When you do, don't fight it. Your body knows what to do."

She nods, the blood draining from her face. "All right," she says, sounding as far from all right as a person can.

"Don't you have something you can give her for the pain?" I say.

He shakes his head. "I'm sorry, but I'm not set up to give her anything strong here. I can give her a local anesthetic, sure. It won't help with the contractions, but it will help with any stretching or tearing of the perineum."

"Do it. Anything to help her through this."

Lia hands me a half-filled bottle of water. "Here. She needs to drink."

Beth is resting at the moment, her eyes closed, and I hate to disturb her. She needs all the rest she can get between contractions. Damn it! I've never felt so helpless in my life. She should be in a hospital, as comfortable as medically possible. Instead, she's been biting her lips until they bleed in an effort to keep from crying out.

"Sweetheart, can you drink some water?"

She turns her head to me, staring at me with pain-glazed eyes. "All right."

I lift her head gently and hold the water bottle for her as she takes a few small sips.

Abruptly, she pushes the bottle away. "It's starting again."

"Get ready," Lia says, stepping in front of Jason to be closer to Beth. "It's okay, princess. Look at me. We got this."

We. Damn, I love my little sister, but I've never loved her more than I do right now. She has stepped up to this situation as well as anyone ever could.

Beth's entire body tenses, and she strains upward in a half-sitting position, her jaw clenched tightly, her face screwed up in concentration. She doesn't make a sound other than faint keening noises coming from deep in her throat. She's so fucking brave. I move in closer, slipping behind her to support her body with mine, my arms going around her, gripping her hands with mine. Her body is tense, strung tight as a bow. I'm desperate to do anything I can to comfort her, but I'm at a complete loss. I look to Lia.

"Just talk to her," she says. "Talk her through it. Let her know you're here."

Feeling so incredibly inadequate, I press my lips against her temple, murmuring mindlessly to her. "Sweetheart, I'm here. You're so brave, honey. I'm so proud of you."

"Breathe, Beth!" Lia says sharply. "Don't hold your breath. Breathe!"

"I have to push," she gasps, her eyes widening.

"Then push, damn it," Lia says. "Push that baby right out."

Jason shoots to his feet and pulls back the sheet, opening Beth's legs to examine her. He reaches between her legs. "I'm going to touch you again, Beth." His gaze meets mine. "Ten centimeters," he mutters to himself. "Cervix is fully effaced, and I can feel the baby's head." He gives me a relieved smile.

It takes me a minute to realize the significance of that statement. He can feel the baby's *head*—that means the baby's in the right position, head first, not breech. Thank God.

Jason has one hand between Beth's thighs and the other on her abdomen, pressing gently as if guiding the baby out. "You're doing great, Beth," he says. "Push when you feel the need."

Beth pushes and pushes, straining so hard that I'm afraid she's going to burst a blood vessel. When the contraction ends, she falls back against me with a quiet sob, her body like dead weight as she tries to catch her breath. I slip out from behind her and gently lower her head onto the pillow so she can rest.

The contractions continue, over and over, each one wracking her body and zapping her strength. Jason gives her an injection of a local anesthetic to take the edge off the pain.

During one of her moments of respite, I brush her hair back from her pale, damp face and give her a rueful smile. "I sure hope Luke likes being an only child, because we're never doing this again."

She laughs shakily. "I don't think now is the time to be making those kinds of decisions."

While Lia gives her a sip of water, I press my throat mic and request an update from Jake. "She's pushing, Jake. What's the ETA on the NICU ambulance? We'll need to evac the baby ASAP. Nearest hospital. Relay that information to Tyler, Ingrid, and our parents."

My ear piece crackles with static, and then Jake's voice comes through. "SWAT team is still negotiating with gunmen. It's pretty hostile in there. Don't be surprised if SWAT goes in on the offensive. Be prepared for a lot of noise."

"Keep our people clear of them," I instruct Jake. "This is their show. Just keep our evac route clear and get me my fucking neonatal ambulance."

"Roger that. Oh, and regarding Tyler, you can tell him all this yourself. He's on his way up. Consider yourself forewarned."

Well, shit.

"Lia, come sit with Beth," I say. "I have to go deal with you-know-who."

Lia glances back at the doorway, and then she rolls her eyes at me. Of course she knows who I'm talking about. We can hear Tyler arguing in hushed tones with Cameron and Killian, who are guarding the stairwell. They have strict orders not to let anyone through the door.

Lia takes my place, and I hightail it back to the other side of the wall before all hell breaks lose. Tyler Jamison must have come straight from work—he's dressed in a dark suit, white shirt, and tie. His expression is equally dark, bordering on murderous.

"Tyler."

Tyler levels his gaze on me, and if looks could kill, I'd be a dead man. My brother-in-law doesn't like me much because I had the gall to fall in love with his baby sister. I brace myself for what I know is coming, but I figure I might as well let him take a swing at me now and get it over with.

Tyler grabs my shirt collar and shoves me into the wall. "What the fuck have you done?" he grates at me in a low voice.

Tyler has a habit of going ballistic on me where his sister is concerned. He once attacked me at a crime scene and had me arrested for assaulting an officer—*me!*—when he was the one who threw the first punch. I was only defending myself.

I sigh. "We don't have time for a pissing contest right now, Tyler. Do you want an update on her status or not?"

Reluctantly, Tyler releases me, but his hands remain fisted at his sides, and I figure he's debating whether or not to take a swing at me.

"Where is she?" he demands, glaring at me.

Cameron gets in Tyler's face. "Keep the noise down, asshole," he whispers.

I nod at the opening in the wall. "Through there." He moves to pass me, but I grab his arm. "Keep it together, Tyler. She's in labor. She doesn't need your Neanderthal shit right now."

He stops, the blood draining from his face. "She's in labor?"

"Yes."

"But it's too soon."

I watch, astonished, as he reins his temper in, morphing from raging hot to ice cold in an instant.

I step aside and let him proceed me through the opening, close on his heels. He goes right to her, kneeling down beside her and laying his hand on her hair, gently stroking her. "Hi, kiddo," he says.

She turns to face him, her pale eyes stark and filled with pain. "Tyler?"

"Yeah, honey. It's me. How are you doing?"

"Okay," she rasps. "I've been better."

"I'll bet." Then he looks at Jason, a questioning scowl on his face. Tyler looks to me for answers.

"Jason works for me," I say. "He's a former Army medic and he worked as a licensed paramedic." To Jason, I say, "This is Tyler Jamison, Beth's brother. Chicago homicide detective."

Tyler and Jason give each other a curt nod. Then Tyler shifts his attention back to Beth. "Everything's going to be okay, Beth," he says. "I promise. You and the baby are going to be fine."

Beth nods, giving her brother a weak smile. Then she closes her eyes and exhales a long, slow breath just as her brow begins to furrow. "Shane?"

"I'm right here, sweetheart," I tell her, lifting her so I can slip behind her and brace her. As I lean down to kiss the top of her head, she reaches out blindly for a hand. Before I can grab it, Tyler does, cradling her hand between his.

She gasps when the contraction hits her, turning her face away from everyone, toward the back of the sofa as if she's trying to hide her pain from us. I talk her through it with my eyes squeezed shut as I try to staunch my own silent tears, my words jumbled together in a barely comprehensible mix of promises and apologies. I'd take this pain for her in a heartbeat if I could.

When I spare a glance at Tyler, his expression is void of any emotion whatsoever. He just stares at his sister, his expression blank. If you didn't know better, you'd think him heartless and unfeeling. But I do know better. This is affecting him every bit as much as it's affecting me. He's shoved it all away, for her sake, because he knows she needs for us to be strong for her right now.

Cameron and Killian step through the doorway carrying our requisitioned supplies. Cameron's holding what I presume is a pot of hot water—the oven mitts he's wearing giving it away. Killian has a metal basin in one hand and a stack of bright white kitchen towels in the other. As quickly as they deposit the supplies, they're gone again, returning to guard duty.

The contractions are coming so fast and furiously now that one seems to blend into the next, with hardly a respite in between. Beth's body is constantly straining, her muscles tense, her breaths ragged, her voice raw. I've lost all track of time. She can't keep this up.

"You're doing great, Beth," Jason says, looming over her, with one hand between her legs and the other pressing on her rippling belly. "He's so close now. Take a quick breath and then push once more, as hard as you can."

She sucks in air, then grimaces as she bears down, pushing with all her might, growling deep in her throat. When the contraction ends, she collapses against me, and the quiet whimpers coming from her tear at me.

I glance at Tyler, whose gaze meets mine head on. He swallows hard, his anger at me gone, replaced by something I can only describe as fear.

"It's okay," I murmur against the top of Beth's head while holding Tyler's gaze. "Everything's going to be fine." The words are just as much for Tyler as they are for Beth.

Beth draws in a shaky breath as I brush back her hair, my fingers gently stroking her forehead. She sighs. "That feels good."

My ear comm crackles with static, then Jake's voice comes through. "How's she doing?"

"She's holding her own," I reply. "Sit rep."

Jake gives me a run-down of what's going on downstairs. The gunmen have shot another hostage—that makes three now—and the SWAT leader has decided they need to go in with full force and take out the perpetrators. He also reports that the ETA of my neonatal transport is fifteen minutes.

"Beth, you might hear some loud noises coming from downstairs," I warn her, shooting Tyler a glance. "Don't be alarmed. The SWAT team is making their move. But we'll be okay up here. We have guards on duty."

She nods, and a moment later, she tenses as another contraction starts. I move into position, supporting her body as she bears down. Every second of her agony kills me, and I hate myself for letting her be in this position. I never should have agreed to this trip. I should have kept her home in comfort and safety. All of this is my fault, and I can't escape the knowledge that I've let her down.

"That's it, Beth!" Jason says, shooting to his feet, excitement lacing his voice. "The baby's head is crowning. Push! As hard as you can, push! He's so close!"

Lia leans over the back of the sofa, catching Beth's gaze. "Push him out, Beth! Push hard!"

"I'm trying!" Beth snaps, sounding more than a little annoyed.

Tyler gives Lia a dirty look, and if the situation weren't so awful, I would have laughed.

"You'd better push harder, princess," Lia says, making a face at Tyler. "Tyler's looking a little green around the gills. I don't think he can handle the miracle of life."

Beth laughs, but her laugh is quickly cut off by a choked cry. Tyler glares daggers at Lia, and she sticks her tongue out at him.

Lia glances down at the juncture between Beth's thighs, and her eyes widen as she gives me a stricken look. To cover her distress, she pats Beth on the head. "Holy shit, princess, I can see his little head. He's got hair."

Jason quietly moves into position. "All right, Beth. It's time. Let's bring your baby into the world."

"Push, Beth!" Lia urges. "One more really good push! You can do it!"

Beth bears down and powers through a concerted effort to bring our child into the world.

"Oh, my God, you're doing it!" Lia crows quietly, looking surprised and elated. "Push! Push!"

Beth makes a strangled sound as her body tenses and strains. It's a miracle she hasn't already broken something.

Jason's hands are between Beth's thighs as he prepares to catch the baby. "You're doing great, Beth," he says. "Just keep doing what you're doing. That's good. His head is out." Jason reaches for a bulb syringe and begins suctioning fluid out of the baby's mouth. "Okay, just one more big push to get his shoulders out, and then the rest is easy."

A loud, wet pop, followed by a gushing sound, heralds the arrival of Lucas Samuel McIntyre into the world. Beth sags against me, exhausted. Jason moves the baby onto a clean towel laid out at the far end of the sofa and quickly administers to him, his movements quick and efficient. Lia watches Jason work, looking both awed and horrified. Beth's eyes are closed tightly, her entire body trembling.

I hold my breath in anticipation as I wait to hear Luke's first cry, but when there's nothing but silence, I start to get worried. Jason is working feverishly at the far end of the sofa, his expression a careful mask of concentration. Beth is shaking uncontrollably in my arms now, and I'm afraid she's going into shock.

"Find more blankets," I tell Lia.

I catch Tyler's concerned gaze as he watches Jason working on the baby. We still haven't heard a sound from Lucas yet, and that sends up all kinds of red flags. Don't babies usually start wailing the instant they're born? "Sit rep," I snap at Jason.

Tyler rises to stand behind Jason, who still hasn't said a word. It's easily been a minute now, and I still don't hear what I expect to hear. Just silence and the sound of Beth's labored breathing.

Lia returns with a heavy comforter, which we drape over Beth, hoping to warm her.

The seconds pass without the sound of a crying baby, and my heart begins to jackhammer against my ribs as the implication sinks in. I slide out from behind Beth and lay her down gently. "I'll be right back," I tell her, but I don't think my words are registering.

She turns her face toward the back of the sofa and closes her eyes. "He's not breathing, is he?" she says, her voice barely audible.

I don't need to be told that she's praying with every fiber of her being.

17

Shane

He's not breathing is he?
Beth's words play over and over in my mind, caught in a loop, as the seconds tick by. How long has it been now? Ninety seconds? A hundred? How long can a newborn infant go without breathing? Jesus, I don't know.

I sidle up next to Jason, who's using a bulb syringe to suction fluid from the baby's throat. The umbilical cord is still attached to the baby, who is incredibly tiny, and yet so perfect. He's perfectly formed, with tiny flailing fists and kicking feet. His little face is all scrunched up, and he looks like he wants to scream bloody murder, but he can't. The only thing I hear is thick fluid gurgling in his airway.

Jason spares me a quick glance. "As long as the umbilical cord is attached, he's still getting oxygenated blood," he whispers. "That will buy us some time to get him breathing."

As the seconds pass, Luke's complexion darkens as he struggles to cry. My heart stops as reality sinks in.

He's not breathing.

My tiny, perfect little son can't breathe.

The pain ... my God, it's indescribable. I'd rather be gutted than experience this all-consuming agony.

I look to Jason, desperate for answers, but he's so intently focused on the baby that he ignores me. Jason turns Luke over in his hands, holding the baby face down, and rubs his tiny back briskly, whispering, "Come on, damn it! Breathe!"

He turns Luke back over and suctions more fluid from the baby's airway. Then we hear it, a faint, wet cough followed by a tiny squawk. Lucas coughs again, a little more forcefully this time, expelling fluid from his mouth, and then he lets out a shaky cry.

I'm so relieved that my knees almost give out on me. I glance back at the sofa, where Tyler is holding Beth, whose body is wracked with tremors. My throat tightens as I watch Beth sobbing in her brother's arms.

After wiping the worst of the mucus and blood from Luke's torso with a damp towel, Jason attaches two clamps to the umbilical cord. Then he hands me a pair of surgical scissors and points to a spot between the clamps. "Cut here, Dad," he says, grinning at me.

After I cut the cord, Jason picks Luke up and motions for me to follow. We step away from the sofa, out of Beth's hearing. "His lungs are likely underdeveloped," he says over the sounds of Luke's labored breathing. "This is not uncommon with preemies." Jason lifts his somber gaze to mine. "He needs a respirator. Where's my NICU ambulance?"

I press my throat mic. "Jake? Where's that transport? We need it now."

After a moment of static, Jake's voice comes back over the comm. "Their ETA is three minutes."

"Three minutes," I tell Jason.

He nods curtly, then glances at Beth. "I've done all I can do for the baby. He needs the NICU team now. They'll take him to the nearest hospital with air flight, and they'll send him by helicopter to the Children's Hospital in Chicago. Your wife is in shock, and we're not done here yet. She still needs to pass the placenta, and then we need to get her to the hospital for treatment—she's going to need stitches. Who's going in the ambulance with the baby? I need to stay here and help Beth." Jason eyes me expectantly as he continues to rub Luke's back, stimulating him to breathe.

I stare at the medic, momentarily stunned when it dawns on me that I can't be in two places at once. I can't stay with my wife and be with our son too. I open my mouth to speak, but nothing comes out. I've never felt so conflicted in my life. There's no way in hell I can leave Beth at a time like this, and yet I can't send our defenseless son off without us.

Cooper appears at my side, his hand firmly gripping my shoulder. "You stay with Beth. Sam and I will go with Luke. We won't leave his side."

"The NICU ambulance has arrived!" Jake says over the comm unit. "Bring him down now."

The ominous silence is interrupted by the plaintive wail of my tiny son, who's about to be whisked away from me before I've even had a chance to hold him. Before his mother has even held him.

I hold out my hands. "Give him to me."

Jason nods. "Hold him against your chest, skin to skin. He needs your body warmth."

I yank open my shirt, sending buttons flying everywhere, and hold Luke's tiny body against my bare chest, his cheek over my pounding heart. With one hand, I cradle his body against mine, and with the other I close my shirt around him, hoping to insulate him and let the warmth of my body seep into his.

"Good. Just like that," Jason says. "Talk to him, Shane. Let him hear your voice. He'll recognize you. I need to check on Beth."

As I stand there holding my son, rubbing his back, Jason and Lia tend to Beth. Luke's making noises now, which is a good sign, quiet, fidgeting sounds and plaintive, breathy cries. And he's wriggling in my arms, surprisingly strong for one so small. I'm relieved to feel his body warming against my chest, but I can also hear fluid rattling in his airway and most likely in his lungs, and that's not good. I realize with a sick sense of dread that he's not out of the woods yet.

Beth meets my gaze, her face pale and her expression gaunt. I'm just beginning to realize how having a child has complicated our lives. I need to be with my wife. I should be the one holding her right now, comforting her, not Tyler. But our son needs me, too, and I know that if I asked her, she would want me to take care of him first. It's no longer just the two of us—Beth and me—we're a family of three now. And no matter how desperately I want to, I can't be in two places at once. The realization is sobering.

I move to stand at the foot of the sofa and watch Jason as he tends to Beth. She's pushing again, straining, although not as hard as before, to pass the placenta. Tyler has taken my place, bracing Beth's body, supporting her and encouraging her in a low, coaxing voice. Jealousy eats at me like acid. It should be *me* holding her. It should be *me* comforting her.

She gives me a small, sad smile as she watches me stroke Luke's back through my shirt. She's not even had a chance to hold her own child, and that breaks my heart.

I start in her direction, wanting to give her that chance, when Jason intercepts me and hands me one of the clean towels. "Wrap him in this and take him down to the paramedics. They will have a portable incubator and a respirator for him. Go now."

Carefully, I wrap him in a white towel and hold him close

to my chest. Cooper follows me as I carry Luke downstairs and out the rear door of the restaurant into the alley. There, the two NICU paramedics are waiting.

The woman takes Luke from me without a word and climbs up into the ambulance and lays him in an incubator, while the man follows her in and takes Luke's vitals. The male rattles off some numbers.

The woman frowns. "His oxygen levels are low," she says as she attaches a breathing mask to his face.

I stand at the rear of the ambulance and watch the proceedings with fear gripping my gut.

The female paramedic jumps back out of the ambulance. "You're the father?" she asks me.

"Yes."

"We're going to transport him to the hospital in Stowe. From there, he'll be airlifted to Children's Hospital in Chicago. They have a first-rate neonatal intensive care unit. They'll take good care of him."

I nod, having expected this.

"Do you want to travel with your son?" she says.

My throat closes up. It kills me to say no, but I can't leave Beth. I shake my head. "I can't leave my wife."

"I'm going with Luke," Cooper says to the paramedic.

The woman looks at him. "And you are?"

"I'm his grandfather," Cooper says without batting an eye.

The paramedic looks to me for verification, and I nod. "If his mother and I can't go with him, this man is his next-of-kin. His grandfather."

"I'm coming, too," Sam says, standing shoulder-to-shoulder with Cooper, staring hard at the paramedic as if daring her to refuse him.

"And you are?" she says.

Sam points to his T-shirt, *I'm With Him*, and then points to Cooper. "I go where he goes. We're a package deal."

"Okay, fine," she says, looking to me for validation.

I nod, thinking it's only fitting as we had already asked Cooper and Sam to be Luke's godparents. "My wife and I will get to Children's Hospital as soon as we possibly can."

I watch helplessly as Cooper and Sam climb into the ambulance with Luke and the paramedics, and the doors close. As the ambulance pulls away, something inside me is screaming to go with them. But Beth is still upstairs, and she needs me. I race back inside the restaurant and up the stairs to the attic room.

Just as I approach the sofa, Jason presses on her abdomen, and she pushes, grimacing as she expels the placenta. She's lying back against Tyler, her eyes tightly shut. Even so, tears are streaming down the sides of her face, and it breaks my heart. It wasn't supposed to happen like this.

I drop to my knees beside the sofa and take Beth's chilled hand in mine, cradling it to my chest. One glance at Tyler tells me he's hurting just as badly as we are. "Sweetheart? I'm here."

She turns her face toward me, noting my open, blood-stained shirt with a frown. "Where is he?" she says, sounding a bit disoriented. "Where's the baby?"

I brush back her hair. "The paramedics took him to the hospital in Stowe. From there, he'll be flown to Children's Hospital in Chicago. They have a top-rate neonatal intensive care unit."

Her eyes widen in horror as my words sink in. "He's gone? They took him?"

I nod, feeling choked with guilt. I got to hold him. She didn't. "I'm so sorry, sweetheart. They had to. He's not breathing well on his own. His oxygen levels are low, and he needs help."

"I didn't even get to hold him," she says, giving in to tears. "And he's *alone.*" She looks absolutely devastated. "We should be with him."

"Please don't worry. Cooper and Sam are with him. They won't leave his side. He'll be safe, and he'll get the care he needs."

"I have to go with him," she says, struggling to sit up, even as Jason is attempting to clean her up.

Tyler gets up from the sofa, and we both use gentle pressure to force her back into a lying position.

"Sweetheart, you can't be moved yet," I tell her.

"She's in shock," Jason says, working quickly to finish up. "Shane, talk to her. Try to comfort her. And get me an ETA on Beth's transport."

Jake gives me an estimate of seven minutes on a second ambulance.

While Jason finishes getting Beth ready to travel, I try to comfort her and keep her calm. When the ambulance arrives, I wrap Beth in a clean sheet and carry her downstairs. The paramedics, who are waiting for us outside the rear door to the restaurant, strap her into a gurney and load her into an ambulance. I climb in after them and sit out of the way as the paramedics take her vitals.

Lia stands at the rear doors of the vehicle, looking uncertain. "What do you want me and Jonah to do?"

"Get our clothes and toiletries from the Escalade and ask Jake to bring them to us in the hospital in Stowe. Beth's purse, too. Then head back to Chicago in the Escalade." I toss her the keys to the SUV. "Update the rest of the families, ours and Beth's."

Lia nods, looking more than a little shell shocked. I think assisting in childbirth really shook her. Jonah comes into view, and the moment she sees him, she tears up.

"Hey, tiger," Jonah says, his voice gentle as he draws Lia into his arms. He holds her close, rubbing her back as he leans down to kiss the top of her head. Her shoulders are shaking as she presses her face against Jonah's chest.

"Everything's going to be all right," he says. "Don't worry." Then he holds her at arm's length to look her over from head to toe. "Are you okay? Are you hurt?"

She nods, wiping her damp face on her T-shirt. "I'm fine. Stop fussing."

Jonah shares a look with me over Lia's head. It's pretty clear to both of us that Lia's far from fine. Jonah pulls her close again and holds her.

"Just get her back to Chicago," I tell him. "We'll regroup at Children's Hospital."

18

Beth

They took my baby.

He's gone.

Everything hurts—my legs, my arms, my back. Every muscle hurts, and the area between my legs burns. I'm so cold, I can't stop shaking, and my mind is numb. I'm slowly sinking into a deep, dark pit of nothingness.

Shane wraps me up in a blanket and carries me downstairs and out the back of the restaurant into an alley where two paramedics wait with a gurney. They load me into an ambulance, and Shane climbs in with me. The ambulance is moving now, slowly, as it makes its way out of the alley and onto the main road. Shane is seated on a bench at the foot of the gurney. That's as close as he can get while the paramedics loom over me, taking my vitals and inserting needles into my arm.

I glance at Shane, stunned by the stark expression on his face. He looks like a man haunted. I've never seen him like this before. He's always so much in control, so self-assured. He watches me intently as the paramedics go about their business, his hand warm and solid on my ankle. Why is he here? Why isn't he with our baby?

The two paramedics take their seats when the ambulance picks up speed. They're hashing over my vitals, talking so quickly I'm having trouble following, not that I really care.

"Your wife is in shock," the female paramedic says. "Her blood pressure is low."

The other paramedic attaches a tube to the IV needle embedded in my arm.

Someone lays a warm blanket on me, I'm not sure who. I've closed my eyes and turned away from their quiet conversation, lost in my own thoughts.

This is all my fault. My baby is at risk, whisked away from me before I could even see him, let alone hold him.

My fault.

I'm the one who wanted to go out of town. None of this would have happened if we'd stayed home. It's certainly not Shane's fault. If he'd had his way, we wouldn't have gone anywhere, and my baby would be safely in my womb, where he should be.

My fault.

Mine.

And now our baby is alone and at risk.

And Shane... oh, my God, Shane must be so angry at me. That's why he's just sitting there, watching me so intently. He looks gutted, and I'm sure he blames me. Why wouldn't he? I can't bear to look at him. I can't bear to see the disappointment in his eyes, the recrimination. And he has every right to blame me.

The female paramedic pats my shoulder. "We're almost there, Mrs. McIntyre. Just hold on. They'll get you fixed up in no time. You're going to be just fine."

I can't stop shaking. I feel so utterly exhausted, and everything *hurts*. I just want to sleep. I just want to drift away and shut off my brain so I don't have to think about what I've done.

"Beth? Sweetheart?"

At the sound of Shane's quiet voice, my heart stops. He sounds hesitant, which is unlike him. I can feel his hand on my leg, stroking me, and I have to fight the urge to pull it away from his touch.

The ambulance makes a turn and comes to a stop. I can hear the paramedics jump to their feet and unlock the wheels of my gurney. Then I sense Shane hovering over me.

"Beth?" His warm hand brushes my hair back. Then his thumb brushes the trail of tears falling down the side of my face. "Sweetheart, can you look at me?"

But I can't. I can't face him. I turn away, unable to bear the accusation I know I'll see in his eyes. My throat squeezes shut, choking me.

"Sir?" It's the female paramedic. "Would you mind stepping out of the ambulance, please? We need to move her inside. Thank you."

Then I'm moving, quickly, as the gurney is slid to the back of the ambulance. For a moment, it feels like I'm floating in air, and then the wheels touch down on the pavement and I'm wheeled into the hospital.

There are a lot of voices, all speaking rapidly, decisively, and I try to shut it all out. I know what's going to happen now. Someone's going to look at me, put stitches in me. I heard Jason telling Shane that I'll need stitches. That means I tore down there. More pain, more injury to an area that's already too painful to bear.

Someone reaches for my hand, pulling it out from beneath my blanket to hold tightly as I'm whisked down a brightly-lit hallway. The light bleeds through my eyelids, blinding me. It's Shane's hand—big, warm, with calloused fingertips and scarred knuckles. I'd recognize his touch anywhere.

"Everything's going to be all right, honey, I promise," he says, squeezing my hand. There's a frantic quality to his voice that scares me. He must be leaning over me because I can feel his warm breath on my cheek. "They're taking you to Labor and Delivery, where an OB can examine you and... finish things up."

We ride up in an elevator, and then travel a long hallway.

I hear metal doors bang open, then close, and finally the gurney comes to a stop. When I open my eyes, I'm in a room—a surprisingly pretty one—with cherry-wood paneling and floral wallpaper. A big picture window takes up one wall, and there's a table with a vase of fresh-cut flowers on it. It looks more like someone's home than a hospital.

Hospital staff members transfer me to a bed, moving my IV bag as well, hanging it on a pole. A woman comes into the room—a nurse, I presume—and listens to a run-down of my condition.

Shane appears beside my bed, his expression tight as he looms over me, trying to catch my gaze. "Honey?" He gently turns my face toward his. "It's going to be all right, I promise. Cooper's been sending me regular updates on Luke. They're on their way to Children's Hospital in Chicago right now. As soon as the doctor here releases you, we'll head back to Chicago, and I'll take you right to him, I promise. But right now, you need to be seen to."

When I finally get up the courage to look at Shane, I'm shocked at his appearance. His white shirt is hanging open and stained with blood. The buttons are gone. His chest is stained with blood, too. He looks completely disheveled, his expression tight, his hair tousled. When I finally bring myself to meet his gaze, I expect to see accusation and resentment, but he hides it well.

"Sir?" The nurse appears at Shane's side. "Would you mind stepping aside, please? I need to take your wife's vitals and get her prepped for the OB. She's on her way."

Shane gazes down at me, a frown on his face. "All right," he says. But before he steps back, he leans down and kisses my forehead. He squeezes my hand one last time before slowly releasing it and stepping out of the way so the nurse can do her work.

Another nurse appears, holding out a blue scrub shirt to Shane. "Sir?" Her voice is hesitant as she eyes his shirt. "Here's a clean shirt for you to wear until you get a chance to change."

Shane glances down at his destroyed shirt and grimaces. "Sorry, I wasn't thinking. Thanks." He takes off his ruined shirt and tosses it into a wastebasket, and then he pulls on the clean scrub shirt.

As the nurse takes my blood pressure and temperature, I close my eyes and lose myself in the numbness.

"Here's something to help you relax," the nurse says as she injects medication into my IV line. Suddenly I feel weightless, as if I'm floating on a sea of warm water.

Feeling nothing is better than feeling so much pain.

19

Shane

Something's wrong.

Beth hasn't said a word to me since we left in the ambulance. She's shut herself off, from me, from everyone, and seems lost in her own world. I know she's been through a terrible trauma, and my heart breaks for her, for all she's suffered... the stress, the anxiety, the pain. And not just the physical pain of a swift and sudden labor, but the emotional pain of knowing our son has been rushed away for emergency medical treatment. It kills me that she never even got to hold him. But there just wasn't time.

In hindsight, I realize I should have used my phone to take pictures of the baby. At least then she'd have something to look at, something to hold onto until we're reunited with him. I could kick myself for not thinking of that when I had the opportunity.

I text Cooper and ask him to take pictures of Luke and send them to me. As soon as the obstetrician is done with Beth, I'll show her the pictures. I know it won't make up for the fact that she didn't get to hold him, but at least it's something to tide her over until we get to Children's Hospital.

A middle-aged woman with short blonde hair, dressed in scrubs, comes into the room, her sharp gaze quickly assessing the situation. She shakes my hand. "I'm Dr. Anderson. I'll be assisting your wife, Mr. McIntyre. I'll make sure all of the afterbirth was delivered, and then we'll see what else needs to be done."

"Thank you. Do you have an idea when she can be released? We need to get back to Chicago to be with our son at Children's Hospital."

The doctor nods. "I certainly understand. But under the conditions your wife delivered, and due to the risk of infection, I'd like to keep her at least overnight for observation. She'll need some pain medication, and possibly an antibiotic, depending on what I find."

The obstetrician examines Beth and gives her a local anesthetic before stitching her up. I stand beside Beth, holding her hand, grimacing every time she flinches or whimpers. Despite the anesthetic, she can still feel the stitches going in.

"Mr. McIntyre?"

I glance up at the sound of my name, feeling a bit disoriented. I've been so focused on Beth, I'd lost track of the time. "Yes?"

The OB smiles at me as she pulls her surgical gloves off. "We're all done here. Your wife will be moved into a maternity recovery room where she can rest. You can stay overnight with her there."

I stand. "Thank you. Is everything...okay?"

The doctor gives me a smile. "Yes, she's going to be just fine."

* * *

The nurse moves Beth's bed to a room just down the hall. Walking through the hospital corridor feels surreal. Today wasn't supposed to go like this. We should have been at the cabin, enjoying some steaks on the grill, kicking back and listening to the insects and birds in the woods. Instead, here we are, a hundred miles away from our son.

Thank God Cooper and Sam are with him. Otherwise, I don't think I could hold my shit together. Luke is in good hands. Our Children's Hospital has one of the best neonatal intensive care units in the country, and his godfathers will watch over him like avenging angels in our stead.

Right now, my job is to concentrate on Beth and make sure she gets the care she needs.

The recovery room is nicely decorated, resembling an upscale hotel room. The room has everything we need, including a sofa and a chair that pulls out into a single bed, and a bathroom with a shower. God, I need a shower. And clean clothes.

I check on Beth, who's exhausted and drowsy from a sedative the doctor gave her to help her relax.

My phone chimes with an incoming message from Cooper.

Cooper: He weighs four pounds, two ounces.

I wonder if that's good or bad. I have no frame of reference. How much is a newborn supposed to weigh? He came six weeks early, so my guess is four pounds is small. Too small? Dangerously so? I have no idea.

Another update from Cooper follows.

Cooper: He's breathing on his own, but they're giving him oxygen.

Then a series of photos arrives, half a dozen pictures of Luke lying in an incubator, looking so damn tiny in an impossibly tiny little diaper. It's painful to see him with all those tubes and wires attached to his little body.

I scroll through the pictures again, more slowly this time, and study my son. He's got ten tiny fingers and ten toes. He's had a bath, and his hair is clean and dry. He's a blond, just like his mama.

He's sleeping in all of the photos, so I have no idea what color his eyes are. Probably blue, since Beth and I both have blue eyes. Maybe he'll have that blue-green shade that Beth has. I think back to when I held him earlier in the afternoon. It was too dark up in that attic for me to clearly see his eyes.

I look down at the palm of my hand and marvel that his entire head fit in my palm, with room to spare. God, he's so small. So fragile.

My phone chimes with another incoming text.

Cooper: He's going to be fine in a few weeks. Tell Beth not to worry.

There's a knock on the door, and I open it to find Jake standing there with our duffle bag and toiletries case.

"Thank God," I say, waving him into the room. "I need to shower and change."

Wordlessly, he opens his arms, and we embrace.

"How is she?" he says, after he releases me with a clap on the back. He eyes my temporary shirt. "Nice shirt."

"I ruined my shirt, so a nurse gave me this to wear."

I give Jake a quick rundown on Beth's condition and the updates that Cooper has sent. "Here, pictures," I say, handing him my phone. While I change shirts, Jake flips through the photos of Luke.

"Damn, he's so small," he says. "The NICU paramedics whisked him away so quickly I didn't get a chance to look at him." Jake studies one of the pictures. "He looks like you."

I laugh. "How in the hell can you tell by looking at those photos?"

Jake shrugs. "I can tell." He pats me on the back. "Don't worry, bro. He's going to be fine. Beth's going to be fine, too."

Jake abandons me to check on Beth, but she's sound asleep.

"The doctor gave her something to help her rest," I say,

reaching for her hand. "And something for the pain."

* * *

Jake leaves us so Beth can rest, telling me he'll be in the waiting room if we need him. I crash on the sofa and watch her
sleep, but my mind is too wired to get any sleep myself.

Sometime later, there's a quiet knock on the door. I open
the door and in walks a woman. She gives me a smile, then observes Beth sleeping. "Mr. McIntyre? My name is Denise. I'm a
lactation consultant. Do you know if your wife is planning to
breastfeed?"

I nod. "She is, yes. Unfortunately, our baby's in Chicago right
now, at Children's Hospital."

"I know. I'm sorry about the difficult circumstances of your
wife's delivery. Since your baby's not here at the moment, your
wife will need to pump to help start the milk production process. I can help her with that. She can save the colostrum she
pumps and take it with her to give to the baby when she can."

"Oh, right." Good lord, I am so in over my head here. "We
have the equipment back at home... a breast pump, bottles, the
whole nine yards."

She gives me a sad smile. "Sorry things didn't work out as
planned. We can give you a hand pump. That will work fine
until you get home. And we have cold packs you can have to
keep the colostrum chilled."

The lactation consultant departs, promising to come back

when Beth is awake. I sit in the visitor chair next to Beth's bed, turning the chair so that it's facing her. I reach for her hand, which is warm and soft, and so very still. I hold it in mine, stroking the back of it. "I'm here, Beth."

I know she can't hear me, but I need to talk to her. I kiss the back of her hand, breathing in the delicate scent of her skin, the familiarity of it making me ache. "I won't leave your side again, honey. I promise." And then I lay my head down near hers and close my eyes.

* * *

I wake up from my impromptu nap when Beth begins to stir, moaning with every movement. If I could bear the pain for her, I would. Gladly.

She shifts under the covers and a whimper escapes her.

"Beth?" I scoot closer, until I'm at the edge of my seat. "Honey? Can you hear me?"

She moans in response, and then her eyelids flutter open. She blinks several times, trying to focus. Then she turns to face me. "Shane?"

20

Beth

Everything comes rushing back like a bad dream, the guilt, the crushing sense of shame that I let Shane down. That I let our baby down. The fear of seeing accusation in Shane's eyes. I can't bear that.

It's all my fault.

"How do you feel?" he asks, as he brushes my hair back and strokes my forehead with the pad of his thumb.

"Better." At least that part is true. I still feel a lot of physical discomfort, but the sharp edge of pain has been greatly tempered. My muscles are sore all over, and the area between my legs is quite swollen and tender. As I shift my position, I can feel the unwelcome bulk of bandages between my legs.

"Would you like to see pictures of the baby? Cooper sent these about an hour ago. He said Luke's doing well." Shane pulls out his phone and slowly flips through images of our baby lying in an incubator, wearing nothing but a diaper, with God knows how many wires and tubes taped to his tiny body.

It's all my fault.

I look at Shane, his image swimming through the tears pooling in my eyes. "I want to go home. Please take me home."

He frowns, his brow furrowing as he watches me far too closely. I look away, staring up at the ceiling, not wanting to see what I'm afraid I'm going to see in his eyes.

"Your doctor wants you to stay overnight for observation," he says. "If everything checks out in the morning, we can head home then."

I'm saved from making a reply when someone walks into the room—a woman, a nurse.

"Hello, Beth," she says, giving me a bright smile. "I'm Ruby. I'll be your nurse tonight."

Ruby does a cursory inspection of my blood pressure cuff and oxygen monitor. Then she checks my chart. "How do you feel, hon?"

"Better."

"Would you like to try using the restroom?" Ruby looks at Shane. "It's important that we know she can urinate. She can't leave until we know she can. It can take a while for the body's functions to start working again after something as traumatic as birth."

Ruby smiles down at me. "Do you want to try to go to the bathroom now? I'll help you."

I'm not looking forward to getting up and walking, but my bladder is full—painfully so. I might as well give it a try. I toss off the blankets and sit up, gingerly swinging my feet to the floor.

"I'll help you, sweetheart," Shane says, offering me his hand.

I shake my head, coward that I am, not meeting his gaze. "That's all right. She'll help me."

Frowning, Shane steps back without a word, giving Ruby and me a clear path to the restroom. I can't bear to look him in the eye.

Pulling my IV pole along with me, I shuffle across the room in my drafty hospital gown to the restroom, Ruby at my side, her hand on my elbow supporting me.

After I'm settled in the restroom, Ruby waits outside the door to give me some privacy while I try to convince my bladder it's okay to let go. I know I need to go—my bladder is killing me. But it doesn't seem to want to cooperate. My body starts shaking, and I'm finding it difficult to relax.

"Any luck?" Ruby says through the door.

"No."

She comes into the restroom and turns on the water faucet to a gentle stream, the water trickling loudly into the sink. I laugh, remembering my mom doing the same thing when I was a little girl. "Maybe that will help."

Ruby goes back to her spot outside the door and waits patiently. I will my body to relax, and finally have success.

After washing up, I shuffle back to bed, with Ruby's help, and lie down once more. On her way out, Ruby promises to bring me something to eat. I haven't eaten more than a protein bar since breakfast that morning, and I'm starving.

Shane's standing at the large picture window, staring out at the night sky, with his back to me. Tension radiates off his body in waves. I imagine there are all kinds of things he wants to say to me, none of which I'm ready to hear.

He closes the blinds and returns to the chair beside my bed, his expression carefully neutral. "How'd it go in there?"

"Fine," I say, staring down at my hands folded on my lap. "It took a while, but I did it."

"Good. That's great. Beth—"

"Ruby's going to bring me some supper," I say, cutting him off before he can say anything more. I'm just not ready to talk. "You should go eat something. I'm sure you must be starving."

He stands, looking dejected, and I feel even worse. "All right. I won't be gone long."

ᘓ 21

Shane

Warning bells reverberate in my head as I head down the hall to the delivery waiting room where Jake is camping out, on standby in case we need him. Something's wrong. Beth's avoiding eye contact—not just with me, but with everyone—and when asked a question, she gives the barest of answers.

I feel a growing sense of anxiety, but I tamp it down. We'll get through this, whatever this is. It's only temporary. Once she's had a chance to recover from the events of today, she'll be okay. We both will. But right now, she feels so far away from me, and moving farther with every passing minute. I'm desperate to pull her back to me, but I'm not sure if that's the right thing to do. Maybe she just needs some space, some time to process everything that's happened.

I know she's tired—more like exhausted—and she's got to be hurting all over physically, not to mention emotionally. I'll gladly give her all the time she needs... but I can't dismiss the red flags I'm seeing.

She didn't ask where Luke is. She didn't ask how he's doing. She didn't ask what his prognosis is. She didn't ask when we can see him. This isn't like Beth. If anything, I would have expected her to be in tears, begging and pleading with me to take her back to Chicago tonight so she can see the baby. Instead, nothing.

In fact, I don't think she's said more than a dozen words to me since we arrived at the hospital.

I find Jake seated in the waiting room, flipping through a racing magazine.

"How's she doing?" he says, tossing the magazine aside as soon as he sees me.

I shrug. "I'm not sure. Physically, she's doing well. The obstetrician said everything looks fine, and that she should be able to go home tomorrow. But emotionally..." I shake my head. "She's struggling."

"She's been through a lot, Shane."

"I know, but this is different. It's like she's shutting down. She's not herself. And she's not showing any interest in Luke.

That's not like her. Before, the baby was all she could talk about, and now...nothing."

I drop down into the empty seat beside my brother. "I showed her the pictures of Luke in his incubator, and all she said was that she wanted to go home."

Jake pats me on the back. "Give her some time," he says. "She experienced a hell of a trauma today. Maybe she's still in shock. I'm sure she'll be back to her sweet and charming self by morning."

"I hope you're right."

But as much as I want to believe Jake's right, my gut tells me differently.

* * *

Jake and I go down to the cafeteria to grab some coffee and sandwiches. When I return to the room, the lactation consultant is just leaving. I take a seat in the chair beside the bed. Beth's sitting up.

"How'd it go?" I ask her.

She shrugs. "Fine."

"Did you try the pump?"

She nods, staring down at her fingers which are fiddling nervously with the blanket. "She said the milk won't actually start flowing for a couple of days, but I'm pumping the colostrum and that will get things going." She grimaces as she shifts position.

"What's wrong?"

"My breasts hurt. They're swollen. But I guess pumping will help with that." Her gaze flickers my way for a brief moment, though she doesn't look me in the eye. "Would you please turn out the lights? I'm tired. I want to sleep."

I swallow hard, debating whether or not it's the right time to address the elephant in the room. I don't know if I should give her more time, or jump into it head first. I figure there's no time like the present. I don't think it's healthy to let this continue unaddressed. "Beth, honey, we need to talk."

There's no mistaking the flash of panic in her eyes as she glances at me, then away. "Talk about what? Can't it wait? I'm really tired."

I sigh, blowing out a heavy breath. I'm so out of my element here. "Sweetheart, something's bothering you, and I think we should talk about it."

She shakes her head as she reaches for the remote control and lowers the head of the bed. She closes her eyes, effectively shutting me out.

I reach for her hand. "I know you've been through an awful experience. You have no idea how sorry I am that this happened. I know you're hurting and you're scared, and you have every right to be. But please, don't shut me out. Let me help you. Luke is going to be fine. He's experiencing some complications because he's premature, but Cooper assures me his doctors said he's not in danger. He just needs a little time to catch up."

I get no reaction from her at all.

I bring her hand to my lips and kiss it, pressing my nose against her soft skin. "Honey, talk to me."

"I'm tired, Shane. I just want to sleep right now. Please."

* * *

Nine o'clock that night, there's a quiet knock on our door. When I open it, I'm not surprised to see Tyler standing there, along with their mother.

"Ingrid," I say, opening my arms to her.

Ingrid Jamison falls into my arms looking like she's a heartbeat away from losing it.

"They're okay, Ingrid," I tell her as I rub her back. "Beth's resting, and Cooper tells me Luke is not in any danger. He's going to be fine. They both will."

"My poor baby girl," she says, her voice muffled against my shirt.

I glance over the top of Ingrid's head, at her son. Tyler may be one self-controlled son-of-a-gun, but he doesn't fool me, not for a second. He's just as worried as the rest of us.

Ingrid pulls back and looks up at me. "Can I see her?" Her voice is little more than a whisper as she peers around me, trying to get a look at her daughter.

"Of course, you can." But first, I step out of the room and close the door quietly behind us so we can speak frankly. "Beth has been through a lot today," I warn them. "She's pretty traumatized, so don't expect a lot out of her. She's not very talkative right now."

"All right," Ingrid says, and Tyler nods.

I open the door and stand aside to let Beth's family precede me into the room. Ingrid swallows hard, her shoulders lifting as she pastes a brave smile on her face. Tyler gives me a considering look as he passes me, saying nothing for the time being. I'm sure he'll have plenty to say to me later, well out of Beth's hearing.

I stake out a position at the foot of the bed and watch as Ingrid sits on the side of the bed. Tyler stands on the side opposite his mother.

Ingrid gently touches Beth's cheek. "Baby, it's Mama. I'm here."

Beth's eyes flutter open, and she stares at her mother. "Mama?" Her eyes fill with tears as she sits up with a whimper, reaching for her mother.

Ingrid wraps Beth in her arms and kisses her temple. "I'm so sorry I wasn't there for you, sweetheart," she says, gently rocking her daughter. "I'm so sorry."

Beth breaks down, sobbing in her mother's embrace. My own throat tightens as I watch her.

"It's all right, baby," Ingrid says, holding Beth as she cries. "Everything's going to be all right. You'll see."

When Beth's tears subside, Ingrid lowers her back down on the bed and arranges the bedding just so, smoothing the blanket over Beth's chest. Beth bites back a pained grimace, and Ingrid pulls her hand back.

"Her breasts," I say. "They're swollen, and she's uncomfortable."

"Oh, right," Ingrid says. "It's been so many years since I had a baby, I'd forgotten. It's a shame Lucas isn't here with you. Nursing would help."

"She has a pump," I say. "She's going to pump until she can nurse him."

And just like that, what little energy Beth had is gone, and she closes her eyes again. "I'm so tired," she says. "I'm sorry."

"Don't be sorry, darling." Ingrid strokes Beth's hair. "We understand. Just rest."

They stay another half-hour, Ingrid sitting on the bed and stroking Beth's hair. Tyler watches from the side, his expression grave. Every once in a while, he makes eye contact with me, and it's clear we're on the same page for a change.

Tyler nods toward the door, and I follow him out into the hallway.

"What's wrong with her?" he says after closing the door behind us.

I sigh. "I'm not exactly sure, but obviously something's not right. Maybe she's still in shock. Clearly, she's traumatized. Maybe even depressed."

He glares at me. "Have you tried asking her?"

"Of course I did. She said she didn't want to discuss it."

Tyler shakes his head. "She's not herself."

"No, she isn't. I'm hoping once I get her back to Chicago and she sees Luke, she'll snap out of it."

"And if she doesn't?"

"I'll deal with that when the time comes."

Ingrid and Tyler take their leave around ten o'clock, planning to head back to Chicago. I walk them out into the hallway.

"I'll be staying in town with Tyler for the time being," Ingrid says, "so I can be close to Beth and the baby. If there's anything I can do to help, please let me know."

"I will." I hug Ingrid good-bye. "I'll take good care of her and keep you posted. I promise."

"Thank you."

I offer my hand to Tyler, who shakes it. But he doesn't say much. I think he's as thrown by Beth's behavior as I am. And equally as worried. He gives me a level stare. "Take care of her."

"I will."

* * *

After heading back into Beth's room, I grab a pillow and blanket from the cupboard and make up a bed on the sofa. The last thing I feel like doing right now is sleeping, but a few hours of sleep tonight would be a good idea. Who knows what tomorrow will bring?

Beth's eyes are closed, and she's breathing evenly, but I suspect she's not asleep. She opened up to her mom, and to Tyler, but she's avoiding me, and I don't know why.

I sit on the edge of her bed and take her hand in mine, stroking the back of it. I want to be in that bed with her so badly, just to hold her in my arms, feel her warmth and breathe in her scent, but I know I can't. Right now she needs some space. "I'll be right over there, on the sofa, sweetheart. Call me if you need anything."

I get no response, but that doesn't surprise me.

"Everything's going to be all right," I tell her. "Please, don't worry."

Still nothing. Until she swallows hard, the corners of her lips turning down just the slightest bit. Her lower lip quivers. Yeah, she's awake.

"I wish you would talk to me, honey. Let me know what you're thinking. I'll do anything to help you, you know that."

Nothing.

I can't for the life of me figure out what's going on with her. She always talks to me about what's bothering her. She always confides in me. Unless....

An unwelcome thought slams into my head, and I have to know. "Do you blame me for what happened today?"

Her eyes snap open, and she stares at me, horrified. "No! Of course I don't blame you!"

"Then what's bothering you? Is it me? Is it something I did? Or something I didn't do? Beth, please, throw me a bone here. Tell me what's wrong so I can fix it."

Her expression falls, and she looks devastated. "You can't fix this."

"Of course, I can. I can fix anything. Just tell me."

She shakes her head, turning away. "Everything that happened today... the baby... it's all my fault. You can't change it or fix it."

I stare at her, completely dumbfounded. "Beth, you can't be serious. None of it was your fault!"

"Yes, it was. The trip was my idea. You didn't even want us to go. You only agreed to appease me. And Cooper didn't want us to go. No one did, but me."

"You cannot hold yourself accountable for a robbery, or for going into labor prematurely. You're assuming those two events are tied together, and you don't know that. You can't blame yourself for any of this."

She shrugs dismissively.

"Sweetheart, no one blames you. I certainly don't. Your family doesn't. My family doesn't. No one does."

"I'm tired," she says. "Can I sleep now?"

I have to fight the urge to crawl into that damn bed with her, pull her into my arms, and hold on for dear life. But I know she's still in a lot of discomfort, and I'll only hurt her if I do. Still, I feel so damn helpless.

Leaning down, I kiss her forehead, my lips clinging to her soft brow. "You listen to me, Beth. None of what happened today is your fault, and I refuse to let you take the blame for it." I straighten, but she doesn't respond. "Please, don't shut me out. I can help you get through anything, but you've got to let me."

Later that night, as I lie on the sofa wide awake, staring at the ceiling, my mind replays the events of the day over and over, in a vicious loop. I'm still awake two hours later when the lactation consultant pays Beth a visit. I can hear Beth's quiet frustration as she tries to get the hang of using the pump. I want to help her, at least support her, but I don't think she wants anything from me right now.

She's too busy punishing herself for something that was not her fault.

* * *

In the morning, a nurse helps Beth to the restroom so she can urinate again. Apparently, everything is working fine in that department, which is good news. It means we might be cleared to leave soon. The obstetrician comes in to examine her one last time, and she gives Beth the okay to be released.

I accompany Beth and the hospital staff member who wheels her downstairs to the main exit, where Jake is waiting for us with a rented SUV. I help her into the back seat and join her there.

"Where to?" Jake says, as he pulls away from the hospital and heads for the highway heading south, back to Chicago.

"Home," Beth says.

"To Children's Hospital," I clarify, reaching for Beth's hand. She's shaking.

Dear God, she's afraid to see her own child.

22

Beth

Every mile we travel brings me closer to something I can't face.

My heart is hammering in my chest, and I can't stop shaking. The shadows are closing in on me, and the air presses inward, suffocating me. Shane has a death grip on my hand, but even he can't help me now. No one can. This is my shame to bear. Mine.

I don't know how in the world I'm going to face that tiny, precious little boy. I feel sick, my heart aching for him. He deserves better than this. He deserves better than me. It's all I can do just to keep breathing—in, out, in, out. My chest is so tight, my lungs feeling squeezed. Tighter and tighter, a band constricts around me, making my pulse thunder and my heart jackhammer.

I can't do this.

I can't face my child.

I can't face my husband.

Oh my God, Shane, I'm so sorry. If I could take it all back, I would. I would undo the damage, make different choices. I wouldn't be so selfish. But it's too late for that. It's too—

Shane reaches across me to grab my purse and haul it onto his lap. He digs around inside until he locates my rescue inhaler, which he pulls out and shakes briskly.

"Open," he barks, holding the device to my lips.

I open my mouth, and he inserts the inhaler, pressing down to release the medication. I draw it into me, sucking it deep into my lungs and holding my breath for a couple moments. Then I force myself to relax and let the medicine do its job.

"She okay?" Jake says, eyeing us in the rearview mirror.

Shane turns in his seat to face me. "Feeling better, sweetheart?"

I cough, my throat scratchy and my breath short. "Yes." The sad thing is, I hadn't even realized I was having an asthma attack. If I can't take care of myself, how in the world can I take care of a vulnerable little baby? My voice breaks on a sob. "I'm so sorry."

Shane cups my face, his warm palms comforting against my

cheeks. I want to dissolve into his touch, just disappear and float away into nothingness.

"Sorry?" he says, giving me a sad smile. "For what? You have nothing to be sorry for, honey."

"I'm sorry about everything. Me."

He frowns, then leans close, brushing his lips against my forehead. "If we weren't sitting in a moving vehicle, I would un-buckle you from that seat and pull you onto my lap—whether you liked it or not—and never let you go. You listen to me, Beth Marie Jamison McIntyre—I mean it, are you listening? You have *nothing* to apologize for."

I can't resist a brief smile, but then reality returns with an ugly vengeance, sucking every ounce of joy out of me. I don't deserve to be happy.

He kisses my cheek, then skims his lips up to kiss my temple. "I am not going to let you punish yourself over this."

* * *

Jake pulls up to the front entrance of Children's Hospital in downtown Chicago, where Sam is waiting for us with a wheel-chair. Sam is a sight for sore eyes, looking so achingly familiar in his ripped jeans, chunky combat boots, and *I'm With Him* T-shirt. He peers through the backseat window looking right at me.

"I don't need a wheelchair," I tell Shane. I've drawn enough attention to myself the past twenty-four hours. I don't want any more. "I'm fine. I can walk."

Shane pats my leg as he opens the door. "I asked him to bring you a wheelchair. You need to conserve your energy."

Sam eyes me cautiously as I follow Shane out. "Hey, princess," he says, looking me over thoroughly. "How are you feeling?"

I force myself to smile. "Fine."

Sam looks at me, his brow furrowing, then at Shane. Then Sam steps forward and wraps me in a bear hug, squeezing me tightly.

"Careful, pal," Shane says, clasping Sam's shoulder. "She's still recovering."

Sam relaxes his hold on me, and whispers, "Sorry. I missed you."

"I missed you, too," I whisper back.

Sam looks me in the eye as he steers me to the wheelchair. "Sit down, rest, and let me take you upstairs so you can meet the most amazing little guy in the world. Just wait until you see him, princess. He's incredible."

I can't help smiling at Sam's exuberance.

Sam straightens and looks to Shane. "Don't worry. Cooper's with Luke. One of us is with him twenty-four-seven. We haven't left his side for a second, I promise."

"I'll park the vehicle and come up," Jake says to Shane. "Do you want me to bring your bags inside?"

"Yes, bring everything. We're staying here until Luke is ready to come home. I'm not leaving without my son."

* * *

Sam wheels me across the hospital foyer to a bank of elevators, and we catch one just as the doors slide open. As the elevator car ascends, my anxiety increases, and I feel sick. Shane grips my shoulders and leans down to whisper. "It's okay. Just relax. You're fine. He's fine. It's all good."

We have to be buzzed in to the neonatal intensive care unit. Once we're signed in, and we've gotten our parental identification bracelets, Sam wheels me down the hallway to our baby's room.

I have a baby, a son, and I've never even seen him up close, let alone held him. This is all so unreal, like a dream that I'll wake up from any minute.

Shane opens the door for us, and Sam wheels me inside a dimly-lit room. The focal point of the room is an incubator surrounded by all sorts of monitors and wires and tubes. There's a padded rocking chair, as well as a few extra chairs, and on the far side of the room is a single bed. I'm surprised—and grateful—to find we have a private room.

Cooper, who's seated beside the incubator, jumps to his feet as we enter. "Hey, kiddo!" Meeting me halfway, he smiles down at me, his gaze searching mine. "How are you?"

I force myself to return his smile. "I'm fine."

Cooper glances over my head at Shane, who's standing somewhere behind me. Shane doesn't say a word, but I can tell from the expression on Cooper's face that the two of them are having one of their silent conversations.

"Wash your hands, honey," Cooper says. "Then come meet your son. He's quite the little trooper."

I leave the wheelchair behind and follow Shane to the bathroom, where we both wash our hands. Cooper and Sam wash theirs as well, a task they've undoubtedly performed a dozen times by now.

I follow Cooper to the incubator and peer down at the sleeping baby inside. He looks... so tiny and so peaceful. Ten little fingers, ten little toes. There's a blue band with his name on it affixed around his tiny ankle.

His skin is a healthy shade of pink, and I'm surprised to see a silky thatch of blond hair peeking out from beneath the blue knit hat on his head.

"What color are his eyes?" I ask, peering down at him.

"Blue," Cooper says. "Blond hair and blue eyes, just like his mama. Although, his nurse said a baby's eye color can change later."

I nod, staring at all the wires and tubes attached to his face and chest and arm. A tiny tube is in his nose, taped to his cheek, and there's an IV attached to his arm. He's naked except for a diaper. "Why doesn't he have any clothes on?" I ask no one in particular. "Isn't he cold?"

"The incubator is heated." Cooper slips his hand through an opening. "Don't worry. He's plenty warm in there."

I stare at the baby, mesmerized by how beautiful he is. How perfect. I reach out, wanting to touch him, but my hand hovers inches from the incubator.

"You can touch him," Cooper says, demonstrating as he strokes the baby's arm gently. "It's okay. You won't hurt him." Cooper withdraws his hand and takes hold of mine, guiding it to the opening. "Reach through here—"

"No!" Startled, I yank my hand back as if burned, holding it close to my chest. "I can't."

Cooper gives me a side-long glance. "Why not?"

I shake my head, trying to clear the loud buzzing in my ears. "I can't. I might—hurt him. I don't know what to do."

"You can touch him, Beth. Touch is good for him. He needs it, especially from you. You're his mama."

To demonstrate, Cooper runs his fingers lightly down the baby's body, over his hips and down his leg. Even in his sleep, the baby responds to the gentle stimulation, shifting and stretching his arms, practically cooing in his sleep.

Cooper smiles. "See? He likes it. Do you want to hold him? We can call a nurse in to help us if you want, and you can hold him in the rocking chair. You could even try to nurse him. We've been feeding him formula from a bottle, but now that you're here, he can try to nurse."

I shake my head as the panic surges inside me, threatening to pull me back into the darkness. "Maybe later. He's sleeping now. I don't want to wake him."

Cooper glances back at Shane, his expression perfectly neutral, then at me.

I press my hands against my aching breasts, which are hard

and heavy. "Shane, we should go. I need to pump."

ᑲ 23

Shane

My heart aches for Beth, as well as for our son. For the first time in my life, I don't know what to do. It's my job to have all the answers and to fix things—but right now, I'm floundering.

I tip my head to the side, and Cooper falls back to join me, while Sam moves in beside Beth and distracts her with a run-down on Luke's progress since arriving at the NICU.

Cooper follows me out into the hallway, and we close the door behind us so we can talk out of Beth's hearing.

"Care to tell me what the hell's going on?" Cooper says, crossing his arms over his chest and glaring at me.

"I'm not exactly sure," I reply. "She's completely withdrawn, and I think it's safe to say she's depressed. She feels responsible for what happened yesterday... all because she wanted to go out of town. She blames herself for all of it... for delivering prematurely... for Luke being here."

Cooper frowns. "That's ridiculous. None of this is her fault."

I scrub my hand over my beard. "I don't know what to do. I don't know how to help her. I've told her repeatedly that it's not her fault."

Cooper looks as pained as I feel. "She needs to hold him, Shane. There's no way she could hold that precious little baby and not fall head over heels in love with him. Let's get a nurse in here and have Beth at least hold Luke. And then she can try to breastfeed."

"Do you think he's able to nurse? He's so small."

Cooper shrugs. "I don't know. We won't know until she tries."

Jake appears, heading down the hallway toward us, carrying our bags and the case holding Beth's breast pump.

"Perfect timing," I tell him. "Thanks."

I carry our things into the room. When I hand Beth the breast pump, she smiles gratefully, pressing a hand to her chest. "Thank goodness. I'm about to explode."

She takes a seat in the padded rocking chair and opens the case holding the breast pump.

I crouch down beside her. "Wait. Before you do that, would

you like to hold Luke?"

Her eyes widen in panic, and she shakes her head as she holds a hand against her breasts. "I really need to pump, Shane. It's been three hours, and they hurt."

"You could try nursing him."

She shakes her head. "I'll pump, and then you can feed him from a bottle. You'd like that, right?"

Quiet voices draw our attention across the room, where Cooper is talking to a woman dressed in light blue scrubs decorated with tiny teddy bears. The woman nods at something Cooper said, and then she approaches us.

"Mrs. McIntyre?" the woman says. The nurse—*Laura*, according to her name tag—smiles at Beth. "I'm so glad you're here. Luke needs his mama."

The nurse offers me a smile too. "And you must be Dad. It's a pleasure to meet you both. Lucas is doing really well. His oxygen levels are improving, and he's been eating well. Mr. Cooper informs me that you want to nurse him, Beth. Is it okay if I call you Beth?"

Beth nods, her hands fidgeting with the breast pump.

"We've been giving him formula," Laura continues, "but now that you're here, he can try to nurse. Would you like to try?"

The blood drains from Beth's face, leaving her ghostly pale.

"Maybe we should start with letting Beth hold him," I suggest, earning an equally appalled glance from Beth.

Laura nods as she observes Beth's reaction. "I think that's a good idea. Would you like to hold him, Beth?"

Everyone's looking at Beth, unfortunately putting her on the spot.

She nods reluctantly. "All right."

The guys quietly leave the room as the nurse gets Luke out of the incubator, which takes a bit of doing as he's connected to so many wires and tubes. He's awake now, squirming and fussing.

Laura brings the baby to Beth. "Would you like to unbutton your blouse, so you can hold him against your chest, skin to skin? That way he can feel your warmth and smell your scent."

Beth slowly unbuttons her blouse, revealing swollen breasts that strain against the too-small cups of her bra. I make a mental note to have someone bring her nursing bras from home.

Laura gently places Luke against Beth's chest, nestled right between her breasts, and helps Beth arrange her hands so that she can cradle the baby securely against her body. Then Laura draws a blanket around the two of them to help insulate their combined body heat.

"Just like that," Laura says, her voice gentle and encouraging. "You're doing great, Beth."

"He's so small," Beth says, staring down at him. "I'm afraid I'll hurt him."

"He's tougher than he looks," Laura says, patting the baby's back gently.

Laura glances at me, as if gauging my reaction. I know I'm hovering, but I can't help it. The sight of Beth holding our son against her skin hits me hard, like a punch to the gut. I'm just sorry that it took so long for this to happen. The desire to get them both home, so we can be together as a family, is gnawing at me.

Luke starts squirming in Beth's hands, his fussing growing louder and more forceful, and she shoots me a panicked look.

"It's okay," I tell her, my hand going to the back of her head to stroke her hair. "You're doing great."

"He's not happy," she says, looking from me to Laura, as if hoping someone will step in and bail her out.

I watch Luke rubbing his face against the swell of Beth's breast where it overflows her bra, his mouth open and searching. Jesus, the kid knows he's in the right place.

Laura leans in to watch the baby's movements and smiles. "He's rooting," she says to Beth. "That's a good sign. It means he wants to nurse. Would you like to give it a try?"

Beth looks at me, overwhelmed. I feel bad for putting her on the spot like this, but maybe it will help her connect with our son. I pull a chair up beside her and sit down. "Go on, sweetheart. Give it a try."

"Here, I'll help you," Laura says, looking at Beth for permission. "Okay?"

Beth nods, looking far from convinced.

"Unhook your bra," Laura says.

Beth unfastens the hook at the front of her bra, uncovering one full breast.

"Let me show you how to hold him," Laura says, grabbing a pillow and demonstrating. "This is one of the best positions for premature babies."

Luke turns his face toward Beth's breast and nuzzles her nipple.

"See, he's interested," Laura says. "That's a really good sign. Now, stroke his cheek like this."

It's a good thing I'm sitting down, because if I wasn't, I'd have already hit the floor, landing flat on my ass. Seeing Luke nuzzling Beth's breast is one of the most beautiful sights I've ever seen.

Luke tries several times to latch on, his mouth open and eager, but impatient and uncoordinated. He doesn't seem quite able to manage it. Laura helps him get latched on a couple of times, but he invariably loses his grip on the nipple. With each attempt, he gets fussier, his cries progressing from thin and breathy to all-out wails. And the fussier he gets, the more frantic Beth looks. Before long, Luke's screeching his head off, and his face starts turning red.

"I can't do this," Beth says, her own voice shaking and her eyes filling with tears. "I can't!"

"It's okay," Laura says, gently taking Luke into her own arms and wrapping him in a blanket. "Let's take a break. Would you like to pump and feed him with a bottle this time? We can practice getting him to latch on the next time. How does that sound?"

Beth wipes her wet cheeks with the side of her hand. "Yes. Thank you."

✧ 24

Beth

The baby's room has everything we need. A private
bathroom with a sink and shower, a mini refrigerator
for storing breast milk, a single bed and a recliner
that unfolds into a bed, in addition to the cozy padded rocking
chair. It's a perfect little family space. So why am I so desperate
to go home?

I want to go home, but I'm afraid to say anything to Shane.
It'll just disappoint him further that I'm not what I should be.

After I pump, Laura helps me transfer what little I produced
into a tiny bottle for Luke. "That's not very much," I say, staring

at the thin, yellow liquid. "It doesn't look like milk."

She smiles, screwing the nipple onto the bottle. "That's because it isn't. It's colostrum. Your milk won't come in for another day or two. But don't worry. This stuff is good for him. It's called *liquid gold* for a reason."

When Laura hands me the bottle with barely an ounce in it, I shake my head and pass it to Shane. "I've already held him. It's your turn. You feed him."

I refasten my bra and vacate the rocking chair for Shane.

"Are you sure?" he says.

"Yes." I trade seats with him. Laura hands Shane the baby, and he nestles the child in the crook of his arm. The baby is so small, he's practically dwarfed in Shane's arms.

Fascinated, I watch Shane as he feeds the baby for the first time. He seems pretty relaxed and comfortable, far more so than I would be. He must be doing it right because Laura's watching over his shoulder and she's not correcting him.

There's so much love and tenderness in his gaze as he watches his son eat, it takes my breath away. Shane's going to be a wonderful father. He'll more than make up for my shortcomings.

Shane and I watch in awe as the baby sucks vigorously on the miniature bottle.

"He's doing really well, isn't he?" Shane says, glancing up at Laura for confirmation.

Laura smiles. "Yes, he is."

When the bottle is empty, Shane holds it up, and the baby starts fussing at the loss of his dinner. "I think he's still hungry," he says.

"I'm sorry," I say. "That's all I was able to get."

"That's okay," Laura says. "You did great, Beth. We'll supplement with formula until your milk comes in."

Laura goes to prepare some formula, leaving me and Shane alone with the baby. I watch Shane gazing down at our son, cradling him so carefully in his strong arms. It's mesmerizing to see such a strong, confident man being so incredibly gentle.

"He's perfect," Shane says, giving me a smile. He slides the baby's knit cap back just enough to expose tufts of pale blond hair. "He's got your coloring."

The baby resumes crying, his voice thin and breathy as he broadcasts his displeasure at having his meal interrupted.

"Hey, little guy," Shane croons, gently bouncing the baby in his arms. "It's okay. More milk is coming. Be patient."

Shane strokes the baby's clenched fist with the tip of his index finger, and the baby opens his fist and latches on, holding on for dear life. Watching the two of them together makes my heart hurt and my throat tighten painfully. We could have lost the baby so easily, before he'd even had a chance.

The door to the room opens, making me jump.

Laura comes in with a fresh bottle, and I brush away the tears on my cheeks as she hands it to Shane. "Here you go, Dad."

Shane looks to me. "Would you like to feed him?"

I shake my head, gingerly rising from my chair to stretch my back and legs. My body hurts all over—but most especially *down there* after sitting so long. "No. You finish it. I need to use the restroom."

"Do you need some help? I'll come with you," he says. "I'm sure Laura wouldn't mind feeding Lucas."

"No, you stay. I'll be fine."

I escape into the bathroom, desperately needing a few moments alone. Just as I'm closing the door, I hear Shane's low voice as he coos at the baby, encouraging him to latch onto the nipple. Alone now, I lean against the door and close my eyes, squeezing them in an attempt to stem the flow of tears. I don't know what to do. I've messed everything up so badly, and I'm afraid I'll make things worse. I don't know how to take care of a newborn, let alone a preemie. This all happened too soon, and I'm just not ready.

I take my time in the bathroom, emptying my bladder and washing my hands and face. I'm so exhausted I can barely stand. When I leave my sanctuary, I find Cooper and Sam back in our room with clothes from home and other necessities. It's only six o'clock, but I feel like I'm about to pass out.

Shane has finished feeding the baby, and he's rocking him, gently patting his back.

I go sit on the bed.

"How are you holding up, kiddo?" Cooper says, patting my leg as he hands me a carry-out bag. "I brought you and Shane some dinner."

"Thanks. I'm exhausted."

"I'm sure you are." He studies me for a moment. "I heard you held Luke."

I nod. "Yes. I tried to nurse him, but it didn't go well."

"Give him time. He's a smart boy. He'll figure it out."

I laugh. "How can you tell he's a smart boy? He's two days old."

Cooper grins. "He takes after his mama. That's how I know."

We both glance over at the incubator, where Shane's getting diapering lessons from Laura, and Sam's looking on, critiquing Shane's technique.

"Everything's going to be okay, honey," Cooper says, rubbing my back. "You know that, right?"

I nod. "Sure."

"No, I mean it. Everything's going to be okay. You just rest and enjoy that precious little boy."

I try my best to smile at Cooper's reassurances, but inside I feel so undeserving. I almost lost my child because of my selfishness.

"Beth?"

I snap my attention back to Cooper. "Hmm?"

"It's not your fault."

Pain and shame cut through me like a knife, stealing my breath. "Yes, it is," I say, my voice barely audible.

"Oh, honey...."

I can't bear to see the sorrow in his eyes, so I look away, hiding from his scrutiny.

He takes my hand, holding it gently in his. "Listen to me, kiddo. What happened was not your fault. None of it."

I snap back to look at him. "He could have died in that attic!"

I say, trying to keep my voice low. "He couldn't breathe! He wasn't supposed to be born then, not at that time, or in that horrible place. If he'd died, it would have been my fault."

Cooper shakes his head. "You were in the wrong place at the wrong time, honey. What you went through was horrendous, and you did a courageous job. No one blames you. You need to concentrate on your son and let this misplaced sense of guilt go."

I want to believe him, I really do, but I can't let it go. It's not that easy. Forgiving myself would be taking the easy way out, and I don't deserve that.

Someone turns the lights down in the room, casting us in semi-darkness. There's a nightlight near the incubator, and I can see that the baby is back in his safe little box, warm and protected.

Shane joins us, clasping Cooper's shoulder. "Thanks for bringing our stuff. And for the food."

Cooper nods. "No problem." Then he stands. "Sam and I will head home and let you guys try to get some rest. Call if you need anything."

As if on cue, Sam appears in front of me and leans down to kiss my forehead. "I can't wait until you and the little dude come home. We're going to have so much fun."

Shane walks Cooper and Sam and Laura out the door, leaving me alone with my thoughts, grateful for the solitude. He's gone longer than I expected, which makes me wonder what they're talking about out in the hallway.

When Shane finally returns to the room, he grabs his toiletries bag and some pajamas and disappears into the bathroom for a few minutes. When he comes out, he's wearing flannel PJ pants and a T-shirt, ready for bed. I'm sure he's as exhausted as I am.

I sit in the rocker, and he sits in the chair beside me, and we eat the sandwiches Cooper brought us. Afterward, we brush our teeth, ready to crash, even though it's only seven o'clock. We both have a lot of lost sleep to make up for.

Instead of unfolding the recliner to make a second bed, Shane climbs into bed with me and lies at my back, sliding beneath the covers and pulling me into his arms.

I stiffen, feeling unsure. "This bed is too small for the both of us," I say, laughing to cover my initial reaction.

"I know." He nuzzles the back of my head, his lips and nose buried in my hair. "I'll make up the other bed in a few minutes. But first, I need to hold you. It's been a rough couple of days."

I close my eyes when I feel his lips in my hair. His tenderness just makes me feel worse.

"Sweetheart, we need to talk," he says a few minutes later, his voice hesitant.

My heart starts hammering painfully and the darkness feels like it's closing in on me. I attempt to pull away, but he holds me firmly at his side.

"No, no. Just relax," he murmurs. "Everything's okay."

"No, it's not."

He sighs, tightening his hold. "We have a beautiful, perfect little boy."

"He could have died, Shane."

"But he didn't. Jason got him breathing in time."

"None of that would have been necessary if I hadn't—"

"Hadn't what?"

"Been so selfish. So stupid!"

"Beth." He sighs heavily, then drops a kiss on my shoulder. "Do you know what I think?"

"What?"

"Remember how your back was hurting when you woke up yesterday morning? How you were having mild contractions?"

"Yes."

"I think you were likely already in labor then, and we just didn't realize it. We assumed those were Braxton Hicks contractions, when in fact, I think they were real ones."

"You're just saying that to make me feel better." I'm stunned by his suggestion. But now that he mentions it, it seems plausible. But wouldn't that make things even worse? I was in labor already when we left home? How could I have been so stupid?

"We'll never know, sweetheart. But whether you were already in labor, or the trauma of the robbery kick-started your labor, it doesn't matter. Luke's here, albeit a little early, but he's doing well. Laura said if he continues as he has been, he could go home in a couple of weeks."

Shane turns me to face him. "None of this is your fault. Do you hear me? None of it." His beautiful eyes, barely visible in the darkened room, search mine. He reaches for my hand and links our fingers together. "I want you to let go of this misplaced guilt and let yourself enjoy that little baby. He needs you, sweetheart."

When I don't respond, he frowns. "How are you feeling? In all the excitement about Luke, your health has been neglected."

"I'm fine."

"Are you?" He lays his hand gently on my belly, which is still quite a bit round and soft. "How do you feel? Really?"

"I'm tender."

"I want you to see your obstetrician for a follow-up tomorrow. I'll call her in the morning to see if she can squeeze us in. I'm sure Cooper and Sam will be more than happy to stay with Luke while I take you to the doctor. Or maybe your mom or mine can come." He leans over and kisses the tip of my nose. "I wish I could sleep with you tonight, but this bed really is too small for the both of us."

Shane slides out from beneath the bedding and gets to his feet, taking care not to jostle me. He unfolds the recliner beside my bed into a makeshift bed and grabs bedding and a pillow from the cupboard. "I'll be right here all night. If you need any help, wake me."

25

Shane

Am I supposed to pretend I can't hear her crying? I can't do it. Even with her face pressed against the pillow to muffle the sound, I can still hear her quiet sobs. And it's tearing me apart.

I don't know how to help her. Should I make an appointment for her to see someone? A mental health therapist maybe? Should I talk to her obstetrician? I'm sure this kind of thing happens to new mothers occasionally. She's been through a traumatic ordeal, and given how she's prone to anxiety, this can't be a total surprise. Laura suggested earlier that she might be experiencing post-partum depression, which is not uncommon, especially in mothers of preemies.

Unable to bear the sounds of her sobs any longer, I rise from my bed to sit at the side of hers and lay my hand on her hip. "Beth?"

The crying stops abruptly, but she doesn't reply, and it's too dark for me to see her face. I slide into her bed and pull her onto my chest, wrapping my arms securely around her. "You're breaking my heart, honey. I can't bear to hear you cry."

I kiss the top of her head, and I'm relieved when she slips her arm around my waist.

"Sleep with me," she says.

"I will." I let out a heavy sigh. "We'll get through this, I promise."

* * *

I awake around seven in the morning with Beth tucked closely into my side, my arms wrapped securely around her. There was no way in hell I was going to let her tumble off the too-small bed in the night. She's still asleep, her body warm and soft against mine.

After her crying spell last night, she slept peacefully until she had to get up and pump. She's pumping about every three hours now, producing more milk each time and managing to keep ahead of Luke, who eats at about the same interval.

Danielle, the night nurse, came into the room each time to

help while Beth pumped and I fed Luke a bottle. I've been hoping Beth would try to nurse him again, but so far she's been resistant to the idea.

"Honey, he won't learn how if you don't give him a chance."

But she shakes her head, adamant. "He's not ready yet. He's too small."

I check the time and realize we have about fifteen minutes or so before Laura comes in to check on Luke. Already I can hear him stirring in the incubator, making a few quiet squeaks and squawks. He's not fully awake yet, but I can tell he's thinking about it.

I hate to wake Beth up, but I need to make some calls. I need to call all the grandparents and invite them to come meet their grandson. I need to get Beth an appointment with her obstetrician today, if possible, for a check-up. And I have to talk to Jake about the meeting with Frank and Annie Elliot, which is scheduled for this afternoon.

Unfortunately, I'm not going to be able to make the meeting with the Elliots—there's no way I'm leaving Beth and Luke right now—so Jake's going to have to meet with them for me. I hate throwing him to the wolves like this, but there's no help for it. I have to take care of my family.

Jake needs to be apprised of what's going on. I'm not looking forward to that conversation, and I honestly don't know how he'll take it. Shit, he might refuse to talk to them, and in that case, I'll need to assign the case to someone else.

Luke escalates things with some light fussing and restless

kicking. I slip out of bed so I can change his diaper and start a bottle warming for him. I'll let Beth sleep a little longer.

"Hey, little guy," I say to my son, reaching into the incubator to stroke his arm. I run my finger tip down his arm to his little fist, and when I brush his fingers, his fist opens and closes on my finger, clenching it tightly. I smile. He's got a pretty good grip for someone so tiny. "Are you hungry, buddy?"

He stretches, his tiny limbs going in every direction with un-coordinated enthusiasm. He kicks his legs, blinking up at me with eyes so much like his mama's it makes my chest hurt. "You know what? I can't wait to get you and your mama home."

I change his diaper, and while the bottle's warming, I carry Luke around the room, bouncing him in my arms and mur-muring quietly to distract him.

When Laura comes in, at the beginning of her day shift, I'm already seated in the rocking chair with the little guy, who's de-molishing his breakfast. The breakfast of champions.

"Good morning," Laura says, observing Luke sucking eagerly on his bottle. "Danielle said he did really well in the night. I'm glad to see he has such a strong appetite."

Laura glances at the bed, where Beth is still asleep. "Has she tried to nurse again?"

I shake my head. "She's afraid he's too small to nurse."

"He's not too small to try," she says. "Babies at thirty-four weeks gestation are sometimes able to nurse. He just needs practice. He'll catch on before you know it. The important thing is that she keeps trying."

I hear a rustling sound coming from the bed. When I glance over, Beth's sitting up, pushing her hair out of her face and rubbing her eyes. She looks exhausted.

"Good morning," I say.

She gives me a small smile. "Good morning." Then she presses her hands to her breasts and winces. "I need to shower and pump. Badly."

"Do you need some help?" Laura asks.

"No, thank you." Beth swings her legs over the side of the bed. "I think I can manage on my own."

She grabs her overnight bag, and I watch as she shuffles slowly to the bathroom and closes the door behind her.

Laura meets my gaze, but she doesn't say anything. It's easy enough to know what she's thinking though. Beth didn't stop to check on Luke. She didn't even ask about him.

"I'm taking her to see her obstetrician, for a check-up. That's the first step—her physical health. Then we'll deal with the rest."

Laura nods.

After Luke finishes his bottle, Laura checks him over and reviews the overnight data from his monitors.

Shortly after, Cooper and Sam arrive. Cooper scoops Luke up to cuddle him while I make my phone calls.

"How's my favorite little guy this morning?" Cooper says, bouncing Luke in his arms.

I look at Sam, who rolls his eyes at me. "I think Cooper likes being a grandpa."

I smile. "I think you're right."

* * *

My parents are the first to arrive. When I hear a quiet knock at the door, I find them standing there, eager to meet their first grandchild. I step out into the hallway with them and close the door behind us.

My mom, who's holding a gift bag and a blue helium balloon that says *It's a boy,* takes one look at me and says, "What's wrong, honey?" She doesn't miss a beat. "Is everything okay?"

I blow out a long breath, unsure what to say, or where to start.

My dad reaches out to squeeze my shoulder. "Just spit it out, son."

"It's Beth."

Mom's brow furrows. "What's wrong?"

"I don't know. Well, I do, but I don't know what to do about it. I don't know how to help her. She's very withdrawn, cut off from everyone and everything, especially Luke. She's held him one time since we've been here. I think she's depressed, and I know she blames herself for the premature labor."

"Blames herself?" Bridget says, frowning in confusion. "That's ridiculous." She sighs, the sound as melancholy as I feel. "I assume you've talked to her. That you've told her it's not her fault?"

"I have. So has Cooper. Now that I look back, I suspect she

might have been in labor Saturday before we even left the apartment, and we just missed it. If anything, this is my fault. I should have insisted she get checked out before we left home."

"Why don't you tell her that?"

"That it's my fault?"

"Yes," Bridget says. "When she hears it coming from your lips, she'll realize how ridiculous it sounds, and that neither of you is to blame. It happened. The important thing is that Beth and Luke are both okay. And make sure Ingrid knows about this. Sometimes a girl just needs her mom."

When we hear footsteps coming down the hall, we all three glance back to see Jake heading our way. And that reminds me of the next item on my to-do list—Annie. This is a conversation I'm not looking forward to.

"You guys go on in," I say to my folks. "I need to talk to Jake."

Bridget shoos me away. "Go talk to your brother. Your dad and I are going to dote on our daughter-in-law and grandson."

I motion for Jake to follow me down the hall. We duck into an empty visiting room.

"How are you holding up?" he says.

"I'm okay, but Beth is struggling, and I'm not sure how to help her."

"Just be there for her. Love her."

I chuff. "I'm trying. You make it sound so easy."

"At least you have the right to be there for her. We aren't all so lucky."

He's obviously thinking about Annie, and that brings me to

the conversation I'm dreading. "There's something you need to know."

Jake frowns. "What?"

"Frank Elliot came to see me Friday afternoon."

"What?" Jake stares at me as if I've suddenly grown a second head.

I nod, wondering what can of worms I'm about to open here. "He wants to hire us."

"To do what?"

"Provide personal protection services. For Annie."

"Protect her from what?"

"Her abusive husband. Or, rather her abusive *ex*-husband. They divorced three months ago, but apparently he's still threatening her."

"Abusive?" Jake looks like he's about to keel over. "How so?"

"Frank said Ted's physically abusive, as well as emotionally. He didn't go into a lot of details. He wants it to come from Annie."

"Why didn't you tell me this sooner?"

"I didn't want to tell you over the weekend because I didn't want you stewing over this. We'll find out the details soon enough. But here's the problem, I can't make this meeting now. I need to take Beth to her doctor's appointment."

"Don't worry, I'll take it from here," Jake says. "You concentrate on your family. I'll deal with the Elliots."

"You don't have to be the one to handle this case, you know. I can assign it to someone else."

Jake scoffs, his expression filled with bitterness. "No. It has to be me."

"Jake, there's more."

He frowns. "What?"

"According to Frank, Annie isn't the only one Patterson abused. You know they have a son, Aiden. It sounds like he's been abused too."

"Jesus," Jake says, his expression darkening ominously.

I know how he gets when he looks like that. If Ted Patterson has any sense at all, he'll stay the hell away from Jake and Annie.

Jake takes his leave, clearly shaken by the news. I feel for him. Annie was his first, and only, love. She's not only divorced now, but she needs protection. He's not going to take this lightly.

When I return to Luke's room, I'm greeted by the sight of my mother rocking my son. There are tears in her eyes as she coos at him. My dad sits beside the rocker in another chair, his hand on my mom's back as he looks on.

I see Cooper and Sam, but there's no sign of Beth. "Where's Beth?"

Cooper nods toward the bathroom, giving me a telling look. I get the distinct feeling my wife is hiding. I think she's a little overwhelmed.

I knock on the bathroom door. "Sweetheart? Would you like to go downstairs with me to get some breakfast?"

"Yes, please."

ॐ 26

Beth

I jump at the chance to go down to the cafeteria with Shane. I'm not really hungry, but I'm grateful for the escape. Being around all those people is making me nervous. I feel like everyone's watching me, judging me, and I know I'm falling far short of expectations.

I'm glad Shane's parents are here, and Cooper and Sam. Shane's mom looked like she was in heaven as she rocked the baby. He looked so impossibly small wrapped up in his ducky blanket.

My milk finally started coming in during the night, and I'm

producing more each time I pump. That's good, because the baby's eating a little more each time, and I'm determined to keep ahead of him. Right now, I'm ahead two bottles.

With promises to return soon, Shane and I head for the cafeteria.

While we're waiting for the elevator doors to open, he cups the back of my neck and I relax into his comforting hold and close my eyes. A moment of respite, just the two of us, which I desperately need.

His arms steal around my waist and I feel his chin perch lightly on my head. "Did you sleep okay?" he says.

I smile, remembering him climbing into bed with me in the night. "Yes. Thank you." I sleep so much better when he's near.

"I love you."

I smile and melt into his embrace. "I love you, too."

The elevator doors open with a ding, and we step into the already crowded car. Shane pulls me close, tucking me under his shoulder. His fingers are warm on my waist as they slide beneath my top and stroke my skin.

He doesn't say much, but I can feel his eyes on me. I wish I knew what he was thinking. He was so sweet last night, holding me while I slept, chasing the bad thoughts away. And each time I got up to pump, he was there with me, handing me what I needed and seeing after the baby, changing diapers and warming bottles.

"What sounds good for breakfast?" he asks when the elevator deposits us in front of the cafeteria. Shane takes my hand

and leads me into the bustling restaurant. "Let me guess...decaf coffee and pancakes?"

I smile. He knows me so well.

"How about some eggs, too?" he says. "You need protein."

After getting our food, we find a table in front of a window overlooking a lovely flower garden and eat quietly, holding hands across the table. He seems to know I need some quiet time, as he doesn't strike up any conversation, or worse yet, press me on anything.

I know we can't stay down here forever, hiding, but it's nice to have a quiet moment of respite.

* * *

When we make it back up to the baby's room, we have quite a room full of visitors, and I'm sure we're probably breaking hospital visiting rules.

Lia and Jonah stop by, and then Liam and Sophie come. My dear friend Gabrielle comes for a visit. And then Molly and Jamie. There's a steady stream of people in and out of the baby's room all day.

Even with all the company coming and going, I manage to pump every few hours, and everyone's only too happy to take a turn feeding Luke his bottle. My breasts are starting to feel better now, not quite so swollen and hot as I express more and more milk. At least there's something I can do right.

A couple times, the baby's doctor comes to examine him and

see how he's doing. And his nurses are in and out of the room throughout the day, checking on him, monitoring his progress. He's eating well, and he's gained a couple of ounces since arriving at the NICU, which is good news.

* * *

That afternoon, we leave the baby under the watchful eyes of my mom and Sam and Cooper, while Shane and I go to my obstetrician's office. While Shane signs me in, I find us two seats in a corner of the otherwise crowded waiting room.

Shane joins me, taking my hand in his as he turns in his seat to face me. "How do you feel?"

I shift carefully in my chair, wincing at the tenderness between my legs. There's still a lot of healing that needs to happen down there. I can't imagine ever having sex again. Just the thought makes me grimace. "I'm okay."

He frowns. "Can you be a little more specific? Are you in pain? Does anything hurt?"

I nod. "A little. You try pushing a four-pound baby through a hole this big." I make a circle with my fingers to approximate what I imagine is the maximum circumference of my vagina. Shoot, sometimes taking Shane is a bit much for me, and he's way smaller than a baby's head.

He bites back an amused grin, saying, "I'm sorry, sweetheart."

His response makes me chuckle. "It's not your fault. It's the plight of all women who give birth. Blame it on the circle of life."

He brushes his thumb across my cheek. "I hate that you're hurting. Physically, and emotionally."

My stomach tightens at the sorrow in his tone, and I don't know what to say. I know I'm a disappointment. He deserves better. The baby deserves better. "I'm so sorry, Shane."

His eyes widen. "What? No!" He leans in closer, his mouth close to my ear. "You have nothing to be sorry for, sweetheart. I'm the one who's sorry."

I pull back, confused by his words. "What are you talking about?"

"I've been thinking about this, and I've come to the conclusion that you were already in labor when we left the apartment Saturday morning. Your backache that morning, the mild contractions... I dismissed them too easily. I should have insisted that you get checked out before we went anywhere. If I had, things would have turned out very differently. You would have given birth in a hospital, where you belonged, under professionally controlled circumstances, not in a dirty, dusty old attic. I'm so sorry, honey."

I can't help staring at him, shocked. "It's not your fault! Are you crazy? Neither one of us suspected I was in labor. It was way too early for that." I reach up and grasp his jaw, holding him to face me. "Don't you dare blame yourself!"

Shane gives me a long, considering look, and I realize what he's doing. "It's not the same thing," I say, my shoulders falling. "I'm the one who insisted on going away in the first place. I'm the one who had to stop and pee. It was all me. Stop trying to steal the blame."

He shakes his head and smiles as he runs his finger down the side of my face. "Do you have any idea how much I love you? I would take every pain from you if I could. I would suffer any torment for you. I refuse to let you torture yourself over things that aren't your fault. Luke wouldn't want you to."

"The baby—"

He presses his index finger to my lips. "Beth?"

"What?"

"Do you realize you always call him 'the baby?' I don't think I've ever heard you call him by his name."

I'm stunned. "That's ridiculous."

"No, it's not. I've been paying attention."

I open my mouth, searching for a suitable reply, but nothing comes out.

"Luke needs you, Beth. You're his mom. You're the most important person in the world to him."

Before I can reply, a nurse comes to the door. "We're ready for you, Beth."

Shane stands and helps me up, and we follow the nurse to our assigned examination room. After giving me instructions, she leaves. Shane helps me undress and climb up onto the examining table, and then he covers me with the thin paper sheet, tucking it around my body for good measure. It's sorely inadequate cover, and I can't help shivering.

"Are you cold?" he asks.

"No."

"Just nervous?"

"Yeah, a little."

He stands by the examination table, stroking my hair. "I'm right here if you need me."

Fortunately, Dr. Shaw doesn't keep us waiting long. After a friendly greeting, she examines me quickly, checks my stitches, and presses on my soft belly. "It looks like you're healing well, Beth," she says, when she removes her sterile gloves.

"How long does this take to heal?" I say.

Dr. Shaw shrugs. "It varies. Another two to four weeks perhaps, maybe longer. If you're still experiencing any discomfort a few weeks from now, come back and see me."

* * *

When we return to Children's Hospital and our NICU room, we find Cooper seated in the rocking chair, feeding the baby. With a burp cloth thrown over his shoulder, Cooper looks perfectly at home feeding his grandson. He would make such a great dad.

Sam's sitting in the chair beside the rocker, watching Cooper with obvious affection, a silly grin on his face, and his hand on Cooper's thigh. I wonder if they've thought about having kids. They'd be such incredible parents. As I stand there watching them, I'm swamped with so much emotion I can barely breathe.

When I sway on my feet, Shane is there to steady me. "What's wrong, sweetheart?" he says.

My mom's seated on my bed, and Tyler's here too, sitting in the recliner. I'm surrounded by family. *My* family, *our* family. And then I look at the baby. *His* family, too.

When my eyes fill with tears, Cooper hands the baby to my brother, who looks less than comfortable with the idea.

"Come here," Cooper says to me, opening his arms wide.

I walk into Cooper's embrace.

"It's okay," he says in a gruff voice, rubbing my back.

I never knew my birth father. A drugged-out robbery suspect took him from me when I was an infant. My mother did her best to make up for the loss of him, as did my big brother. But as a child, I craved the notion of having a father, like most of the other kids had. When I met Cooper, we found that we needed each other. I needed a dad, and he needed a family, since his own family had abandoned him when he was a teen because of his sexual orientation. So, Cooper and I adopted each other.

"I'm sorry," I say, laughing to make light of my reaction. "I'm so emotional lately."

"You're doing great," Cooper whispers.

I squeeze him tightly and ask him something I've been wanting to ask him for a while now. "Would you mind if I call you *dad*?"

"Oh, Jesus, honey," he says, his voice thick with emotion as he holds me close. "I would be honored."

When he releases me, I glance at my mom to see how she's taking my request. To my surprise, there are tears in her eyes and a smile on her face.

Sam pulls me close for a hug. "So, what does that make me? Your uncle?" He shakes his head, grinning. "This is one very confusing family tree."

I laugh through my tears. "That's what you get for marrying my dad!"

Sam squeezes me. "Hey, never underestimate the old guys, right?"

When I feel Cooper's arms steal around both me and Sam, something becomes a little more right in my world.

ꙅ 27

Shane

Ingrid and Tyler stay for a while longer after we get back from Beth's doctor visit. They come with us down to the cafeteria for supper, while Sam and Cooper stay upstairs with Luke.

After we eat, Beth's family heads home, promising to come back soon. I coax Beth into taking a walk with me outside in the flower garden.

"I'm sorry you didn't get your overnight trip to Harbor Springs," I say, holding her hand as we walk through the garden.

Night is falling, but the garden path is well marked by strings of twinkling lights threaded through the trees. We stop by a stone fountain lit by colored lights and listen to the hypnotic sound of the water splashing.

"That's all right," she says. "It's inconsequential now. The baby's all that matters."

"I know. But I'm still sorry our plans didn't work out. When Luke's home, and it's safe for him to travel, we'll take a trip somewhere, okay? Anywhere you want to go."

She smiles. "That's okay. We don't have to go anywhere. Besides, he's so young. He probably shouldn't be traveling much."

We walk a little more until we find a swinging bench suspended from a wooden frame. "Come sit with me," I say, leading her to the swing.

I pull her down beside me on the swing and wrap my arm around her, drawing her close. The evening air has cooled down considerably, and she doesn't have a sweater or jacket. She shivers.

"I'm worried about you, sweetheart," I say as I set the swing gently in motion.

She gazes across the path at some purple flowers planted at the base of a lamp. "Why? I'm fine. Dr. Shaw said—"

"I'm not so worried about your physical health. Dr. Shaw said you're healing fine. I'm more worried about your emotional health."

The chains creak softly overhead as the swing glides back and forth. I wait patiently for Beth to respond, hoping she'll open up to me about how she's feeling. Her hands are in her lap, her fingers twisting and twining nervously. I wait, wanting to give her plenty of time.

But she doesn't say anything more.

The longer she sits there silently, the more worried I become. "Beth?"

"Hmm?"

"I think you're depressed."

She sighs and looks away. "I don't know what's wrong with me."

"But something is wrong?"

She nods, pressing her trembling lips together to still them.

"Can you talk about it?"

Her gaze returns to the flowers directly across the path from us. She's looking anywhere but at me. "I don't know what it is." She sighs again. "I just feel...numb."

I lean over and kiss the side of her head. "You've been through a lot, honey."

She looks up at me, her blue-green eyes radiating pain. "I feel like I'm drowning in quicksand. Everything's so hard. Everything's such a chore. I feel smothered, trapped, and I can't breathe. The air's too heavy. I have trouble sleeping because my heart races all night long, and when I wake up, everything comes crashing back in my head, and I start panicking."

"How do I help you, sweetheart?"

"I don't know. Last night I dreamed I was still in that attic. It was so hot, I could barely breathe. The baby was there with me—it was just the two of us. He was having trouble breathing, too." She leans into me, laying her head on my shoulder. "I'm sorry I'm such a disappointment."

"Sweetheart, you could never be a disappointment. Not for one second." I hug her tighter. "I love you. Our son loves you. We both need you, Beth. You're the center of this family."

She's quiet then, saying nothing more.

We swing for a while longer, just quietly taking in the night sounds, crickets and other nocturnal insects, a few quiet bird calls.

"We should get back," she says, breaking the silence. "It's getting late. Cooper and Sam probably need to head home."

I stand and pull her to her feet. "Okay. Let's go."

"Will you sleep with me again tonight? I sleep better when you're near."

"Of course I will."

* * *

When we arrive back at Luke's room, Sam is rocking a sleeping baby, while Cooper looks on.

"Hey, guys," I say. "Sorry it's so late. I know you must be tired."

"Not too tired for this little guy," Sam says, continuing his rocking.

"We just changed his diaper and gave him a bottle," Cooper says. "He's ready for bed."

"Thank you," Beth says, then excuses herself as she disappears into the restroom.

Cooper and Sam both give me a look, but don't say anything. I just shake my head.

Sam hands me Luke, who's out like a light, and I walk them to the door. "Thanks, guys," I say. "We appreciate everything you've done."

"Are you kidding?" Sam says. "Baby watching duty is the most fun I've had in a long time."

After they leave, I lay Luke in the incubator. Then I make up the bed for both of us and wait for Beth to come out of the restroom. She's ready for bed, wearing a nightgown. I get myself ready and climb into the single bed with her, snuggling close.

She lies on her side facing me, with her arm across my chest and her head on my shoulder. I rub her back, saying nothing. I've pushed her enough this evening. I don't want to add to the pressure she's feeling.

"Sweet dreams," I tell her, kissing her forehead.

She rises up on her elbow and looks at me. I wish I knew what she was thinking.

"What?" I say.

She shakes her head, then leans closer to kiss me, her soft lips brushing against mine. Her gentle kiss is electric, and I allow myself to deepen the kiss for just a moment.

When she pulls back, there's a smile on her face. "Thank you for this evening. For the walk in the garden. It was lovely. I wish we could have a garden like that at the penthouse. And thank you for the talk. It helped a lot just to say those things out loud."

Her eyes tear up. "I'm trying, Shane."

"I know you are, sweetheart."

She lays her head back down on my shoulder. "I love you."

"I love you more."

She laughs softly. "I loved you first."

Now it's my turn to laugh. "I seriously doubt that."

* * *

In the middle of the night, we're awakened by the sound of a shrill alarm. The noise is shockingly loud, startling us both into full wakefulness. Careful not to toss Beth onto the floor, I shoot up out of bed, my pulse pounding like a jackhammer as I orient myself.

Beth sits up and swings her feet to the floor. "What is it? What's that sound?"

The door to our room opens and Danielle comes in, flipping on the light before heading straight for the incubator. I meet her there, staring down at Luke, who's sleeping.

"What's wrong?" I say, my heart in my throat.

Beth is standing beside the bed, a blanket wrapped around her. She's pale and her eyes are wide with fright. She looks as frantic as I feel.

"That's the low-oxygen alarm," Danielle says, scanning the data on the monitor. "And his heart rate is slow. Those two things usually go hand-in-hand. It's pretty typical for his gestational age." She reaches into the incubator and rolls Luke onto his side and starts rubbing his back. "Come on, little guy," she says. Then, to us, she says, "He just needs to breathe a little deeper. This happens quite often at his age. It's nothing serious."

Beth sidles up beside me, and we both watch as Danielle rubs Luke's back. The numbers on the monitors go back up into the normal range and the alarm stops.

Danielle returns Luke to his back. "He's fine," she says, smiling apologetically at us. "It's a scary alarm, I know. Parents hate it. But he's fine now. No need to worry."

Danielle wishes us a good night and leaves the room, turning off the light on her way out. Beth remains beside the incubator, staring down at Luke. I wait quietly by her side until she's ready to return to bed.

Without warning, Beth bursts into tears.

I sweep her up into my arms and carry her back to bed, laying her down and crawling in beside her. "It's all right," I tell her, holding her close. "He's okay."

She doesn't say a word. She just lies there crying, her wet face pressed into her pillow. I rub her back until she finally falls back to sleep.

$\curlywedge$ **28**

Beth

Ten days later, the NICU doctor gives us the okay to take our son home. He's breathing fine on his own now, and his oxygen levels have stabilized. All those tubes and wires have been removed from him, and he's doing great. He's eating and gaining weight as he should be. He's wetting his diaper like a champ and meeting all the milestones a premature baby needs to meet in order to go home. I'm so relieved. He's at thirty-six weeks gestation now, and at the rate he's going, he'll be caught up in no time.

Shane and I pack up our belongings, and the baby's. We say

a tearful farewell to his nurses, Laura and Danielle, and to his doctors.

Cooper and Sam arrive in the Escalade to transport us home. Cooper waits out front behind the wheel while Sam brings up the baby's car seat. I watch, trying valiantly not to laugh as Shane and Sam strap the baby in. How many adults does it take to strap one baby in a car seat?

Shane carries the baby down to the front entrance, and Sam and I carry the rest of our things.

After Shane secures the baby's seat in the back, behind the front passenger seat, I climb in to sit beside him, in the other seat. Sam climbs back to the row of seats behind us, and Shane sits up front with Cooper.

It's not far to our apartment building, but with each passing block, I can feel a heaviness begin to recede, making it easier for me to breathe. We're going home. Finally. *He's* going home. That's got to mean he's doing well. Surely his doctors wouldn't let him leave the hospital if he was still in danger. And that means I can breathe just a little bit easier.

I find myself staring at the baby, marveling at how small he is, how perfect. Maybe I'm biased, but I think he's incredibly adorable. Like really, really adorable. He's got blond hair peeking out from beneath his knit hat, and when he opens his eyes, there's so big and blue. The splotchy red complexion he was born with has evened out into a healthy complexion. He's sleeping through his first car ride, looking angelic and peaceful. I'm sure that will change when he wakes up hungry.

After parking in the underground garage, we pile out, collecting all our belongings. Cooper brought the stroller that goes with the car seat, but before he can pull it out of the rear of the vehicle, Sam unbuckles the baby from the car seat. "I'll carry him," Sam says, cradling the baby and his blanket to his chest.

On the ride up in the elevator, I find myself sneaking glimpses at the baby, marveling all over again. He's a little miracle. He was born before he was supposed to be, and under terrible conditions, but he pulled through it like a little trooper. He's going to be okay.

Sam shifts the baby to the crook of his arm, and the baby's eyes open. His gaze is all over the elevator ceiling as he stares at the sparkling lights reflecting off the mirrored walls and the shiny gold fixtures overhead.

With a familiar chime, the elevator doors open and we all head through the foyer into the apartment. It feels so good to be home! I set my purse down on a side table and stand there, staring around the great room and feeling a little lost.

Shane comes up behind me and steers me toward one of the sofas. "You sit down and rest," he says, "while I put our stuff away."

Sam joins me, laying the baby on the sofa between us. The baby's unfocused gaze darts all over the place, from me to Sam and back again.

"Welcome home, little dude," Sam says, grinning at me.

Shane leans over the back of the sofa and kisses the top of my head. "I'll be right back. Cooper and I are going to move

Luke's bassinette into our room, so he can sleep near us."

I tilt my head back for a quick kiss. "Thank you."

Shane points to the floor behind the sofa. "The cooler with milk is here. He's going to be hungry soon."

I laugh and press my hands against my heavy breasts. "I know. I can tell it'll be time to pump soon."

Shane gives me an enigmatic smile before he walks away. He didn't say anything, but I know what he's thinking. I know what they're all thinking. I should be trying to nurse the baby. I should be trying to get him to latch on and suck. I want to, but I can't bring myself to try again. I'm afraid I'll fail at yet one more thing.

Right on schedule, the baby starts fussing, kicking and squawking on Sam's lap.

"He's hungry," Sam says, looking at me expectantly.

I nod. "I need to pump. Do you want to feed him?"

"Sure. If you don't mind."

"Of course not. You feed him, I'll pump."

I get up from the sofa and hand Sam the diaper bag. He pulls out a bib—*I Love My Uncle*—and snaps it around the baby's neck. While Sam entertains his new little best friend, I warm up a bottle and get ready to pump.

Occasionally, as I pump at the breakfast counter, I glance over my shoulder to watch Sam, who's making silly faces and cooing at my child as he feeds him. It should be me. I should be the one feeding him. But the truth is, when he offered to feed the baby, all I felt was relief.

My phone chimes with an incoming text message from my brother.

Tyler: Are you home yet?

Me: Yes.

Tyler: Can we stop by?

Me: Sure. Come on over. Mom's with you?

Tyler: Yes. On our way.

It's barely noon when I finish pumping and put the bottle of milk in the fridge. I got quite a few ounces this time, which is good. This milk should last us at least two feedings because the baby still doesn't drink that much yet.

The baby's done with his bottle, and Sam's changing his diaper when I return to the sofa to join them.

"You would make such a great dad," I tell Sam, watching him securing the clean diaper and tucking the baby's feet back into his sleeper.

Sam gives me a wistful smile, making me wonder how much he's thought about it.

"Do you want kids?" I ask him.

He nods. "Yeah. But Cooper thinks he's too old to be a dad."

I laugh. "That's ridiculous. He'd be a fantastic father. You both would."

Sam shrugs. "Maybe one day, once we're married."

The elevator chimes, announcing the arrival of my mom and brother.

"Darling," Mom says, joining me on the sofa. She gives me a

hug, then sits back to study me. "How are you feeling?"

"Fine."

"Are you? Really?"

"Yes."

She tucks some loose strands of my hair behind my ear. "How's my adorable little grandson?"

Sam wraps the baby securely in his fuzzy blanket and hands him to my mom. "Fed and freshly changed. He's all yours, Ingrid."

Tyler sits on the back of the sofa and watches Mom fussing over the baby as she rocks him in her arms. "I think he's grown," he says.

"He has," I say. "He's gained eight ounces since he was born."

Shane walks into the room, followed by Cooper. "Hey, Tyler!" he says. "Are you volunteering for babysitting duty?"

Tyler gives Shane a level stare. "Funny."

"Well, I volunteer for babysitting," Ingrid says, making kissy faces at the baby.

"Hello, Ingrid." Shane leans down to kiss my mother's cheek. "You are welcome to babysit anytime you want. But this guy here..." Shane nods toward Tyler. "We're going to need some referrals first, before we consider him for babysitting duty."

Ingrid rises from the sofa and lays the baby in Tyler's arms. "Don't let him fool you, Shane. Tyler is great with babies. He helped me raise Beth."

I watch, completely mesmerized, as my big brother holds my baby in his strong arms, smiling down at him and whispering. I realize I've never seen him with a child before. But Mom's right, he did help raise me, so of course he has experience with kids, although it was quite some years ago. But I guess it's like riding a bike—you never forget.

Shane pats Tyler on the back. "You're not such a tough guy now, when you're holding a two-week-old infant in your arms, are you?"

"Don't test me, pal," Tyler says, giving Shane a dark look. But his expression softens when he gazes down at his nephew once more, cooing and smiling, bouncing him gently as he pats the baby's back.

"Who's hungry?" Cooper says, coming out of the kitchen. "Ingrid, Tyler, would you like to stay for lunch? In honor of her homecoming, and Luke's, I'm going to whip up one of Beth's favorites, chicken and dumplings. You're welcome to join us."

"We'd love to," Mom says. "Thank you."

That's the one thing I really missed while we were in the NICU. Cooper's cooking.

∼ 29

Shane

My son has no shortage of attention during lunch. Everyone takes turns passing him around the table while we eat. Even Beth takes a turn, holding him close and talking quietly to him as the rest of us enjoy our meals. He stares up at her, mesmerized by the sound of her voice. Of course, he must recognize her. She's his mama. He spent the better part of seven months in her womb, listening to her voice, hearing her laugh. My throat tightens as I watch the two of them together.

"All right, it's my turn," Tyler says, holding out his hands to his sister.

Beth smiles at him, then hands him the baby. Her expression is wistful as she watches her brother cuddle with her son.

It amazes me to see how attentive Tyler is with Luke. I think I've underestimated the homicide detective. I think he has a softer side after all. He seems actually quite comfortable holding and entertaining a newborn.

"Anybody need a refill?" I say, rising from the table.

* * *

After Ingrid and Tyler leave that evening, Beth and I order Cooper to go sit down and relax on the sofa with Sam and Luke while we take care of the dirty dishes and the kitchen.

"I was surprised to see Tyler so comfortable with Luke," I say. "I think your brother's bark is worse than his bite."

Beth smiles as she loads dishes into the dishwasher. "He's a big teddy bear at heart. I remember, when I was young, he'd be the first one there to pick me up when I fell off my bike and bandage my scraped knees." Her expression falls as her eyes fill with tears. "He always came to my rescue."

"Oh, sweetheart, come here." I pull her into my arms. I know exactly what she's thinking, and I could kick myself for making her remember.

"Tyler was the first one to find me," she says, her face pressed against my shirt.

A chill crawls through me when I think about how close she

came to being horrendously abused. She was just six years old when Kline abducted her. If the cops hadn't found her so quickly, God knows what might have happened to her. And yes, Tyler Jamison, at that time a rookie Chicago street cop, had been the one to bust down that cellar door and find his little sister bound and gagged, lying naked on the cold, dirt floor in the pitch-black darkness.

"I'm sorry," I murmur against the top of her head, before kissing her there. "I didn't mean to bring back bad memories."

"It's all right. I'm fine, really."

"You've been saying that a lot lately, but I'm not so sure it's true."

"Shane—"

"I know," he says, threading his fingers through my hair. He pulls me close and kisses my forehead. "You've been through a lot. You need time."

After we're done in the kitchen, we join Sam and Cooper in the living room. With his head in Cooper's lap, Sam's lying on the sofa with Luke on his chest, the baby's little knees drawn up beneath his body.

"You're pretty good at that," I say.

Sam laughs as he pats Luke's back. "What can I say? I'm a natural." He kisses the top of the baby's head. "Luke and I are buds."

I reach down and squeeze Sam's shoulder. I haven't forgotten for one second that Beth and I owe Sam everything. There's no way we can ever repay him for his selfless act—for sacrificing his own safety to protect Beth's...and likely saving our son's life before we even knew Beth was pregnant.

Sam pats the baby's well-padded bottom. "I just changed his diaper, after Cooper gave him a bottle. He's all ready for bed."

Beth yawns, drawing lots of chuckles.

"I think Luke's not the only one who's ready for bed," I say as I put my arm around Beth. "I think we could all use some sleep."

"Bed sounds good to me," she says.

Sam hands me Luke, and with my son cradled in one arm, and my other arm around my wife, we head for our own room.

* * *

As I carry Luke to our suite, I can't help lowering my face to his head, smelling his hair and his skin. I guess this is what they mean by the new baby smell. It's oddly addictive, which is undoubtedly nature's way of ensuring that parents take care of their offspring.

I press my cheek to the side of his head and pat his diaper-padded little butt. "Welcome home, son. You'll have no shortage of people only too happy to love you and take care of you, not least of all your mama and me."

At the mention of his mama, I feel a pang of sadness. I know she's not fully on board yet, and she's suffering all kinds of emotions she doesn't need to suffer. I'm hoping that getting her home will help, but if it doesn't, we'll have to take further steps, like counseling.

Luke stays asleep as I put him into his nighttime sleeper and lay him in the bassinette. No pillows, no blankets, on his back, just like the nurses at the hospital drilled into our heads. I watch him for a few minutes to make sure he's actually going to stay asleep. But he's got a dry diaper and a full belly, and he's likely worn out from being passed around by adoring relatives all day. He should be ready for bed.

When I'm sure he's out for the count, I join Beth in the bathroom, where she's getting ready for bed. While she brushes her teeth, I grab a quick shower.

As I climb into bed, I close the distance between us and slip my arm around her waist. "God, it feels good to be home, in our own bed." We've been gone almost two weeks, quite unexpectedly. Being back home again feels a little surreal.

Beth's arm slips over mine, and she clasps my hand.

"I wasn't sure if you were still awake," I say quietly, my mouth just inches from the back of her head.

"I'm exhausted, but I don't think I can sleep."

She doesn't elaborate, and I don't push her. I'll give her a few more days to settle in, and if she's not better, then I'll push. I'll push as hard as I need to—whatever it takes to bring her back to us.

ꝏ 30

Beth

I can't sleep. Even though my body is worn out, my mind is overthinking everything. My thoughts keep racing, and my heart is thrashing in my chest like a caged rabbit. Every breath is a chore, and I'm afraid I'm a heartbeat away from another panic attack.

"Hey." Shane slips his fingers into my hair and starts combing it, gently separating the strands, sending tingles down my spine that make me shiver.

"It's okay, Beth," he murmurs as he continues to play with my hair, stroking it and gently tugging on the strands. "I know, and I'm here."

I groan softly as his fingers grip my scalp, beginning a firm massage, the kind he knows I love. Then his hands slide down to my shoulders, massaging my tight muscles and making me moan with pleasure.

"Can you lie comfortably on your front?" he says.

I roll onto my belly, careful not to put too much pressure on my breasts.

He sits up and pulls the bedding down to my waist. Then he pushes my nightgown up to my shoulders. His hands come down on my bare skin, warm and heavy, and begin a slow, gentle massage. He chuckles softly when I moan shamelessly.

"Your muscles are so tight," he says.

I make an unintelligible sound, and he laughs. "Just relax and let me work my magic."

Now it's my turn to laugh, the sound quietly muffled by my pillow. I close my eyes and try to think about nothing but the pleasure of his hands on me.

Like a wicked master of touch, he massages my shoulders, then my back, his fingers traveling slowly down my spine, chasing the tension out of each individual muscle. He works my back methodically, not missing an inch, until he reaches my hips. Then he pushes the bedding aside exposing the lower half of my body, making me shiver.

His warm hands chase the chill away as he massages my butt cheeks, making me giggle, then continues down each thigh and leg, one at a time, until he reaches my feet. I'm little more than a puddle of sensation now, all of the aches and pains of the past week momentarily forgotten. All I can focus on is how good his hands feel on my body, how gentle he is, how attentive.

Hot tears form in my eyes, spilling over onto my cheeks, and I wipe my face on my pillow. I don't deserve such tender, selfless attention from him. I've been a terrible wife, and an even worse mother, leaving him to shoulder the brunt of the work alone.

I roll to my back, tears streaming down my face. "I'm sorry," I say, my voice choked. "I'm so sorry."

"Shh," he says, brushing the wetness from my cheeks. "You have nothing to be sorry for." He leans down and kisses me gently, his lips clinging to mine. "My love for you doesn't come with any conditions."

He tugs my nightgown back into place, then leans down to brush my hair back so he can kiss my forehead. He settles down beside me, and I roll to my side so he can spoon against me, our favorite position for sleeping. His arm snakes around my waist, and he tucks me close to him.

"You sleep," he says, burying his nose in my hair. "I'll get up with Luke."

* * *

A few hours later, I awake instantly as the baby starts stirring in his bassinette. He's not crying exactly, not yet, but he's definitely awake and making quiet mewling sounds.

I roll to my back and glance at Shane, but he's sound asleep. I can't blame him. He's been pulling far more than just his weight lately. He's been pulling mine too.

The baby starts fussing louder, making faint crying sounds as he ramps up. I carefully slip out of bed and walk to the bassinette, leaning over it to peer at him in the semi-darkness.

"Shh," I say, laying my hand gently on his torso. "Are you hungry?"

The baby's eyes widen, and at first he's satisfied with simply staring at me. But before long, his little legs start moving, followed by his arms. His little face screws up and he takes a deep breath in preparation to make himself heard.

"Shh, it's all right," I say, reaching down to pick him up. I hold him against my chest, the way I've seen Shane do, one hand supporting his butt and the other supporting his back and head. My goodness, he's so small. Technically, he's not supposed to have been born for four more weeks, and I can't help wondering how much bigger he would have been at birth if he'd arrived at the right time. "I guess we'll find out in four weeks, won't we?" I whisper.

When he nuzzles his face against my breast and opens his mouth, my heart starts hammering. Then he starts crying in earnest, his faint, broken cries growing louder with each breath. I feel a sudden flush of heat in my breasts, and they start aching, feeling way too full. I need to pump.

"Do you want to try nursing him?" Shane says quietly from the bed.

I glance his way, surprised to see him sitting up in bed,

watching me with a small smile on his face.

"No!" I flinch at my too-hasty response, realizing how frantic I sound. "I can't. I need to pump now."

Shane nods. "Sure," he says. "Or, you could try to nurse him. If you're successful, then you won't have to pump."

The baby has worked himself up into a pretty good cry now, his increasingly frantic wails piercing the quiet. "He's hungry," I say, my gaze imploring Shane to step in and do something.

As if reading my thoughts, Shane swings his legs over the side of the bed and rises. "Why don't you hold him while I go warm up his bottle? Then, while I'm feeding him, you can pump."

He indicates the little seating area across the room, next to our little kitchenette and fireplace. I feel panic nipping at my heels, but when Shane lays his hand on the center of my back and steers me toward the sofa, I manage to walk across the room without dropping the baby.

I sit on the sofa, cradling the baby in my arms trying to entertain him, and watch as Shane takes a bottle out of the fridge and puts it into the bottle warmer.

"I'll go wash my hands before I feed him," Shane says, heading to the bathroom, leaving me alone with the baby.

I watch Shane's back until he disappears into the bathroom. Then I look down at the fussing baby. "Shh, it's okay," I tell him, bouncing him in my arms. "Your daddy will be right back to feed you. Just hang on."

Rocking him in my arms seems to help, so I keep it up until Shane returns with a blanket and a burb cloth. He checks the bottle, testing the temperature of the milk on his forearm, then sits beside me on the sofa and reaches for the baby.

"Are you sure you don't want to try?" he says, giving me a curious smile. "I can help you. I watched the lactation consultant enough times to know what to do."

I shake my head as I get up from the sofa to fetch the pump. "No, that's okay," I tell him. "I'll just pump."

Half an hour later, after a diaper change, the baby is back in his bassinette, sound asleep with a full belly. I wash the breast pump and put it away for the next time. I join Shane at the foot of our bed, and the both of us stand over the little crib watching our baby sleep.

Memories of childbirth assail me. I can remember it so clearly, the searing pain, the crushing pressure on my abdomen, Jason working so frantically and diligently to get the baby to breathe. The helpless look on Shane's face as he stood watching Jason work on the baby.

"He almost died," I say, my throat closing up on me.

Shane's arm slips around my waist. "But he didn't, sweetheart. He's fine."

Before I can pull away, he lifts me gently into his arms and carries me back to bed, setting me down on the mattress and covering me with the blankets. Then he climbs into bed and settles down beside me, pulling me into his arms.

"Luke is fine, and that's all that matters," he says. He kisses my forehead. "I'm so proud of you."

"For what?" I ask, genuinely surprised at his words. I've done absolutely nothing to deserve any praise. On the contrary, I'm a pathetic disaster as a mother.

"For pumping. It's hard work."

"Oh. Well, it's the least I can do."

He chuckles under his breath. "Maybe you could try nursing him again."

I feel a pang of guilt that I haven't made more of an attempt to nurse him. I've tried a few times, but gave up too easily. "All right, I'll try again tomorrow."

"Good."

* * *

Later that night, or I guess early the next morning before the sun has even risen, I awaken to the sound of Shane's low voice as he croons to the baby. Shane's standing across the room in the kitchenette, rocking the baby in his arms as he waits for a bottle of breast milk to warm. I watch him, mesmerized at the sight of him, so comfortable as he entertains our son. I can hear the baby fussing quietly, and Shane talking to him, telling him his breakfast is on its way.

I need to get up too, to pump. My pumping schedule pretty much mirrors the baby's feeding schedule, and so far I've managed to stay two bottles ahead.

Cradling the baby in one arm, Shane pulls the tiny bottle out of the warmer, gently swirls the milk, then tests the temperature on his forearm. He does all this so naturally, without missing a beat, and I'm amazed by him.

I climb out of bed, feeling weary and exhausted, and join them. "Is there anything you don't do well?" I ask, smiling up at him.

"I had six younger siblings," he reminds me. "I know how to take care of babies. Didn't you ever do any babysitting when you were a teenager?"

Thinking back, I realize I've never been around children. "No. Never."

"For years, as a kid, I was either helping my mom diaper or feed a baby. Dad worked two jobs to support the family, so that left me as the oldest one at home to help out."

Shane pops the bottle into the baby's mouth and takes a seat on the sofa while the baby drinks his milk. I grab my breast pump and join him there, watching him watch the baby guzzle down his breakfast.

Shane talks to the baby, smiling and cooing at him as he sucks on the bottle. Halfway through, he lifts the baby up to his shoulder and pats his back until a surprisingly loud burp startles us both.

"That's my boy," Shane says, smiling proudly. He leans down and kisses the baby's forehead, then settles Luke into his arms to resume the feeding.

"How can you be so chipper at four o'clock in the morning?" I say, shaking my head.

Shane shrugs. "Our son is awesome. What can I say?"

* * *

Three hours later, I'm awakened again by snuffling little cries of hunger. When I sit up, I'm surprised to see Cooper standing beside the bassinette.

"Shh," Cooper whispers, holding his finger to his lips. "I'll take this one. Is there a bottle in the fridge?" He points at the fridge in our suite.

"Yes."

"Go back to sleep, honey. I'll change him and feed him."

I fall back to the mattress, my eyes so heavy I can't keep them open. Shane groans in his sleep and pulls me close.

It really does take a village to raise a baby.

ℰ 31

Beth

Just three hours later, the baby is fussing again, ready for another feeding. I realize I didn't pump at his seven a.m. feeding which means we're short a bottle now and my breasts are so full, they're about to explode. The sound of the baby's crying causes that warm flush to hit me again, making my breasts ache as my milk suddenly comes down.

I glance over at Shane, who's still sound asleep. I don't blame him. Our days and nights have been turned upside down the past couple of weeks, and he's been running himself ragged, taking care of me, taking care of the baby. Shane needs sleep.

Since I'm wide awake, I might as well get up and take care of the baby so Shane can rest.

I head to the bathroom first to empty my bladder and brush my teeth. When I reach the bassinette, Luke's staring up at me with wide eyes, kicking his legs and waving his arms.

He's so cute I can't help smiling. "Hello there," I whisper.

His gaze is wide and unfocused, but at the sound of my voice, he turns his head in my direction and stills, as if listening.

I reach down and stroke his cheek. "Do you recognize my voice? I'm your mama."

He starts kicking again, his arms moving all over the place, and I smile. "I bet you're ready to eat, aren't you?"

He extends one of his little arms in the air, then draws it back toward his face. As his fist brushes against his lips, he opens his mouth and begins squawking.

"All right, keep it down. Let's not wake up your daddy."

I pick him up, his little body warm and cuddly in my arms, and carry him to the nursery. I know there's a nursing pillow in there, and of course the delightfully comfy rocking chair. Since we're short a bottle and my boobs are about to burst, I decide I'd better give the nursing thing another try.

"But first, a diaper change," I murmur, laying him on the padded changing table.

I haven't actually changed very many diapers yet. There's always been someone ready to jump to the task, and I've taken the coward's way out and let them.

"I'm sorry," I say, as I remove the baby's sleeping gown. "I guess I haven't been a very good mom to you so far."

I untape the wet diaper and pull it back just enough to take a peek inside. "You aren't going to pee on me, are you?" I've heard all kinds of horror stories about what can happen when you change a little boy's diaper.

Keeping him partially covered, just in case he decides now would be a good time to pee, I clean him thoroughly with a wet wipe. I also check his umbilical cord stub to make sure it's healing well.

After I put on his clean diaper and a fresh onesie, we nestle together in the rocking chair. I prop my feet up on the foot stool and position the baby on the nursing pillow, just like the lactation consultant showed me.

I unfasten my bra and offer him a nipple, coaxing him into what I think is the right position. "Here you go," I tell him, practically holding my breath as he opens his mouth wide and nuzzles my nipple. *Come on, sweetie, you can do it.*

He tries valiantly to latch on, but he keeps slipping off me. *Come on, Luke. Please.*

He makes another go at it, and I try to help by holding my breast still for him. By now, he's frustrated and hungry, and done messing around. He hasn't quite worked himself up into a crying spell, but he's getting close.

Because he's stressing out, now I'm stressing out, which probably isn't helping the situation. But still, I keep trying. When he finally latches on and starts sucking, I relax into the rocker as I feel my milk coming down in a rush. I sigh in relief and watch him suckle.

I rock us gently as he nurses, a few minutes on one breast, then a little break to burp him—the importance of which he doesn't seem to appreciate—then a few minutes on the other breast. He's nursing like a champ now, pulling and tugging on my nipple with glee.

I stroke his soft, silky tufts of hair. "I'm sorry I haven't been the best mom," I tell him, my voice little more than a whisper. "It's sort of complicated, but I promise to do better."

He glances up at me, his little fist pressing against my breast as he suckles.

I hum as he nurses, picking out the gentle melody of a lullaby I remember from my own childhood. Gradually, the sucking slows, his little tongue fluttering against my nipple, and eventually his mouth goes slack and he releases me. I watch him for the longest time as his eyelids open and close, fighting gravity as sleep pulls him under.

I hear a quiet sound behind me and glance back to see Shane standing in the nursery doorway, watching us with a very satisfied, if sleepy, smile on his face. He's dressed only in a pair of boxers, and his hair is sleep-tousled. He must have just woken up.

"I'm sorry. Did we wake you? I tried to keep him quiet."

Shane comes into the room and kneels beside the rocking chair, one hand on the back of my neck while he gently strokes the baby's forehead with his other. He lifts those beautiful, bright blue eyes to me and gives me a handsomely crooked smile. "God, I love you so much."

I smile, feeling my cheeks heat and figure I'm probably blushing. "I wanted to let you sleep," I tell him. "You've been doing so much for me, for us. We came in here so we wouldn't wake you."

He smiles at me, his eyes suspiciously damp. "Watching our son nurse at your breast has got to be the most moving thing I've ever seen in my life."

Now I'm definitely blushing.

He tucks a strand of my hair behind my ear, then traces the shape of my ear with his fingertip, sending delicious tingles down my spine. At least part of my body has come back online.

"Jamie just called," he says. "He and Molly want to know if they can come over this afternoon for a visit."

I nod. "Of course they can. Luke needs to spend some quality time with his Uncle Jamie and Aunt Molly."

Shane lights up as he grins at me.

"What?" I say, laughing at his expression.

"You just called him *Luke*."

"So? That's his name."

"Honey, that's the first time I've ever heard you call him by his name."

I open my mouth to contradict him, but then I snap it shut, as now that I think back, I'm afraid he's right.

He smiles and leans forward to press his lips gently against mine.

* * *

While Shane takes a shower, I bring Luke with me to the kitchen so I can make a cup of French Vanilla decaf. When it's ready, I carry my son and my coffee to the sitting area so we can relax while we wait for Shane to join us for breakfast.

Oh, my. When I come around the sofa, I spot Cooper and Sam lying there sound asleep, spooning in their PJs. Cooper's arm is around Sam's waist, and he's holding him close, probably to prevent Sam from falling off the sofa as it is hardly deep enough to accommodate two grown men comfortably.

Quietly, so as not to wake them, I sit in one of the chairs and sip my coffee while I hold Luke in the crook of my other arm.

I'm sure both Cooper and Sam have been run ragged the past couple of weeks, running errands for us, helping with the baby. When Luke was in the NICU, they spent most of their waking hours at the hospital helping us watch over him.

About the time I finish my coffee, Shane comes into the great room wearing sweatpants and a T-shirt, a damp towel thrown across his shoulders. "I don't know about you, sweetheart, but I'm starved. What sounds good for breakfast?"

"Shh," I whisper, holding a finger to my lips. I point at the sofa, and he comes to investigate, peering over the back of it at the two sleepyheads.

"Well, isn't that cute?" he says.

"What time is it?" Cooper grumbles, lifting his wrist to check his watch. He groans. "I must have fallen back to sleep after the seven a.m. feeding."

Cooper's hand slides down to Sam's hip and he gives it a squeeze. "Wake up, sleeping beauty."

Sam opens his eyes and groans, then rolls up into a sitting position. His top knot has come loose, and his red hair is mussed. Quickly, he finger-combs his hair, and then twists it back into a neat bun and ties it off with a hairband. "Hey, princess," he says, smiling at me. "How's my little buddy doing?"

"He's fine." I smile. "He nursed this morning."

Cooper and Sam both eye me in blatant surprise.

"He nursed like a champ," Shane says, coming over to me to lean down and kiss the top of Luke's head. Then to the guys, he says, "Jamie and Molly are coming over this afternoon. FYI."

Cooper groans as he rubs Sam's back. "Afternoon? Crap, we haven't even had breakfast yet." He gives Sam a quick kiss, then heads for the kitchen. "Omelets okay, guys? Coffee and toast?"

"Sounds good to me," Sam says.

"Sure," Shane says. "Thanks."

"I'll help," I offer. I'm a parent now, so I really do need to learn how to cook.

Sam comes to me, his hands outstretched as he reaches for the baby. "Come to Uncle Sam."

I follow Cooper to the kitchen. "What can I do to help?"

"For starters, grab a dozen eggs out of the fridge."

While I get the eggs, he pulls a large mixing bowl out of the cupboard and a giant whisk from the cutlery drawer. "Crack the eggs into that bowl and start whisking." He watches me a moment, then says, "I'm proud of you."

I smile. "For what?"

"For nursing your son. Good job."

"I wanted to from the beginning, but it was just too stressful when he couldn't latch on. Plus, I felt like I had absolutely no idea what I was doing."

"Well, you figured it out, the both of you." Cooper heads to the fridge and pulls out cheese and veggies and begins prepping the ingredients. "You have a beautiful son, Beth. Congratulations."

I blush. "Thank you."

Shane walks into the kitchen and grabs a coffee mug from the cupboard and pours himself a cup from the pot. "I think I had something to do with that."

"With what?" Cooper says.

"Making that beautiful baby boy." Shane leans over and kisses the top of my head. "Of course, Beth helped."

Shane sits at the breakfast bar and drinks his coffee, reading a copy of the *Chicago Tribune*, while I help Cooper prep the ingredients for the omelets. Sam sits across the room making baby sounds with Luke cradled in his arms.

This moment is perfect, a sublime picture of domesticity. I close my eyes, thanking my lucky stars that Luke is okay and out of the hospital. When I glance at Shane and catch him watching me, I smile.

While the omelets are cooking, I excuse myself to get dressed. We have a few minutes before breakfast will be served, so I take a quick shower. It's so good to be home. Our walk-in shower is decadent, and I've missed it. I wash all over, gently and carefully in certain places. My belly is still soft, but it's tightening up a little bit more each day. The lactation consultant at the hospital said nursing would help with that.

As I wash, I touch myself experimentally, just to gauge how well my body is healing. I'm still very tender *down there*, but each day it's a little better. Right now, I can't imagine ever wanting to have sex again. I really hope that passes.

Once I'm dressed, I head back to the great room to find the dining room table set. Someone carried in the portable baby swing from the nursery and set it by the table so Luke can nap while we eat.

Shane sets the swing between his chair and mine, so we can both keep an eye on the baby. Halfway through the meal, when Luke wakes up and starts fussing, Sam is the first one to jump up and get him.

"You're going to spoil that baby, Sam," Cooper says, shaking his head. "You can't jump up every time he whimpers."

"Yes, I can," Sam says, returning to his seat with Luke in the crook of his arm. "He needs to know we're here and that he can count on us."

Pressing my lips together in an effort not to laugh, I sneak a glance at Shane, who's shaking his head. "Cooper's right. That baby's going to be so spoiled."

The elevator chimes, and a moment later Molly and Jamie walk into the great room, their arms linked as Molly guides Jamie toward us. Molly's holding a little gift bag.

"Who's going to be spoiled?" Jamie asks.

Shane stands and picks up his empty breakfast plate. "My son, that's who. He's got four adults waiting on him hand and foot."

"Make that five," Molly says, as she hands me the gift bag. "I'll wash my hands so I can hold him."

While they're washing their hands, I open the gift bag and pull out an adorable stuffed teddy bear, very soft and floppy, and a darling blue sleeper. "Thank you, guys," I say, when they return to the table.

"You're very welcome." Molly holds out her hands to Sam. "My turn," she says, grinning.

Pretending to grumble, Sam hands Luke over to Molly.

"Hello, you adorable little thing," Molly says, rocking Luke in her arms, patting his bottom. She leans down to kiss his forehead. "You smell so good."

Jamie, who's seated next to Molly, holds his hands out after a few minutes. "It's my turn."

Molly carefully transfers Luke to Jamie's arms. Everyone watches, captivated, as Jamie gently explores Luke's face with his fingertips, his touch light as a feather as he maps out each little feature.

The smile on Molly's face as she watches Jamie with Luke is bittersweet. I can guess what she's thinking. Jamie will never see his nephew's face. The explosion in Afghanistan that stole his eyesight took so much more from him than just his vision— it took these special milestones from him, too. Ones that the rest of us take for granted.

Jamie kisses Luke's forehead. "Congratulations, you guys," he says. "I'm sorry for what you went through, but I'm grateful that you and the baby are all right."

With the same aplomb as he does everything else, Jamie looks perfectly at ease holding an infant in his arms.

Molly moves to stand behind Jamie, so she can put her arms around his neck. She leans closer and kisses his cheek. "You look good with a baby in your arms," she says to him, winking at me from across the table.

"Is that a hint, Molly?" he says, kissing Luke again.

✌ 32

Beth

Can we see the nursery?" Molly asks.

"Sure," I say. "Follow me."

Shane carries Luke, and Jamie follows Molly and me to the nursery, his hand on Molly's shoulder.

While Molly and I gush over the adorable outfits hanging in the closet, Jamie joins Shane in the doorway, and the two brothers talk quietly.

When Luke starts squirming in Shane's arms, I check the time. "It's not time for him to eat again."

Jamie lays his hand on Luke and pats his diaper. "I think he's due for a diaper change."

"I think you're right," Shane says, laughing as he wrinkles his nose.

"I'll do it," Jamie says.

Shane looks at his brother. "You'll do it?"

"Sure. I've never changed a dirty diaper before. This will be a new experience."

"Just watch out he doesn't pee on you," I say, as Molly and I escape to the great room, leaving the guys to deal with a stinky diaper.

* * *

We grab some glasses of freshly-squeezed lemonade, courtesy of Cooper, and sit out on the balcony to enjoy the sunshine and watch the boats on Lake Michigan. We have a lot of catching up to do.

"How are you, really?" Molly asks, reaching over to touch my arm.

My throat tightens as recent memories resurface. "Actually, as of this morning, I'm doing a lot better. Luke and I had a breakthrough. He finally latched on, and I was able to nurse him."

"Oh, good. That must be a huge relief."

I nod, sipping my drink. "It is. I mean, everyone's been really helpful, taking turns feeding Luke from a bottle while I pumped, but it's a lot easier if I can simply nurse him." When

I realize what I've said, my stomach drops, and I feel the blood drain from my face. How could I be so thoughtless? "Oh, my God, Molly, I'm so sorry. I can't believe I said that."

"Said what?"

"I wasn't thinking. You know, talking about breastfeeding." The fact that Molly's had a double mastectomy completely slipped my mind.

She makes a dismissive gesture. "Oh, please, don't even give it a thought. I knew going into my treatment that, if I were ever blessed with a child, I wouldn't be able to breastfeed. Please don't feel bad. It doesn't bother me one bit to hear you talk about nursing your precious little boy." She reaches over and squeezes my hand. "I'm happy for you, Beth. Honestly."

I appreciate Molly's gracious response, but I still feel bad. "Do you and Jamie want to have kids?"

She smiles as she sips her lemonade. "We do. Jamie's a little hesitant about having kids, given his blindness. But honestly, there's nothing that man can't do, sighted or not. Case in point, he's in the nursery right now changing a dirty diaper, with Shane's help of course. He's testing himself."

"You'd both make wonderful parents."

"Right now, we're just enjoying being together. Our work and remodeling our respective apartments into one larger unit is taking up a lot of our time. And then, we've got to think about—" Molly stops, and suddenly her face lights up in a grin. "Jamie proposed to me last week."

"What!" I set my glass down on the little table between us.

"Oh, my God! That's so wonderful. You said yes, right?"

She laughs. "Of course, I did! I'm not letting that man get away."

"Why didn't you say something sooner?"

"You've had your hands full, with the baby in the hospital, and with recuperating. We figured our news could wait."

"No, it cannot wait! We need to celebrate! I want to host an engagement party for you guys."

"What about your party? The baby shower? It's still scheduled for Saturday, right?"

In all the excitement, I'd forgotten all about the party. Shane's sister Sophie has taken charge of the baby shower. "It seems kind of late for that now, don't you think? Since Luke's already here."

"Oh, no, it's not too late. Trust me, knowing Sophie, the baby shower is still a go. In fact, last I heard, Hannah's flying in to attend."

"I guess I'd better call Sophie then."

"Has there been any word on Jake?"

"Jake? What about Jake?"

Molly pales, and it's clear she realizes she just said something she's not supposed to.

"Molly? What about Jake?"

"I'm sorry. I shouldn't have said anything. I didn't realize you didn't know."

"Know what?" I say, my pulse racing.

The glass doors open behind us, and Shane and Jamie walk

out onto the balcony, Jamie's hand on Shane's shoulder. Shane's holding Luke.

"What's this about Jake?" I ask Shane. "What haven't I been told?"

Shane's expression is perfectly neutral as his gaze darts from Molly to me.

I know he's hiding something from me. "Shane?"

"I'm so sorry, Shane," Molly says. "I just assumed she knew."

"Knew what?" I say, staring at Shane for answers.

Shane pulls up a chair beside mine and sits, settling Luke in the crook of his arm. "I didn't want to say anything while you were recuperating. Besides, there's not much to tell. No one knows much of anything at this point."

"What are you guys talking about? Is Jake okay?"

Shane sighs. "Do you remember hearing anything about Annie Elliot?"

I nod. "She was Jake's high school sweetheart. What about her?"

"She recently divorced her husband—her *abusive* husband. He's been threatening her and their five-year-old son, Aiden. Annie's father hired us to protect Annie and her son. Jake took the case, and he and Annie and the boy have disappeared. We don't know where they are. They've gone off grid."

Thinking back, I realize we haven't seen Jake in a while, over a week now. I'd just assumed he was busy at work, making up for Shane's absence. "Can't you contact him?" I say.

Shane shakes his head. "He's completely off grid. No phone,

nothing we can track. I'm sure Cameron and Killian have a way to reach him. They're doing surveillance on the ex-husband."

"And you have no idea where they are?"

He shrugs. "Well, I have a couple of ideas. But don't worry, sweetheart, Jake knows what he's doing. If he needs help, he'll ask for it."

My mind is racing, wondering how things are going. It's got to be awkward for the both of them to be thrust together like that, after their history. Plus, there's a child involved now. That's got to complicate things too.

Shane reaches over and pats my leg. "Don't worry about them. They'll be fine. We'll hear from him eventually."

* * *

After Molly and Jamie's visit, I nurse Luke and change his diaper, then wrap him up in a blanket.

"I'm going down to Lia's," I announce to Shane and Cooper and Sam, who are watching a baseball game on the big screen TV in the great room. "Just for a quick visit. I need to see her."

"Do you want me to come with you?" Shane asks, rising from the sofa.

"No, I'm fine on my own. You guys stay here and enjoy your game. I won't be gone long."

Luke and I ride down in the elevator to Lia's floor. When I knock on her door, it opens immediately.

"Hi, Beth," Jonah says, opening the door and waving me in.

He reaches out and brushes the top of Luke's head. "How's the little guy doing?"

"He's doing really well. He's nursing now, like a champ."

I glance past Jonah to the living room, where Lia's sitting on the sofa. "Is this a bad time?" I ask.

"No, of course not," Jonah says, closing the door. "Come on in."

"Hey, princess," Lia says, scooting over to make room for me to sit beside her. "How's it going?"

"It's all good." I unwrap the blanket and set it aside, holding Luke in the crook of my arm. He's wide awake, his eyes darting all over the room as he listens to us talking.

Jonah offers to get me something to drink, but I decline. So he sits in the recliner facing us.

I spread the baby blanket on the sofa and lay Luke down between us. Lia reaches for his hand, grinning when he latches onto her finger.

"He's got a strong grip," she says, surprised.

Lia and Jonah visited us several times in the Children's Hospital, but I haven't seen her since Luke was released a few days earlier. There are things I need to say to her. Important things. I'm just not sure how to say them.

"Is everything okay?" she says, eyeing me curiously.

"Yes." I take a deep breath, steadying myself. "It's just that I need to talk to you."

"Spit it out, Beth. You're making me nervous."

I laugh. "I'm sorry. It's just—Lia, I don't know how to thank you for what you did. You saved my life. You saved Luke's. You were so amazing during the whole ordeal...the way you got me out of danger. I was so scared, so overwhelmed, I couldn't think straight." My throat tightens painfully, and I find it difficult to speak.

I brush the tears from my cheeks, my hand shaking. "I'm sorry. I knew this would happen."

When I glance up at Lia, she's tearing up too. "You don't have to thank me."

"Yes, I do. Lia, you saved us. Literally. I'm afraid to think what would have happened if you hadn't been there with me."

She sucks in a breath, then blows it out. "Really, you don't have to thank me." She swallows hard. "You're the best friend I've ever had, Beth. There's nothing I wouldn't do for you. And for him," she says, pointing at Luke.

I give her a teary smile. "Do you want to hold him?"

She shrugs, sparing a quick glance at Jonah, who's watching intently, a smile on his face. "Sure."

I scoop Luke up in my hands and hand him to her. Awkwardly, she takes him in her arms and cradles him to her chest, holding onto him for dear life.

"I've never held a baby," she says, looking sheepish. "If I'm doing it wrong, just say so."

"You're doing fine." I scoot closer to her and lean into her side. My head ends up on her shoulder, and when I break down sobbing, she passes Luke off to Jonah and wraps her arms around me.

"I was so scared, Lia."

"I know you were." She tightens her arms around me. "Trust me, I was too. But we did it. We got through it together."

"I can't thank you enough. There just aren't words…"

Jonah brings Luke back to the sofa, and we scoot over to make room for him to sit on Lia's other side. He hands the baby back to Lia, and she cradles him in her arms.

"Hey, little dude," she says, smiling down at him. "I'm your Auntie Lia. You and I are going to have so much fun."

Jonah chuckles as he winks at me. "I can just imagine."

Lia elbows Jonah. "Don't jinx this for me."

When there's a knock at the door, Jonah gets up to answer it. Shane walks into the apartment, his gaze searching for me. When he sees me, he smiles. "There you are." Then he joins me on the sofa, taking in my teary eyes and wet cheeks as he pulls me close. "What's wrong?"

"Nothing's wrong. I just wanted to thank Lia."

Shane smiles at his youngest sister as she cuddles with our son. "Saying 'thank you' doesn't seem to cut it, does it?" he says.

"Oh, stop!" Lia says, hastily brushing a few errant tears from her cheeks. "You guys are going to make me blush." She leans down and nuzzles Luke's face. "Who's my favorite nephew?"

Shane laughs. "He's your only nephew."

"Oh, shut up," she says, laughing a bit shakily. "You know what I mean."

ॐ 33

Shane

I awake to the sound of a hungry baby Saturday morning at seven a.m. I'm absolutely exhausted. I was up and down all night with Luke, who just couldn't settle down. He finally fell asleep in the great room at about five this morning, in the baby swing, so I got a couple of hours sleep on the sofa beside him. But sleeping time is over. The boy is hungry.

"All right, come on," I tell him, scooping him out of the swing. We make a pitstop in the nursery so I can change his wet diaper. Then we head for mama, who's asleep in our bed.

I crawl into bed and lay Luke down between me and Beth.

"Good morning, Mommy," I murmur to Beth.

She rolls to face us and smiles sleepily. "Good morning."

Luke ups the volume on his request for breakfast.

"Guess who's hangry?" I say.

"Hangry?" Beth laughs. "Gee, I wonder who." Then she pulls Luke close to her and nuzzles his cheek, kissing him. "How's my sweet boy this morning?"

Luke is getting excited now that he's figured out breakfast is imminent. He starts kicking his legs vigorously, flailing his arms, and his mouth opens wide like a baby bird's. This kid has no shame when it comes to getting what he wants.

Beth opens the bodice of her nightgown and rolls to face Luke, rolling him onto his side, too, so that he's facing her. I watch, fascinated, as she offers him her nipple, and he latches on hungrily. Beth closes her eyes, a contented smile on her face as Luke suckles.

I love to watch her nurse our son. Maybe that makes me a voyeur—I honestly don't know, or care. There's something incredibly satisfying about watching her feed our son this way. I reach out and tuck a strand of hair behind her ear, and she sighs. She's still half asleep, making those sleepy noises she makes, which happen to make me hard. Damn. I am a voyeur—I'm certainly perverted. It's got to be highly inappropriate for me to get a hard-on while she's nursing.

Sex is off the table right now, naturally. My God, I've lost count of how many days it's been since we've had sex. I adjust the bedding, so she doesn't accidentally catch sight of my erection. Because that would be bad on my part. My wife is recuperating from childbirth, for God's sake. Sex is probably the last thing on her mind right now.

But I'm a guy, and I can't help it. I see her beautiful breast on display like that, full and plump and rosy-tipped, and I get hard. Fuck.

No sex, I remind myself. No. None. Get the thought out of your head. Dr. Shaw said it would take at least six weeks for her to heal. I should add a few more weeks to that estimate just to be on the safe side. Besides, I'll let her tell me when she's ready.

A bit more awake now, she sits up and props her pillows against the headboard so she can hold him to the other breast. Jesus, she's beautiful. On that note, my hard-on isn't subsiding anytime soon. "Hey, while you're doing that, do you mind if I grab a quick shower?"

"Sure, go ahead," she says, as she strokes Luke's hair.

She's completely oblivious to my suffering, which is how I want to keep things. I hop out of bed and head for the bathroom, hoping a cold shower will put me back to rights.

Twenty minutes later, when I come out of the bathroom with a towel wrapped around my waist, the bed is empty. So is our room. She must have taken Luke to the nursery to change him.

I pull on a pair of sweats and a T-shirt and leave our suite. The door to Luke's room is ajar, and I can hear Beth in there singing softly to him as she changes his clothes. God, it does my heart good to see how she's bonded with him. She's come so far since his shaky birth.

Leaving them to their quality alone time, I head for the kitchen in search of coffee. "Hey, good morning," I say to Cooper, who's poking around in the fridge.

Cooper straightens and closes the fridge door. "Good morning." He peers around me. "Where's Beth?"

"In the nursery with Luke."

"Oh, good."

"Do you need her?"

"No! I mean, no. Actually, I wanted to talk to you. In private."

I glance around the great room, and there's no sign of anyone but the two of us. "Shoot," I say, grabbing a coffee cup from the cupboard and pouring a cup of Cooper's hand-ground Columbian Roast.

Once I'm seated at the breakfast counter, Cooper stands on the other side, opposite of me, and sucks in a breath. Then he lets it out in a long, drawn-out sigh.

"Just say it," I tell him. "Whatever's on your chest... just get it off."

He frowns. "I owe you an apology, Shane."

"What? What are you talking about? No, you don't."

"Yes, I do. I was shitty to you about going out of town, and I was shitty to you in Galford, during her delivery. I said things I shouldn't have said. I was out of line, and I'm sorry."

I shake my head. "You were right. I shouldn't have taken her out of town so close to her due date. I did, and I fucked up. That's on me. You don't have to apologize for being right, Dan."

"I said some terrible things to you, and I'm sorry. I'm sorry for trying to lay the blame on you. I know it wasn't your fault. It was no one's fault. Sometimes shit happens. But God, Shane, I was scared shitless for her. If anything happened to that girl— and that baby—" He stops, swallowing hard as he gets ahold of himself.

I nod. "I know, and I understand. Completely. I still have nightmares about it. But it's in the past. She's fine, and he's fine. We have to let it go."

Setting my coffee down, I sigh. "You and I have been through a lot together, my friend. I totally understand where you were coming from, and I don't blame you one bit. What kind of father figure would you be for Beth if you didn't look out for her best interest? And that includes chastising her husband when you think he deserves it. I know you love her, and that gives you the right."

Cooper shakes his head. "You didn't deserve it. You're a good husband, Shane."

"You're a good dad to her, and I'm glad she has you. Keep watching out for her."

Sam walks into the room in his pajama bottoms and a T-shirt. He walks right over to Cooper and pulls him in for a kiss. "Hell, yeah, he makes a great dad." Sam brushes his hand over Cooper's buzz cut and smiles at me. "I keep telling him that." And then Sam winks at me.

Beth walks in, wearing a robe over her nightgown, and holding Luke, who's dressed in a white sleeper with tiny giraffes on it. "Good morning, guys."

"Good morning, kiddo," Cooper says. "What time is the baby shower this afternoon? Do I have time to go to the shooting range this morning?"

Beth kisses Luke's fist when he shoves it into her face. "The party is at two, so yes. You have plenty of time. Just make sure you're back in time for the party."

"Yes, ma'am," Cooper says. Then he looks at Sam. "You wanna come with me?"

"Yes, sir!" Sam says, grinning at the exasperation on Cooper's face. "Maybe you can teach me something I don't already know."

"Watch your mouth, smart ass," Cooper says, smacking Sam on his ass. "Go get dressed, or I'll teach you something you won't soon forget."

ℰ 34

Beth

Sophie and Hannah arrive an hour before the baby shower to decorate and organize the catering. Gina Capelli very graciously offered to provide the snacks and cupcakes.

"Is there something I can do to help?" I ask Shane's sisters.

"No, you go sit down and relax," Sophie says, shooing me toward the seating area. "You're the guest of honor, sweetie. You get to sit and watch."

"I thought Luke was the guest of honor," Lia says, walking into the great room, along with Jonah.

Lia lights up when she sees her sister Hannah. "When did

your flight get in?"

"Late last night," Hannah says, as she wraps silverware in napkins. "How are you doing? Beth and Shane told me all about your harrowing experience during the robbery. Sounds like you were the hero of the day."

Lia scoffs. "I was just doing my job, that's all. It's no big deal."

Now it's my turn to scoff. "Don't listen to her, Hannah. She saved my life. And Luke's."

The closer it gets to two o'clock, the elevator chimes non-stop as more guests arrive. We're going to have a full house today. Shane's family is coming, and mine. Plus, my friends from the bookstore, namely Erin and Mack, and also Gabrielle. Some of the McIntyre Security guys are coming, and Peter Ca-pelli, Gina's older brother and the owner of Renaldo's, the five-star restaurant where Gabrielle works as a sous chef.

Everyone's here, except for Jake. His absence is sorely felt.

Sam and Cooper arrive in plenty of time and set themselves up as bartenders for the afternoon.

My mom and Shane's mom, Bridget, join me on the sofa, waiting for an opportunity to hold the little guest of honor. Shane brings me Luke, whom I just recently nursed before guests started arriving. Shane changed his diaper and his clothes.

Calum intercepts Shane and reaches for Luke. "Here, son, let me hold the little guy, before the ladies hog him all afternoon."

Shane hands Luke over to his dad.

"Calum, you need to wait in line," Bridget says to her husband. "Ingrid and I were here first."

"You two aren't good at sharing," Calum says. "Besides, a boy needs to spend quality time with his grandpa."

Calum walks away with Luke, heading over to the bar to hang with the guys. Bridget rolls her eyes at me, shaking her head in exasperation. "That man! I swear." And then she gets up and follows her husband.

Erin O'Connor, my dear friend and assistant manager at Clancy's Bookshop, comes to join us, taking Bridget's vacated seat. "You look amazing, Beth," she says, displaying a darling set of dimples that make her look far younger than her twenty-two years of age. "When are you coming back to work?"

"In a few weeks maybe," I say. "If Shane will let me. I would like to come visit the store this week and bring Luke with me. I'm planning to convert the storage room next to my office into a nursery so I can bring Luke with me to work. I'll need to hire someone to help out with childcare."

"Oh, my goodness, it would be fantastic if you brought him to work with you," Erin says.

"Beth?"

I turn to see Hannah standing behind the sofa. Her hair— the same rich chestnut brown color as Shane's—hangs in a single braid down her back. Dressed in a University of Colorado hoodie, jeans, and well-worn hiking boots, she looks every inch the wilderness adventurer she is. I'm so glad she came. We don't get to see her very often.

"We're ready, Beth," Hannah says, nodding toward the dining room table, which holds a feast of hot and cold hors d'oeu-vres. At the center of the table is an elegant display of frosted cupcakes decorated with tiny gold beads.

I follow Hannah to the table, where Gina and Sophie are making last minute touches. "You guys, this is so fantastic. I can't thank you enough."

Sophie hugs me. "It's our pleasure, sweetie." Then she ad-dresses the room. "Food is served, everyone! Come fill your plate and get something to drink. Make sure you get a cupcake, but don't bite into it until we tell you to, or there will be hell to pay."

Erin joins me at the table, and we get in line. I skipped lunch, so I'm starving, and I'm really eyeing those gorgeous cupcakes, wondering what Sophie and Gina are up to.

I glance around the room, looking for Luke, and find him nestled in his Uncle Tyler's arms.

Shane comes up behind me in the food line. "Do you need some help?"

"No, I'm fine. Thank you."

Erin puts a tiny quiche, a few broccoli florets, and two baby carrots on her plate, then steps aside.

"You forgot your cupcake, young lady," Mack says, appearing out of nowhere and placing a cupcake on her plate. He looks at her plate and scowls. "Erin, that's not enough food to keep a bird alive."

Erin's cheeks turn pink, and she glances around, mortified that someone might have overheard him. "Mack, please!"

Mack's holding a plate piled high with food, and a cupcake, but he needs all those calories to fuel his six-foot-plus body packed with muscle. "I'm serious," he says. "You need to *eat*."

He looks expectantly at me, as if wanting me to back him up. I had noticed that Erin looked like she'd lost some weight. Her round cheeks are a little less round, and her clothes are fitting looser. Still, she's adorable.

"Leave her alone, Mack," I say. "It's a party."

Erin gives me a grateful smile and returns to her spot on the sofa.

Mack remains at my side. Once Erin is out of earshot, he says, "She's practically starving herself, Beth. I hardly ever see her eat anything. It's not healthy. The girl needs to eat."

I feel bad because I've been away from the bookstore for quite a while now, leaving Erin to manage things on her own. She's doing a fantastic job as acting manager, but I know it stresses her out. I think it's time for me to return to work, at least a few days a week to give Erin a break.

"Is she doing okay?" I ask him. "Managing the store, I mean. Is it too much?"

"She does a great job," he says. "She's a natural leader, and the store's running smoothly. She just has it in her head that she needs to lose weight, when she sure as hell doesn't. She's perfect just as she is."

"Have you told her that?" I ask him, giving him a small smile. It's no secret that Erin is crazy about Mack. The only problem is, he's quite a bit older than she is, and Shane has warned him to stay away from her.

Mack frowns as he observes Erin across the room. She's busy chatting with my mom and my brother, who has Luke in his arms. Erin laughs as Tyler hands Luke over to her.

"No, I haven't told her that," Mack says. "It will only make matters worse. I don't want to lead her on."

I don't think I'm imagining the longing in Mack's gaze. "If you told her she was perfect the way she is, would you be leading her on? Or would you simply be telling her the truth?"

Mack looks down at me. He's a big guy, well over six feet tall, and built like a Mack truck. He's all muscle and brawn, and even I can admit he's hot as can be. And for such a big, strong guy, he looks a little bit lost at the moment as his gaze fixes on Erin.

"Mack? Are you okay?"

He shakes himself free of his thoughts and looks at me. "I'm fine."

"Shane told me he warned you off of Erin. But honestly, Mack, if you have feelings for her, then you should tell her."

Mack shakes his head. "She's so young, and so inexperienced. She doesn't know the first thing about men."

"Then maybe you should teach her. Somebody's got to be the first, otherwise women would stay virgins their entire lives. I was a virgin when I met Shane. If he thought the way you do, I wouldn't be standing here right now, happier than I've ever been in my entire life, and that precious little baby over there wouldn't even exist."

Mack turns to me, shocked. "Jesus, Beth, I can't. She's so

damn innocent. The things I'd want to do to her. Christ, I can't even have this conversation."

"Yes, you can. She's crazy about you, Mack. If you think you might have feelings for her—"

"I don't just think it, Beth. God, I need a drink. I'm sorry," he says, excusing himself as he heads across the room to the bar.

After everyone's had a chance to eat, Sophie stands and taps a spoon against her glass, capturing everyone's attention. "Time for cupcakes," she says, a grin on her face. "Does everyone have a cupcake? Good. One of these cupcakes has a surprise in it. A tiny plastic baby figurine. Take a bite of your cupcake, and if you find the baby, then you'll be the next one to either get pregnant, or get someone pregnant. And if you win, the filling inside your cupcake—either pink or blue—predicts what you're going to have."

Lots of chuckles fill the air. Some eagerly unwrap their cupcakes, while others shy away from taking a bite while they watch the others.

Shane plucks my cupcake off my plate and hands it to his father. "Nope. No more babies for a while. We're still recovering from the one we have."

"Hey! I want a cupcake!"

"I'll get you a safe one," he promises. "After the coast is clear."

Many of the guests take tentative bites out of their cupcakes and are relieved to find their treats baby-free.

Lia bites into hers, then spits her mouthful of cupcake into a napkin, her lips stained with pink filling. "Oh, no!" she cries, dropping her cupcake onto her plate. "I'm not having a baby. No way! Not going to happen."

Jonah reaches over and snatches the remaining cupcake off her plate and shoves it into his mouth.

"You spit that cupcake out right now!" Lia demands, grabbing the back of his neck. "We are not getting knocked up, pal."

"Oh, come on, tiger," he says, leaning over to kiss her with pink frosting on his lips. "It'll be fun."

* * *

The baby shower is a great success, with lots of fun and raucous laughter. Everyone gives Lia a hard time about the baby cupcake. Mack makes himself scarce, staying as far away from Erin as humanly possible, and she makes sad doe eyes at him all evening. It's enough to make me want to shake him!

After playing a few more silly baby shower games, opening gifts for Luke, and eating up lots of food, folks start heading home, until just a handful of people are left. Shane takes Luke to the nursery to change his diaper, while I help Gina and Sophie and Hannah clean up.

"I can't thank you guys enough," I tell them. "It was a wonderful party. I'm very grateful to you."

Sophie puts her arm across my shoulder and gives me a squeeze. "Are you kidding? You're the one who did all the hard work—having Luke. Compared to that, planning a baby shower is a walk in the park."

Shane and Luke return to the great room, along with Killian. "Luke's ready for bed," Shane says, bringing the baby to me so I can kiss him goodnight. Then Shane carries Luke to our suite to put him in his bassinette.

"Hi, Killian," I say. "I'm so glad you came today. It's always a pleasure to see you."

"Thanks. It's good to see you too. And it's really good to see Luke doing so well." He gives me a hug and pats my back. "I'm happy for you guys."

I notice his gaze keeps darting across the room at something. When I look in that direction, I see Hannah clearing off the cupcake tower.

"Have you met Hannah, Shane's sister?" I ask him.

"No, I have not." And before I can say another word, he marches right up to Hannah, bold as can be. "Hello, cher," he says, holding out his hand to her.

She shakes his hand, staring at it as if she's afraid he's hiding a rattlesnake up his sleeve. I can't hear what they're saying, but Hannah's looking up at him with a highly skeptical expression. He says something more, and she shakes her head, biting her lower lip in an effort not to smile at him. Finally, he grabs a cupcake off the display with a flourish and walks away.

"She shot me down faster than a gator chasin' his Sunday supper," he says to me as he heads for the foyer, a big grin on his handsome face.

Oh, my God, did he just hit on Hannah?

"Night, Miz Beth!" Killian calls back to me, sounding pretty pleased with himself despite the fact it appears Hannah gave him the brush-off. "See ya around, cher."

After Killian's gone, I join Hannah at the table. "What did he say to you?"

She shakes her head. "How arrogant! Like he's God's gift to women."

I laugh. "You did notice that he's hotter than hell, right?"

"Who's hotter than hell?" Shane says, returning to the great room.

I smile at him. "You are, dear. You are."

Six Weeks Later

Beth

I can stare at my baby for hours, marveling at how perfect he is, with his sweet little face and big blue eyes. His blond hair sticks up in little tufts, reminding me of his daddy after he wakes up. Luke's nearly caught up with his gestational age now. He's right on track.

Our nursing time has become a special ritual and the highlight of my days and nights. When it's time for him to eat, we disappear into the nursery and snuggle in the cozy rocking chair, and I stroke his face gently as he nurses. His tiny fist rests on the swell of my breast as if he's holding onto me.

When I think back to his birth, to that traumatic day that nearly cost me my son, I can barely breathe. We came so close to tragedy. Thanks to Lia and Shane and our friends and family, we made it through that dark day, and the days that followed.

The door opens quietly, and I glance back to see Shane come into the room, closing the door soundlessly behind him. With a satisfied smile on his face, he takes a seat on the footstool, facing me, and watches his son nurse.

He strokes the baby's round little cheek. "I'm envious, pal," he says. His gaze moves from my breast up to my face, and he offers me a sheepish look.

The suggestive comment makes me blush. It's the first remotely sexual thing he's said to me since Luke was born. Oh, he spoons with me every night, sleeping plastered to my back with his arm securely around my waist. When I awake each morning, I feel him nuzzling my hair as he kisses the back of my head. He holds my hand when we walk to the kitchen. The physical contact between us has been perfectly platonic since Luke was born, and I was starting to think he'd lost interest in sex. Perhaps not.

He traces Luke's arm, from the tiny fist up his arm to his shoulder and over to his cheek. Then his blue eyes lift to mine. "Would you like to go on a date with me tonight?"

His invitation catches me completely by surprise. We haven't left the apartment, other than to take Luke to his doctor appointments, since we got home from the hospital. "Tonight?" My heart starts racing. Leave the apartment? Leave Luke?

"Yes, tonight. I'd like to take my wife out on a date tonight. Cooper and Sam have offered to babysit."

Even though I'd love to go on a date with Shane, I don't want to leave Luke. I'm not ready for that. It's not that I don't trust Cooper and Sam to take care of our baby, because of course I do. I trust them with his life. It's just that...I don't want to leave my baby. But I also don't want to disappoint my husband. "Um."

"Um?" He grins. "Is that the best you can do?"

"I'm sorry. I don't want to leave Luke."

He gives me a sympathetic smile. "What if I told you we weren't leaving the building?"

"Really?"

"Yes, really."

"I don't understand."

"It's a surprise, so I'm not going to explain. You have to trust me."

"But we're not leaving the building? Really?"

He nods. "Yes, really. I promise."

"Okay then." I grin stupidly, excited by the prospect of going on a date with my husband.

He leans forward and drops a quick kiss on my lips, and then he rises, towering over me. "After you're done nursing, Cooper and Sam will take over with Luke so you can get ready. I'm going to go grab a shower now and get dressed."

I grab his hand. "Wait—what should I wear?"

He smiles down at me, looking suspiciously pleased. "Whatever you feel like wearing. Dress comfortably."

Excitement bubbles up in me as I wonder what Shane is up to. I don't see how we can go on a date and still stay in the apartment building. Nevertheless, I'm excited. We've been keeping a low profile here at home since we brought Luke home from the NICU. The thought of doing something special with Shane gives me goosebumps.

"I wonder what your daddy's up to?" I whisper to Luke, whose eyelids are getting heavy.

When he finally releases my nipple and closes his eyes, I hold him against my shoulder and pat his back until he gives me a good burp. Then I carry him into the great room, expecting to find Sam or Cooper, but neither one of them is there. I head to their suite and knock on their door.

A moment later, Cooper comes to the door, dressed in jeans and a T-shirt, his hair damp, and a towel slung around his shoulders. "I was just about to come find you," he says, smiling at me as he reaches for Luke. "We're ready to babysit."

Cooper rocks Luke gently in the crook of his arm as Sam walks out of the bathroom wearing nothing but a towel around his lean waist. "Oh, hey, there you are," he says, smiling at me. "You ready for your big date?"

"No. I need to change. Do you know what Shane has planned? He wouldn't say a word to me—he said I had to trust him. And that we're not leaving the building."

Cooper grins. "I guess you'll find out soon enough." He makes a shooing gesture with his free hand. "Go get dressed."

"I don't know what to wear."

"Wear something girly," Sam says, coming up behind Cooper to rest his chin on Cooper's shoulder as he peers down at Luke. "Something that shows a bit of cleavage." And then he winks at me.

When I head back to our suite, Shane is in the bathroom, so I go to our dressing room to scan my wardrobe for something suitable. It's difficult to choose when I don't know what we're doing. I end up choosing a backless sundress with spaghetti straps. It's one of Shane's favorites because the aqua print matches my eyes—plus it shows a bit of cleavage. And thanks to nursing, I still have some cleavage to display.

When he comes out of the bathroom wearing nothing but a towel around his waist, Shane stops in his tracks, his gaze eating me up. "Holy—wow," he says, giving me a heated look. "You look insanely gorgeous."

"Oh, stop." I point toward the bathroom. "I just need to freshen up a bit, and I'll be ready to go."

While I'm in the bathroom brushing my teeth and hair, Shane gets dressed. When I rejoin him, he's wearing dark gray trousers and a white dress shirt with the collar open, looking at once both casual and debonair.

When he turns to me, my gaze latches onto the strong column of his throat and the portion of his chest visible through the opening of his collar. My belly clenches in anticipation as heat washes through me. It's been so long, and suddenly my body feels like it's roaring back to life.

I go up on my tiptoes to kiss him. "You look very dashing."

He gives me a warm, lingering kiss, his breath scented with peppermint. I press my nose against his throat and breathe in the warm scent of his skin, fresh from a shower. Shane doesn't wear cologne because of my asthma, but the natural scent of his skin and his soap is an aphrodisiac.

"Are you ready?" he says.

"Yes. As ready as I'll ever be. Cooper and Sam have Luke."

Shane offers me his arm. "Shall we go, then?"

I link my arm with his and let him lead me to the great room. Sam and Cooper are on the sofa now, a muted Cubs game on the big screen TV. Luke is asleep on Cooper's chest, and Sam and Cooper are holding hands. Seeing them like that chokes me up for a moment.

"There are two bottles of milk in the fridge," I tell them. "In case he gets hungry before we get back."

Cooper nods. "Have fun," he says, keeping his voice quiet so he doesn't wake Luke. "Don't worry about this little guy."

"I'm not worried," I say, although that's not exactly true. I hate the idea of leaving him, even for a short while.

"Call if you need us," Shane says, as he steers me toward the foyer. "We'll be back in an hour or two."

I'm wondering where we could possibly be going in our own building when he summons the elevator, pressing the *up* button, which takes me completely by surprise. The *up* button goes to the roof.

"We're going up on the roof?"

"Yes."

"Whatever for?"

"You'll see."

As owners of the building, and as occupants of the entire

penthouse floor, we have exclusive use of the roof, but we rarely go up there. There's a basketball court up there that the guys make use of, and a barbecue pit, but that's about it.

The elevator doors open out onto the roof, and we step out. The sky is still a deep indigo, and twinkling stars are just beginning to flicker into view. The view of the city skyline and the lake is amazing, but that's not what catches my attention.

The roof has been completely transformed. What used to be mostly a utilitarian space of cold concrete and steel is now a lush garden filled with grasses and ferns, potted trees, and a colorful profusion of flowers. Strings of flickering clear lights meander along a wooden boardwalk. It's something out of a fairy tale.

"Go ahead," he says, extending his arm in invitation. "Take a look. Explore."

After taking a few steps, I stop abruptly and turn back to him. "How did you do this?"

He smiles. "I have my ways. You enjoyed the garden at the Children's Hospital so much, I wanted to recreate a space like that for you and Luke here, so you can visit it anytime."

"It's incredible. Thank you!"

He offers me his hand. "Come with me."

We continue along the meandering path until we arrive at a seating area. There's a low, square table surrounded by padded benches on three sides. A few feet away is a three-tiered fountain with water cascading down into a circular pool. Overhead, a wooden pergola creates a magical canopy from which a dozen glass lanterns hang, lighting the area. On the table is a large metal tub filled with ice and an assortment of chilled bottles... everything from beer to fruit juices to water.

"I can't believe you did this." My throat is tight with emotion.

"You never did get your trip out of town," he says. "I thought having a garden might make up for that just a little bit. You can come up here any time you want some fresh air and a change of scenery. And the entire garden is surrounded by a six-foot acrylic wall, so you don't have to worry about Luke when he's older. It'll be safe for you two to explore up here."

"How did you manage to do this?"

"I've had landscapers working up here for the past month."

I wrap my arms around his neck and pull his face down for a kiss. "Thank you. It's absolutely stunning."

He sweeps me up into his arms and carries me to the seating area, dropping down onto one of the thickly padded benches and sitting me on his lap. "Would you like something cold to drink?"

I am parched, so I grab a bottle of chilled water and take a drink. He reaches around me to help himself to a bottle of beer, popping off the cap and taking a long pull.

Seated on his lap as I am, it's impossible to miss the swell of his erection beneath my bottom. Instantly, my belly clenches tightly and anticipation washes through me, settling between my legs. It's shocking to experience such strong feelings of arousal again. I guess my body's coming back to life, and it has *needs*. I want him, here and now, in this magical place. I'm not sure if my body is ready for this, but I want to try.

The wooden screen surrounding this little sunken entertainment nook provides more than ample privacy, so I rearrange myself so that I'm straddling his lap and lean forward to kiss him. It's a deep kiss, filled with intent and heat. His mouth opens to mine immediately, with an intensity that thrills me.

His hands go to my waist, his fingers squeezing and flexing. "Beth."

"Hmm?"

With every kiss, every shared breath, my body is coming back online, rediscovering needs that have been dormant for a while now. I grip his shoulders, holding onto him, needing him close. But it's not enough. I need more, so I free the top button of his shirt, and then the second, watching the material fall open to reveal more of his gorgeous chest. He swallows hard, the muscles and tendons of his throat clenching and releasing.

I quickly release the rest of the buttons, and his shirt falls open, exposing a feast for hungry eyes. I lay my hands on his chest and explore the planes, skimming over his firm pectorals. My thumbs brush the flat disks of his nipples, and he arches his back, groaning loudly. The sound he makes spurs my own arousal, and I feel myself growing wet between my legs.

In case my intent isn't clear, I rock my sex against the firm ridge of his erection, right through his slacks. His hands clamp down on my hips, holding me still. "Beth—"

"I want you." I skim my hands down his torso, letting my fingers play over the ridges of his abdominal muscles, following the trail of hair that leads into his waistband.

He groans low in his chest and tips his head back, gritting his teeth. His chest is heaving. "Honey, are you sure?"

I meet his gaze. "Honestly, no. I'm not sure I can. But I want to try. I *need* you."

He releases a heavy sigh. "Sweetheart, the feeling is mutual, trust me. But I don't want to rush things. If you're not ready—"

"I won't know if I'm ready unless we try."

He grimaces. "But I don't want to risk hurting you."

"You won't. My body is throbbing, on fire, so it must be ready, right? I need you inside me, Shane. I'm aching for you."

His moan is all the green light I need. I slip off his lap and trace the thick length of his erection through the fabric of his slacks.

"God, Beth." He throws his head back, the sounds coming out of him rough and a bit desperate as he captures my hands. "Sweetheart, I'm not going to last long this first time. I'm already so close."

He leans in to kiss me, his lips gentle as they cling to mine. He nudges mine open and slips his tongue inside, stroking the inside of my mouth, teasing my tongue.

Then he stills. "Damn it, I don't have a condom, honey. I didn't bring you up here for sex. That wasn't even on my radar screen."

Condom? Oh, right. I'm not on the pill now, not while I'm nursing Luke. We'll need to use condoms until I go back on it. "How long would it take you to run downstairs and grab a condom?"

He grins. "Four minutes. You can time me."

I slide off his lap, laughing. "The clock is ticking."

He's gone in an instant, and I lean back against the cushions to catch my breath. My breasts feel full and incredibly sensitized. The thought of Shane's mouth on them makes me shiver. I reach between my legs and press against my heated flesh. The pressure feels amazing, and I don't notice any tenderness. Maybe I am ready for this.

I slip off my panties and touch myself, reassured by the slippery juices coating my sex. Everything seems to be working right again. I rub my clitoris, and it feels good. Then I skim my finger down to my opening and let it sink inside. No pain, just lots of happy nerve endings and tingles and slippery arousal. I think my body is definitely on board.

Shane returns, breathless, with a blanket and a strip of condoms. He tosses the condoms onto the low coffee table. "Three minutes, forty-eight seconds." He grins triumphantly. "And for the record, Cooper and Sam are never going to let me live this down."

"They saw you?"

"Oh, yeah. They saw me."

He pulls me into his arms. "Are you sure you're ready, honey? We don't have to do this tonight."

"Yes, I'm sure."

When he glimpses my panties lying on the coffee table, he raises a brow. Then, he pulls me close and kisses the daylights out of me, reaching between my legs to test my readiness. He groans, loudly. It looks like he's on board too.

Taking a step back, I unbuckle his belt and pull the leather free from his belt loops, dropping it onto the table. He strips quickly, shucking off his slacks and boxers, shoes and socks in record time. Then he grabs the hemline of my dress and carefully pulls it off of me, leaving me completely naked. He drops my dress onto the table with the rest of our hastily discarded clothing.

He spreads the blanket he brought up over one of the padded benches and sits. "I'll let you call the shots," he says, as he tears one of the condom packets off the strip. He opens the packet and expertly rolls the condom down his length. Then he guides me onto his lap, my thighs spread over his hips. "If anything hurts, tell me and we'll stop, okay? Promise me."

"I'm fine. Don't worry."

He reaches between my legs and touches me carefully, his fingers sliding easily through the slippery folds. Then he inserts a finger into me, slowly pushing deep. As his finger withdrawals, stroking my sweet spot, he groans, then mutters a curse that makes me blush.

I bite my lower lip and grasp his erection, positioning the tip of him at my opening. Slowly, I sink down on him, sucking in a deep breath as the broad crown parts my wet flesh, pushing through swollen tissues and opening me up to him. Carefully, I work myself down on him, letting gravity ease my way. I feel the stretch as he fills me, but it's not painful. Instead my body feels hyper-sensitized, and every slide of his flesh against mine makes me shiver.

"Doing okay?" he says.

His hands skim up and down my back, as if he's petting me. Gripping his shoulders, I use him for leverage as I rise and fall on his length, sinking lower each time. My arousal coats him, making the slide easier. I feel only a slight burn now as he fills me.

Once my thighs are resting on his, we both take a deep breath. He reaches beneath me and cups my bottom, supporting me as I start to move on him. "Make yourself come on me," he coaxes. "Don't rush it. Just do what feels good."

I close my eyes and listen to my body, positioning myself so that he rubs over that delicious spot inside me with every rise and fall of my body. With each stroke, the pleasure deep inside me intensifies.

He cups my full breasts, his thumbs teasing my nipples, making them tighten into hyper-sensitive buds. When he leans forward and swipes his tongue against one of the tips, the sensation makes me gasp. Then he draws a nipple into the warm heat of his mouth and gently suckles. At the insistent pull of his mouth on my nipple, my milk comes down in a rush, making me shiver.

He groans at the taste as he draws on my milk, swallowing it down. When he finally releases my nipple, he chuckles as he presses his forehead to my sternum. "I've been wanting to do that for so fucking long."

"Taste my milk?"

"Yes. I am a very perverted man, sweetheart. Watching you nurse our son makes me so damn hard."

His hands grip my butt cheeks, squeezing and releasing, upping the pleasure teasing my nerve endings. I rock on him, taking my time and chasing that elusive pleasure. When I feel the tip of his slippery finger teasing my anus, I shudder. "Shane!"

He reaches between my thighs and rubs my clitoris with the pad of his thumb, firm, quick circles that ratchet my pleasure even higher, making me cry out as pleasure rolls through me, stealing my breath and making me tense.

When I come, my cries carry on the night breeze. Shane tenses beneath me, his own hoarse cries joining mine as he bucks up into me, once, twice, a third time. His hand cups the back of my head and he pulls me close for a deep kiss, our shaky breaths mingling with a mixture of pleasure and relief.

When my body settles down, I raise up onto my knees and slip off him. He turns me and sits me on his lap, holding me close. His lips are on me, trailing kisses everywhere he can reach... up my arm, across my shoulder, along the column of my throat to the ticklish spot behind my ear.

When I turn to him, his lips settle over mine, and he kisses me tenderly, reverently. "Are you cold?"

"No. Your body is like a furnace."

"Are you okay? Was it painful?"

"No, I'm fine." I lean into him, every muscle in my body limp as a noodle. "I'm wrecked. I can't move."

Laughing, he rises to his feet and sets me down on the blanket so he can get dressed. Then he helps me slip on my dress and panties.

He picks me up and carries me to the elevator. "Come, Mrs. McIntyre. I'm taking you to bed so I can kiss every inch of your delectable body and make you come on my tongue."

I sigh with great contentment and turn my face toward him so I can kiss his throat, tasting a light sheen of clean male sweat. "That sounds wonderful."

The end... for now.

Redeemed

Jake McIntyre

I've been pining my entire adult life for the one who got away, my first and only love. When she broke our engagement a week before the wedding, she broke my heart in the process and left me a shell of a man. That was a decade ago, and I've never gotten over losing her. I'd go to my knees for just one more day with her. When I discover the horrors she's experienced in those lost years, I am determined to keep her safe... her young son, too. I'll win her back, no matter what it takes.

Anne Elliot

I made the biggest mistake of my life ten years ago, and I've lived to regret it every day since. My heart still aches for the intense, dark-haired boy I abandoned. Now, when I desperately need help, he comes running, just like the hero he is. I know I don't deserve him. I don't deserve his protection or his forgiveness. But I don't want to make the same mistake twice. I will do anything to redeem myself.

Books by April Wilson

McIntyre Security, Inc. Bodyguard Series:

Vulnerable

Fearless

Shane (a novella)

Broken

Shattered

Imperfect

Ruined

Hostage

Redeemed

Marry Me (a novella)

Snowbound (a novella)

Regret

With This Ring (a novella)

Collateral Damage

A Tyler Jamison Novel:

Somebody to Love

Somebody to Hold

A British Billionaire Romance:

Charmed (co-written with Laura Riley)

Audiobooks by April Wilson

For links to my audiobooks, please visit my website:
www.aprilwilsonauthor.com/audiobooks

Coming Next

Stay tuned for more books featuring your favorite McIntyre Security, Inc. characters! Watch for books for Jake, Erin and Mack, Hannah, Killian, Chloe and Cameron, Liam, Tyler, and many more!

Please Leave a Review on Amazon

I hope you'll take a moment to leave a review for me on Amazon. It doesn't have to be long... just a brief comment saying whether you liked the book or not. Reviews are vitally important to authors! I'd be incredibly grateful to you if you'd leave one for me.

Stay in Touch

Follow me on Facebook or subscribe to my newsletter for up-to-date information on the schedule for new releases. I'm active daily on Facebook, and I love to interact with my readers. Come talk to me on Facebook by leaving me a message or a comment, or share my book posts with your friends. I also have a very active fan group on Facebook where I post weekly excerpts and run lots of giveaway contests. Come join us!

Acknowledgements

So many wonderful people supported me on this journey.

As always, I owe a huge debt of gratitude to my sister, Lori, for being there with me every step of the way. She's read *Hostage* so many times, she must surely be sick of it by now. Her support and encouragement are priceless.

Thank you to NICU veteran nurse Laura Bonacker, who kindly and patiently answered my endless questions about premature babies and the neonatal intensive care unit.

Thank you to Sue Vaughn Boudreaux for her tremendous assistance and support. With her many excellent skills, Sue is an invaluable help and instrumental at keeping me on track.

I want to thank Rebecca Morean, my dear friend and writing buddy, and author extraordinaire, for her feedback and critique. Thank you, Becky, for your amazing friendship and camaraderie.

Thank you to my beta readers: Sue Vaughn Boudreaux, Julie Collier, Sarah Louise Frost, Lori Holmes, Keely Knutton, Tiffany Mann, Becky Morean, and Brooke Smith.

Finally, I want to thank all of my readers around the globe and the members of my fan group on Facebook. I am so incredibly blessed to have you. Your love and support and enthusiasm feed my soul on a daily basis. Many of my readers have become familiar names and faces greeting me daily on Facebook, and I feel so blessed to have made so many new friends. I thank you all, from the bottom of my heart, for every Facebook like, share, and comment. You have no idea how thrilled I am to read your comments each day. I wouldn't be able to do the thing that I love to do most—share my characters and their stories—without your amazing support. Every day, I wake up and thank my lucky stars for you all!

With much love to you all... April

Made in United States
Orlando, FL
22 April 2022

17100436R00186